S0-DJY-611

Miriam at Thirty-four

Alan Lelchuk

McGRAW-HILL PUBLISHING COMPANY

New York   St. Louis   San Francisco   Bogotá   Hamburg   Madrid   Milan
Mexico   Paris   São Paulo   Tokyo   Montreal   Toronto

NOVELS BY ALAN LELCHUK

American Mischief
Miriam at Thirty-four
Shrinking
Miriam in Her Forties
Brooklyn Boy

Previously published in paperback by New American Library, 1975.

1 2 3 4 5 6 7 8 9 FGR FGR 8 9 2 1 0 9

ISBN 0-07-037161-X

LIBRARY OF CONGRESS CATALOGING-IN-PUBLICATION DATA

Lelchuk, Alan.
    Miriam at thirty-four / Alan Lelchuk.
        p.   cm.
    ISBN 0-07-037161-X
    I. Title.
PS3562.E464M48   1989
813'.54—dc19

89-2690
CIP

Post coitum omnia animalia tristia sunt.
(After coitus, all animals are sad.)
—LATIN MEDICAL PROVERB

To my mother

Miriam at Thirty-four

One

▪▪

SHE SAT NEXT TO JAMIE, in the vinyl bucket seat of his 380-hp copper Cougar, speeding along Memorial Drive on the way to his apartment. What had been an ordeal during the marriage which had taken up most of her adult life was now, a year later, a pleasure— love-making, going out and eating, driving in a car. Cambridge near twilight was easing by, with its changing streets of mystery (her camera discovery), and her hair blew wonderfully with the windows down. (Like running for a pop fly and losing her Cleveland Indian cap as a tomboy shortstop?) Such simple pleasure from what used to be, with husband Stan, a complicated irritation and neurotic chore. Out of habit, she took her camera and began recording the thrusting concrete energy of the city, buildings being demolished and scaffolding climbing up, skyscrapers-to-be by the Charles. Before arriving at the static respectability of red-brick Harvard.

"Can't stop doing that, can you?" said Jamie, amused by her compulsion.

"I'm hooked for life, I guess," she responded, clicking away, "or at least until a better addiction comes along." But wasn't he driving her to a fine one? "Got any ideas?"

"How about religion?"

"Know any good ones?"

She snapped a few more pictures, then relaxed in her "bucket" (her literalness), car-dreaming. If miracle, mystery, and authority were man's greatest needs, as Dostoevsky claimed, who would have dreamed that Ford and Leica would eventually contribute to such needs? Big companies replacing the big religions? she wondered. Leica for Judaism, Ford for Christianity, Westinghouse for Mohammedanism? Would her Leica save her, for example (Materialism the Final Coming)? It was already *making her,* wasn't it? Clearly she thought too much, even if the thoughts were as airy and frivolous as now—the result of not speaking, just keeping a steady private monologue through all those conjugal dinners, evenings, years. Now she had her camera and her journal, not to mention her men to talk to. Be with.

What a drag, Scheinman! she admonished herself.

"Hey," she asked, "where's my music?" Jamie pointed to the radio. "I thought you were the gentleman, friend." She turned it on and found 740 on AM, WCAS, a folk-rock station, a habit from another friend. That's what she liked so much about this beauty next to her: what he promised was not talk or thinking but other pleasures. She lay back and delighted in the cool wind coming off the Charles River, this golden boy next to her in his open-necked shirt (no undershirt!) and cashmere sweater, the prospect of good love-making coming up. He liked to drive, he glittered while holding the wheel at the bottom and banking sharp curves or scooting past cars, he made driving a comfortable sport. Like sex. She sat up and snapped him once, twice. Then relaxed, smoked, carried along.

4

Sex before dinner, another first for Miriam in this year of firsts. Driving with and toward pleasure, she felt on top of things. So what if Jamie Parsons was now droning on about an important bank loan he had finally secured? Wasn't it enough with Richie Havens on the radio, the sky turning deep pink and mauve, the air traveling through her dress to her body?

Not really, but that was another matter.

In his bedroom overlooking the river, they were undressed and fucking within minutes, and he was making up for all those boring words. Rising and falling swiftly, he took her with him, with masculine ease and natural skill. "Now you just stay still, just like that, only lift yourself more, that's a girl, while I do the moving. *That's a girl.*" A light smile played upon his lips, while he rotated slowly, bringing her more perfect and prolonged pleasures. During these bouts of the senses, her mind revolved on one thought: this ordinary fellow bringing her these extraordinary joys. Deceiving flesh, prostitute body. Fickle skin of a *realer* Miriam? "Do you like that?" he was asking, the veneer of tenderness only barely covering his exquisite vanity—vanity which even she admired, so perfect was its growth. "Yes," she nodded, "yes, yes. That's . . . good." He smiled, content. And said, "Glad you're not a writer with your gift of gab." But why talk, when it was so good just like this, her body massaged that way, her genitals tuned up, say? She glanced at his lake-blue eyes, saw little of interest there, and moved on to the blue-gray walls. "All right, you move now," this Ford of Sex directed. "You move around slowly, or fast, and I'll just stay up here, on my hands and enjoy it. And you, of course."

Of course. Well, it was nice to be locked in with a master at this frequently awkward exercise, a man who knew the business inside out, as her dead dad would have said. As she followed his orders, the brain, released from sex circuitry, switched to the thought that

5

it had taken her one, two, three men at least to have found this sex master, this automatic stud machine, this naïve American Apollo who, once horizontal, gave in to the years and years of his unconscious self-adoration. Even now, just as her own new vaginal tricks were spurring him to acknowledge aloud *her power,* or the power of another person to please, she realized how very poignant he was outside the sheets, when he tried his best, Jamie Parsons from Wausau, Wisconsin, to care deeply for her. Consciousness during sex had always been anathema to her, but recently, during this year of changes, she had taken a new view of it. Especially with Jamie, who knew so well his way around the sex stops of the body. Once the body got going into its intricate rhythms, you could just leave it alone, like the engine of a car, worrying only about direction, speed, stops, and turns. Though you could travel through your life without ever getting the sweet rhythm. Her body, which at first she had ignored or despised, then began to amuse her, like a new toy. Yet even now, through these bouts of pleasure, it confused her, at times hurt her. For it whispered to her again and again how much she had missed out on, how little she had experienced. It was difficult for her, an intellectual, to concede the body's powers, its rights. So it was this pleasure, among her newfound ones, that was so hard to come to terms with, as a way of life, as an open and serious pursuit, after a thirteen-year marriage, and thirteen years of repression as routine, duty as pain, anger muffled and converted to grief; all the sort of behavior that had been defined as *civilized,* adult. Now she knew what she knew: that this renewal of her sex drive freed her spirit as much as her body, and sprung something open in her work too.

And as she moved around slowly, exquisitely, her body working easily toward a release of itself, toward liquid space, toward a splitting of tensions, she knew

6

too what it was like to be locked away in a dark prison hole and then allowed out, to white sands, open space, yellow sun. It took adjusting; and even then there were those who couldn't take it, wanted back to their cells. Miriam knew that she would have to be dragged back, with chains and court orders and shrieking cars like some madwoman of Cambridge; it was the only way she'd leave her white sands, her Cougars and Jamies.

Okay, new stage, he was coming back to and with her, gonna show old Miriam some new tricks with his baptized piece, his masculinity pole, gonna dazzle her head by means of her hole ("Cunt, Miriam dear," instructed other lover Harry), so that it was of little use now distinguishing things or thinking thoughts. With that instinctive signal for release between them, she smiled and felt her face spread, and opened herself deeper as her Jamie "Cagney" Parsons thrust and drove her to higher heights, soon to soar, while he (she read), above and observing, basked in his powers. Well, splendid pal, she said to him in her mind, I'll give you something to bask in all right, and she began to put it to him, no longer awkward wife Brown or body-ashamed Scheinman but a deep driven woman, a Miriam of dominion now, making her pelvis into some sort of crazy angry ring holding fast this sharp piston, and with the smart control she had learned (from him, in part) taught him back, paid him back, taught him about *basking*. Somewhere along the locked whirling ride, she a calf bucking a smartassed cowboy, she opened her eye narrowly, saw a crystal of perspiration upon his forehead (where's his ten-gallon hat?), and felt a private sense of accomplishment. Jamie P. didn't sweat much, in hot weather or sex, got his work done without all that fuss. She closed the eye then; she labored and pleasured and used that pelvis hard and round and teasing true, and thought, with satisfaction, how anyone could be a master once you got in with

7

one. And then, with overwhelming satisfaction, the basking for both of them grew and grew and grew.

She held him and faced the white ceiling, her body a feather.

"From looking at you, you'd never tell what a tiger you become in bed." he said. She ran her hand down his back in appreciation, held him close to her—once he had tried to move off immediately for some reason and she wouldn't permit it, she wanted these moments, they had become almost as powerful as the moments before. And thought again, Was it all a fantasy? She had to keep pinching herself; just now she stuck her fingernail in her flank, to convince herself that it was real, not made up or dreamed of, this boy above her, her body sated, she a free woman and a tiger in bed. A fantasy of Miriam 2001 was here and now, Miriam 1973. And she knew that if anyone had told her of this transformation a year ago, she wouldn't have believed it, or understood its terms. (Shrewd Dr. Levanda simply asked questions, didn't prophesy, predict, or ever look surprised.) Wouldn't have been able to conceive of what independent spirit or bold desires and accomplishments meant. Wouldn't have had a Martian's notion (or, more precisely, a smart Jewish girl born in 1939's notion) of what the experience was like. No, she would have laughed and called this tiger-Miriam a delightful fantasy figure, and then returned quickly to add up the payments and penalties of emancipation. She remembered reading the diary of an old heroine, Ruth Benedict, telling what it meant to an ascetic lady to be kissed seriously for the first time, acting in her late twenties like a junior-high-school girl. Oh Ruth, would you blame me now if I felt the same way, just for these few quiet moments?

In ten minutes he dressed and she watched. He was handsome to the point of beauty, like some thoroughbred colt. She had gotten to the bold point of wanting

8

to photograph him this way, nude, but shy and proper. Jamie wouldn't have it. "Oh no, you don't, I'm not for public show!" He had laughed. "All right, I'll take a rain check." Hairless lean body, strong legs, and full shoulders leading down to halfback waist (a high-school flash, until hopes for a career were torn up with knee ligaments in a freshman game at the University of Wisconsin), the blond hair fashionably long, and those blue eyes that reminded you of every mountain lake you had ever seen (not the crazy icy blue, which frightened her). A model for a man, or a young business tycoon, or a blond yearling? He was all three, actually. Adoring his pale-blue boxer shorts (after years with jockey briefs), Miriam smoked, propped on her pillow, quilt held over her smallish breasts by her knees from the old training in shyness, and wondered how in the world or why, exactly, this six-foot Mr. Everything wanted her, Miss Nothing. Well, Miss Little. Miss Five Foot Four (almost!). Or, as they say, Ms. Little, Ms. Five Foot Four. Short, dark; all right, she had fullish hips and small but well-formed tits, but neither was spectacular, with a mess of black frizzy hair on top. And when he called her his Elizabeth Taylor of *National Velvet,* she returned the compliment with her Cagney tag. With that high forehead and great curl of hair slipping down, he resembled that boyish film gangster of the thirties. He caught her eye. "What are you thinking with that busy brain?" His ingenuous smile reminded her of her own Jonathan's smile, at age six, a smile of narcissism and mischief. No little girl smiled like that! (Traitor to her gender that she was.) "Just thinking that you're better-looking than I am," she observed. "From your point of view," he said, pulling up his trousers. "But from mine"—and he bounded the two steps to the bed and lifted her up in his arms. "No, don't"—but he had, and exclaimed, "You're the raving beauty!" shifting her around and

9

staring at her affectionately, surprised—she thought—
by his own emotion. Oh, he *delighted* her, like an adventure in his Cougar or like some delicious ice-cream
cone (with jimmies) from Brigham's, say; this simple,
sensual boy who would never really love anyone but
himself, even though he wanted to, at times desperately. "I'm a raving beauty," she offered, not against
the idea, being there in the air that way. "Can I get
down now?"

As he obliged, she thought how chivalric he was really, how old-fashioned beneath the flare trousers and
wide ties. And who else ever took her in his arms and
swirled her about in front of the Charles as if she were
a teenage bride?

Set down, she searched about for undergarments.
And thought how different he was from the others.
From Stan, ex-husband / neurotic psychologist, or current friends: Harry, the painter-compulsive, or Adrien,
the young eccentric. Jamie was a simpler, purer creature, a Trobriander smuggled into the beds of Cambridge.

"Where would you like to eat?" he asked, smoking
on the edge of the bed. "Italian, French, Greek?"

Just like a real adult. Going out, spending money,
having late dinners with candlelight and wine. All the
things that other adults took for granted, which she
never had (Stan's excuses: he didn't believe in wasting
money on restaurants and was too hungry to eat later
at night; actually, food was not that important to him,
unlike money or authority). Oh, it was pretty good
becoming adult, Miriam leaving prolonged girlhood to
be a woman. "Italian," she said. Adult, she meant.

He bowed like a knight, told her that her wish was
his command, and slipped into his small red-checked
shirt. No, my dear boy, it's not because I'm a raving
beauty or even a dark brainy semi-suffering Jewess—
though this has helped with you, sweetheart—that you

10

like to hang around me and these parts. No, it's because I can do *without* you, am *not dependent* on you, and don't adore you totally like the others, that you find me so refreshing. What a relief for you, isn't it? Even though you can't help trying to seduce me into worship. Go ahead, try. Feel free, lover.

"Come on, Moonstruck, let's get your ass into gear."

She saluted, coughed as she rose, and when the fit continued while she dressed, he brought her a glass of water. A cough that was a leftover from when she was Miriam Brown, Stanley's wife. A leftover from cigarette smoking and the exhausting hell of the last few years of the marriage. "Thanks," she said, drinking the tasteless liquid, grateful that she didn't require it. She walked over to the mantelpiece, where the brochure for her May photography show was propped. "Looks okay, doesn't it?" she said, as much to herself as to Jamie. "And Miriam *Scheinman* sounds a little better, too, than Miriam Brown or Green or Gold. Who'd ever dream that I'd get to love the name Scheinman again?" But erasing the name was easier than erasing the rest. Jamie, reading her mood, showing off the course in irony he had taken from her, said, "Would you like to do some suffering for us, Ms. Scheinman?" The teacher moved closer to her student at that, into his arms, nice and comfy. "No, just this, my wise goy," and he jumped, screaming "Oww!" at her reward. "Scheinman doesn't suffer," she said casually. "She pleases and pinches, remember?" In consternation, rubbing his assaulted buttock, he loved her for the moment. She finished dressing, his sex scent strongly on her, which she liked. So much so that sometimes she didn't bathe for a day, to keep it with her. Back at the bed, she slipped into the dress that she had brought along with her, the long, yellow, Italian-designer sheath he had bought her. At Phillips Book Store she had purchased a High Sierra Wilderness volume for him, and he had turned

11

around and tricked her into going next door, to Settebello, and had her try on this *chic thing*. It was for his sister, he claimed. The price tag of $139.50 surprised her, but his American Express card on the counter, along with his words, shocked her: "Congratulations, you own a dress." She protested, desperately. ("You can't—please, it's not fair!") She had never in her life owned a hundred-dollar-plus dress, and it was hard, nearly impossible, to accept. "Oh, stop carrying on," he said, enjoying it. "It was made for you." Getting a good dress, not a hand-me-down or Goodwill / Shady Hill charity-bin castoff, hadn't happened to her in fifteen years. In the car she had kept her tears hidden, from herself if she could have.

They drove to Boston for dinner. Following the hypnotic stretches of Storrow Drive, she returned to those names again, Scheinman for Brown. Was a name a name only? Didn't the mask at some point begin to mold the face and character? Sensing a new self being gradually formed buoyed her every morning; and not one of those brand-new Madison Avenue–Esalen overnight-identity selves, but rather a Scheinman who was the true development of the young girl from Cleveland Heights High and undergraduate University of Chicago days, who had one hundred aspirations and could do anything! Nowadays, almost half a lifetime later, that old naïve optimism had surged back. Except that now aspirations were narrowed; "anything" defined: taking her pictures, caring for Jonathan and Rosie, getting her M(inimum) D(aily) R(equirement) of freedom and men. Four hours a day of the first, say—not counting the psychological freedom to pursue her own new desires—and a weekly quotient of her male friends. But what hurt and haunted was the knowledge of the wasteland of her past thirteen years—the claustrophobic emotions, the steady low-grade depression, the daily (and nightly) sense of unfulfillment that lay

12

on the horizon of her memory like the charred remains of a battlefield defeat.

Could she erase that memory, turn past defeat to present use?

"Come on," she implored Jamie suddenly, as if he had been doing the thinking, "tell me about growing up in Wausau."

"You don't really want to hear about that."

"That's true, I always ask for what I don't want," she said, and he looked over. "Is there really a dream place like that? Come on, *talk*, all I ever hear is bits and pieces about it and you."

His voice was like a Chablis, she thought as he began, and, despite his wanderings, it pleased her greatly to hear him talk about his youth: taking care of horses for his builder-father and hating it, and him; playing football at the high school but preferring soccer, and dating not the cheerleader but a girl who loved drawing and crafts; canoe trips on the Brule River in northern Wisconsin and wanting to be a national park ranger and naturalist; winding up at the Tuck Business School because of tobogganing in the Dartmouth region. And as he went on, her own youthful aspirations returned—to be an anthropologist like the woman who wrote *Patterns of Culture,* or a painter like the man who did "View of Delft," or the dignified sufferer who wrote *The Need for Roots* or like another tormented soul, the Amsterdam painter who did those incredible self-portraits. And then later she aspired toward the other alter-egos, the critic who wrote *The Liberal Imagination* and the novelist who wrote *The Adventures of Augie March,* and still later toward the photographer who captured the withered faces and bodies of famine in India and the one who did the bent-over English miner walking his bicycle on the long empty curving path (she still had that 1950's Penguin paperback). She had wanted it all, everything, at one time or another:

13

eloquent literary criticism and field work with Zuñi Indians, powerful faces on canvas and lusty red-blooded characters in novels, social injustice in photographs and humanistic philosophy stemming from personal experience. Yet when Jamie asked her at one point, "And what'd you want to be when you were twelve?" she answered unhesitatingly, "Lou Boudreau." He looked at her, "Huh?" "You never heard of the greatest shortstop who ever lived?" Well, she explained, the one her father loved and took her to see at Municipal Stadium. Not Benedict, Vermeer, Weil, or Rembrandt had popped out, but Boudreau. See, Daddy, I'm still faithful, she acknowledged privately. And asked aloud, "And did you have any real skirmishes with animals when you camped out? Like with bears?" He did a slight double take and said, "How do you keep up with yourself?" To which she responded, "I keep a journal. Now, any bears?"

One bear story and canoe tale later, they were having dinner upstairs at Felicia's, in the North End. For Miriam, it was a special treat (like the dress). Graduate school and the years with Stan had intensified a somewhat introverted and ascetic, morbid nature, so that dining out was like having a party when she was very little—when was the last one, at six or eight? Oh, it was a fine, leisurely evening, a kind of party or prom night amid dark murals and candlelight, red-linen tablecloths, and a waiter who knew Jamie and immediately took to Italian-looking Miriam.

Later on, lying in her own bed and smoking a last cigarette, she contemplated her year's tropism toward enjoying herself. Miriam, in Italian-designer dress, eating linguine and clams and laughing over wine, was a new species to her, purer, simpler, happier. A species that, like the sexuality, was still difficult to accept.

Before going to sleep, however, she had her homework to do. Assigned to her by her teacher, Dr. Esther

Levanda, her former psychiatrist and present friend, who was away for the year in Israel (working with a pilot group of female analysts). Miriam had seen the sixtyish (and stylish) Russian lady for nearly two years, before they both agreed, last summer, that Miriam was fit to be on her own and could see Dr. L. when she wished. (Their exchange of several notes and postcards provided a nice contrast, Dr. Levanda reporting about Israeli women patients who were suffering from the absence of men, or living with the anxiety of loss [sons, husbands, fathers even], while Miriam would write back on the satisfactions provided by the presence of men.) Before leaving, the smart Levanda had suggested, as a "prescription for sanity," that Miriam keep what the doctor herself used, a regular journal / diary to keep up with her life. So Miriam had begun, finding it difficult at first but then getting into it, making the time and creating the habit. Telling the doctor how gratifying it was, Miriam also asked in one note if she would like to read it when she returned. "You ask your doctor this? Just be careful not to make me into a reader-censor. As for yourself as a writer-censor, I assume our old sessions will not have been forgotten, or in vain." Forgotten indeed!

So she picked up her five-by-eight-inch hard-backed friend, with NOTEBOOK printed in gold on the front, and started to think about the evening with her blond friend. In this, her self-therapy kit, her doctor-between-covers, her book of reason, reflection, questions, she wrote:

Evening with Jamie—lots of ego-gratification. Adores me, flatters me. Doesn't hurt at all that he's slow or less sophisticated, or what. (Old Superiority at work again?—other side of Miriam Inferiority?) And is he? Could I ever steer a canoe down the Brule? (The Brules, a new expansion team?)

Or keep my cool when facing a bear? Do I know how to bring back to health failing million-dollar companies, the poor dears?

I'm a child with him, what's wrong with that? Dr. L., childhood is something I abandoned too early on, after Mom died—we've been through that. Dear Momma, with soft brown hair and hazel eyes. And then, after mothering Daddy for a while, there was Stan—more mothering, for a longer time. Can't I be a child with Jamie, then? Along with my fine adult genital-intercourse duties? (That's the way you used to make it sound, my dear Esther! But of course, after my late conjugal years of *no intercourse,* you were right, it was a *duty.*) Adolescent boy and girl having fun together—Cougars, clams, dresses, sweaters, bodies? Can't I be his sweet savage, his Katuyausi, he's my Ulatile, after all. (Can you visit us here in Cambridge and watch us at courtship play, Mr. Malinowski?)

There is something uplifting about being around innocents. Jon and Rosie are great proof of that. They *saved* me during the last yrs of the marriage and during the breakup. In a messed-up life, they can be the best tonic, along with a smart friend. Innocence in an adult is also uplifting, though in a different way. You feel freer, easier. All the things that weigh down adults—superconsciousness, bitterness, guilt, neurosis, destructive competitiveness, backbiting, complacency—he's free of.

Is the innocence boring? If taken in too big a dose, too steady a diet, yes. But this way, a couple of times a week, it's invigorating, and what everyone needs. Meaning what MS needs.

A partner of innocence, a playboy at 34, is especially useful if you yourself are overadult. Or have too much superego operating. Friends and enemies, please let me introduce myself, Ms. Superego is my name.

16

It's not even the sex with him, as much as the looseness, the good-naturedness of the innocence. I remember the first time I spoke to you about him, Dr. L., I complained about how I couldn't really "talk" to Jamie. You smiled, that wonderful ironic smile, and asked, "Why do you want to 'talk' to him? What do you think you pay me for? Don't you have other friends you can talk with? Do you enjoy yourself with him? Have a good time? These are the relevant questions, no?" Yes, my good doctor. Just my old habit of destroying my good times by working overtime on them with my criticism, to make sure I didn't have them. One of my self-destruct. habits (SDH's?) you let me in on, thank you.

So onward and upward with Cougars and Jamies. Let it be, Miriam dear. As the other children's favorite song team would say, Let it be.

Miriam put the pen and notebook down, turned out the light, and sought sleep.

The older species of Miriam appeared more easily the next day, starting with getting Jonathan (six) ready for first grade and Rose (three) ready for day-care center. She dropped Rosie off first, on this side of town, then crossed over, heading for the Peabody School, where she had used a false address—that of her friend Nathalie on Upland Road—to get Jon in. It was the only good public school in town, and they couldn't afford—and Miriam didn't want—the Shady Hills and Buckingham Schools. An old-time prejudice, which she held on to, aided by the scarcity of money. "So what's on the agenda today, big shot?" she asked her son, in his clean shirt and trousers. "Aw, not much. What day is it, Mom?" "Friday, why?" "Well, then I get to play baseball. Dad promised, remember?" She nodded, hoping Dad remembered. "Maybe we can practice in recess today. At least maybe Margie and me can have a catch, then." "Is she good?" she asked about

Jon's best friend, the daughter of her own good friend, Elizabeth Morrison. "She's okay." He shrugged, rather professionally. "For a girl." Professionally baseball, or professionally male? she wondered, amused. She left him off in front of the school, got her hug (which lost its force out in public this way, the little cheat!), and watched him run the few steps to instant recognition, jealous of the three kids who immediately turned to him. A mogul at six.

She drove off to her own version of school, parking just off Brattle on a side street. She loved this ritual: the walk through the oval courtyard of Agassiz, white a few months ago and now budding green; the circle of red-brick buildings, enclosing and comforting; and, looming ahead and high, the Radcliffe Institute. The plush but anonymous corridor to the elevator, decorated with Women Achievers; the smooth, swift flight upward, to floor 4. The only thing she dreaded was meeting other women in the morning; she could do nothing more than nod hello, the last thing she wanted being real talk or lunch invitations. Finally, inside her room, with her papers, notebooks, photographs, and clear space with a city view, she was at home. Instinctively she plugged in her electric hot-water maker, lit a Benson & Hedges (her last pack of English ones), looked out at the streets of Cambridge, that apparently innocent territory whose secrets her Leica eye had begun to uncover and reproduce.

She cherished the institute, even its boring sides. There was little doubt that it had saved her, in a way. She had gotten the fellowship just as she was breaking up her marriage, and it provided her with just enough money, in cash and day-care expenses, to make it through. (Combined with Stan's child-support payments and her work at text editing.) It gave her four to five hours away from the kids, a blessing making her love them more and better. Equally important, it gave

her a room to work in, where she could plan her pictures, her work; a room away from pots, dishes, laundry, garbage, from telephone calls about child development, education, art pretensions—three subjects which
she had had her fill of. This was her office, and it gave
her a feeling of place in society; it allowed her to waste
or use the time. For Miriam, of course, there was little
choice. She was a compulsive worker, whether it was
the writing and painting she had first started out to do,
or the photography that she had switched to, some
four and a half years back. (It was on the basis of her
two shows, one a group show, the other a solo at a local
gallery, plus the high regard of her Boston teacher,
that she had received the fellowship.) She had two
rooms here actually, one a kind of closet which she
used as a spare or emergency darkroom, the other a
more proper room with desk, chairs, calendar, and
rooftop view. One real life was out there, in the streets,
in confrontations; another was here, in her rooms (and
in her darkroom at home). Here, she was a turtle with
her head pulled in, where no one could get at her. She
liked that anonymous feeling. A lot.

Thus she disliked it when certain women at the institute, many of them female academics on sabbatical,
tried to get her involved on Vital Questions. That project, that duty, was a great pain in the behind. Not that
they were all that way, not at all. There was a tall and
beautiful woman named Hannah Lichtenstein who was
tops—smart, civilized, an exciting painter. (Huge col-
lages modeled upon Brueghel just now.) She had an
energetic physicist husband whom Miriam greatly enjoyed the few times she had seen him, out in Arlington.
Then there was a historian from Wellesley, Sally P., a
smart slim lady, tough-minded but generous, a believer
in common sense and experience. Maria Galliani,
thirty, taught Miriam about jeans and polo shirts as everyday dress, this floating risky spirit who came at life

19

like a raft on the open sea. Next, a poet from Rome, a spicy combination of American-bitchy and European-style, a cross between Mme de Staël and Pauline Kael. Perhaps not coincidentally, these women, with the exception of Hannah, had been divorced once or twice, banged around a little by life. So there were enough women to give the place some flesh and blood, which it badly needed. For among other things, the skeletons of Harvard professors hung about everywhere—as judges of prospective applicants, revered guests at shows, authorities on contemporary art. This was a scandal, dreadful. (Was it her business?) Instead of saying fuck off to Harvard, which looked upon artists in general as did a business with academic, not artistic, needs—Harvard University was also the Harvard Corporation—and relying on painters and writers from the outside world for judgments, the institute invited the professors to play a significant judging role. (A few were fine, like the Czech painter in Visual Arts, the lovely man with full shock of white hair and gutsiness, but most were like the young art-historian lecturer and critic, a bloodless wet-behind-the-ears boy who pronounced judgments in the art magazines with Final Certainty, relying wholly on the one-track express of his art-authority figure, forty years his senior. How easy it was to be a critic under such conditions! If you were on the track of field color and design, you were the future; if not, if you were interested, say, in drawing or in the human figure, you belonged to the past and were ignored. Simple, this one-note criticism.)

Again, the institute did have its share of duds in one way or another, women afflicted with self-importance, parochialism, dullness. Selfish neurotic types posing as sensitive poets and tough painters. (And when you added a strain of women's lib formulas to some, the virus was disconcerting. Like Carol L., given a grant to study who was sexist in literature and who not; Jarna

20

D., there to write "militant women's poetry"; or pixie-faced Mary de J., narrating her "retraining" of her academic husband, as if getting him to vacuum was the latest obstacle in her boot camp. Why, Miriam wondered, did Red Guard views of reality have to dilute what may have been authentic problems?) But even here, in relation to the dullness, Miriam found she didn't mind it that much. One reason was that there was civility involved. Meaning decency, common courtesy—enormous virtues, she discovered, in Cambridge nowadays. (Fortunately, she didn't have to hang around the place or deal behind the scenes in any way, which, as she gathered, was much less decent than it might be.) And secondly, she didn't really mind this boredom; wasn't it exactly what she was here for? Outside in the streets, with her camera, life was too hot, too convulsive; and with her men, it was hot too, full of changes and surprises. But here, at the institute, she could slow down, cool off, avoid distractions, encounters. So boredom was a kind of relief, and a greenhouse for reflection and work. For thirty-odd years she had thought it was an enemy, the culture announced it as the Great Enemy, and here she discovered a brand of boredom that was a blessing, an ally.

With the boiling water she made her first cup of coffee. Instant Yuban in the a.m., if she was around then, decaffeinated in the afternoon. She sat at her desk and gazed absently at the wall calendar, showing nature photographs alongside literary quotes. On her desk was a recent institute notice, about a conference seminar to be led by Helen H. Life at the academy, all over again. She had had all that with Stanley, thirteen years of it as he had climbed the career ladder from graduate student to research associate to associate professor in psychology at Tufts. He had turned from biochemistry to experimental psychology, which should have been some sort of tip-off to her. It wasn't, at first. His

21

reaction to her success, modest as that was, was a clearer sign. As long as photography, like painting or writing, had been a hobby, he was enthusiastic, encouraging. (She had given up writing because she was too imperfect for its demands, she acknowledged; that "hobby" took a patience, a steadfastness, a stamina, that she finally was not up to. She would spend hours over a single paragraph describing a man's face or hands, and as a result produced few paragraphs and fewer pages.) But once the photography hobby reached the stage of a real one-woman show, as it had two and a half years ago, she became a threat. Especially when she began to attract notice from his friends and associates. And then, once she began to resist giving or attending dinner parties or other social functions with people or colleagues she was bored by or despised, things got unmanageable.

Her mind clicked off the present successful Stan, with his professional beard, and back to the pre-bourgeois grad-student Stan, whom she had met at Ann Arbor. Smart, aggressive, lean, with a wild mop of hair and horn-rims she loved, he was compulsive, Mediterranean-handsome, bursting with energy; since she was taking anatomy that term, she also noted that he had the finest facial bone structure around. Old Testament prominent. She had met him in a cross-discipline grad seminar in Greek tragedy, where he argued, against his professor, that Antigone was just as self-willed and arrogant as Creon. When it turned out that he was a biochemist who was interested in making a major breakthrough into DNA cancer research, as well as someone who read Dostoevsky—her youthful criterion for human relations!—and who argued against professors' views, she was slightly in awe of him. The first awe since her father's days, when love had outweighed awe. There she was, an English Lit. grad student on a Hopkins Writing Fellowship, thinking about Frye and the shapes of fiction, and this Stanley Brown (real name Roshnashevsky, thank God!) would explain to her about the shapes and functions of enzymes; how vague and unimportant Frye's ideas seemed next to Watson or Kornberg, or her own hopes next to Stanley's. It was like being out on a sailboat to stroll the lazy streets of studenty Ann Arbor, with the big gabled houses and spreading elms and maples, and hear him go on like an astronomer describing a new galaxy; all that leafy Midwestern laziness swaddling their Eastern intensity. In three weeks' time she was crazy in love; Stan became the second man she went to bed with. It was good, she thought then. That summer they went to Europe together, with hitchhiking maps, Eurailpasses, knapsacks, ideals, and Michigan passion. They walked the Lake Country in England; visited the museums in London, Paris, and Amsterdam (and The Hague actually had her picture, Vermeer's "View of Delft"), plus Rembrandt's somber house, which moved her terribly; down the Yugoslav coast to Dubrovnik and over to the tiny isolated islands in the Adriatic. Making love in cheap, charming hotels with bidets, gas fires, huge bathtubs, Slavic toilets without water (until the flush), or in sleeping bags in the deserted countryside. Improvising, on a shoestring, hungry for everything in Europe, students in love, they—or she—believed it was a perfect union of minds and, at times, bodies. The qualities that disturbed her at first she immediately transformed, by means of her ardor, into attractive vulnerabilities or hidden strengths; or even into her own intolerances. The fierce temper, for example, meant that he had nineteenth-century Russian-novel passion; the stinginess signified years of economic struggle; the instinct to dominate was a sign of his intellectual energy and passion for ideas. Through those endless nights of talk (and sometimes love-making) and long days of walking and thumbing and sight-seeing, she believed they were not Americans that summer but something much finer—prospective Artist and Scientist. They returned to Michigan in the fall and married on a hazy gray September day, her favorite sort. A good omen, she decided.

What had gone wrong in the marriage? (She was standing by the window now, seeing the odd rooftops.) The question was wrong because it presumed a single or simple answer. There had been no one incident, no dramatic flare-up or betrayal, no adultery. In fact, she didn't even know that it was bad, that it had become boring being with Stan, until the last few years when she had gotten out and met a few more people, through her own work mainly. And then everything she had taken for granted about the marriage and him was slowly overturned. She hadn't realized the way provincialism had crept up on her, prejudicing beliefs, suffocating feelings. But once she had a questioning eye, it was really all over, though it lingered for nearly three years. Just as he had lost interest in working on cancer research and abandoned biochemistry, so he had gradually grown less interesting himself, less vital. What was once passionate intellectual curiosity was now career interest. And all this was not even his fault (wholly); there was no single decision which showed him a sellout. You just didn't stop trying to be a great scientist and turn to teaching, administrating, academic career in a single day. It was more a matter of creeping convenience, handy practicality (you had to support those children you wanted), well-kept fears. Besides, not everyone was destined to be a Salk, right?

The trouble was twofold to Miriam's mind. Stan *was* destined to be a Salk, in his field; at least the two of them, plus his dissertation adviser, looked in that direction. And by not giving himself a fighting shot at it, he had grown more ordinary and uninteresting, more like everyone else. Old notions and old theories replaced

24

real thinking and new ideas. Ironically, it was only in their bursts of family fighting that the old passion and compulsive drive revealed itself, only in those explosions did the old potential Salk emerge. But, she thought now immediately—wanting to dive through that window, it got her so angry—where were those explosions in bed? There . . . anger became pain, and she turned away. Walked about the room. So who finally was to blame for it all? Stan alone? What about family, circumstance? And what about lily-white Miriam and her taking it all lying down—useful slip, as Dr. L. would have noted—through all those years? Hadn't Esther gotten her to see her part in—

Click. Thoughts off, radio on. RKO and the top forty, which she alternated with Morning Pro Musica and WCAS. But she was too unnerved by now, the room a memory chamber, and so she got on her sweater and hunter's shirt-jacket, and left. Outside, it was fresh, cool, bright. Companion Leica 35 mm. around her neck, she walked up Brattle aimlessly, snapping several pictures of lawns and pretty houses before she took stock of herself. What was she doing? So she walked the other way instead, across the overpass and along Broadway toward Inman Square and ethnic Cambridge. Past the Portuguese grocery and Italian bakery and into the shop with the rags over the handle. Joseph, the white-haired tailor with the beautiful unblemished skin, stood up and welcomed her with a kiss. At seventy-six, Joseph from Bessarabia still walked to work every morning at 6 a.m. and left at 6 p.m.; and this steamy shop, his thirty-five-year-old enterprise, had helped put three children through college and law school. "Nu, how's my pretty *maidele*?" he asked, flashing perfect-teeth smile and loving her in part because she knew some Yiddish. "Not too bad, and yourself?" and as he spoke, she began shooting, Joseph, the flaking walls, the huge piles of clothes, and

25

his collection of Jewish newspapers (mostly *The Forward*). "There you go, always with that click-click-click!" They were not great pictures, nothing like some beauties she had of him, seriously at work, unaware, but she was not here for that now. He just made her feel good. And after a fifteen- or twenty-minute visit, which she made every two weeks or so, she received her customary pinch on the cheek and warm kiss and hug, and was off. "You'll come for a bite one day soon, you hear?" "I hear." "And don't forget to tell me when that show of yours is on!" She waved and left. She still had a solid hour left before she was due to be with the kids (at three), so she headed for Green Street, another of her "family study" sites of the past few years.

Carrie Carouthers was thirty, just separated, with two small children, a Cambridge Brahmin dropped into poverty, and a Harvard M.A. parachuted out of the Ph.D. "Oh hi," Carrie said, rubbing her eyes, "come on in, nice to see you, but NO PICTURES TODAY, I'm a wreck—and don't tell me you like it this way, that it's ME, 'cause *I* don't." Miriam laughed and entered, getting a great kick out of this perpetually frantic girl, with the long pretty face, the makeshift skirts, and the fine ways buried beneath an ocean of disorganization and domestic duties. Miriam knew the two-story dump by heart, having shot here for the past year and more, and she admired the way Carrie dressed up the place with plants, odd remnants and materials, old lamps, bright colors; they went well with the ingenious shelving and odd pieces of furniture made by husband John, who remained on friendly terms with Carrie. They had a cup of tea, Miriam didn't shoot, just laughed and played with David, who was beginning to walk. Carrie was clever and funny, and the forty-five minutes there buoyed Miriam immensely. "And I've also begun to paint again," she said at the end in her most timid voice, reminding Miriam of her friend, another female closet-artist case, a poet. "Three cheers! Will I see some? Or will anyone?" "I'll show something to you, I promise. Just as long as you don't photograph it, or me—*you* have to promise that. I know how loose that trigger finger of yours is!"

Walking home, Miriam felt better, even though the day had been more or less wasted. And she didn't have that many left before the Show at City Hall in May. But at least that awful attack of memory had been dissolved. Also, she knew that the pictures for the Show were mostly taken already, awaiting printing, developing, selection. The toughest work, the agonizing pictures out there in the Cambridge fields, so to speak, had been completed; and a good part of the tedious but necessary time in the darkroom had been put in. Besides, a day off usually gave her more impetus for the next day. And with the kids about to go off to Medford for a weekend with their father, she had clear sailing for the next two days to make up for lost time.

When Stan came by later to pick them up for the weekend, Jonathan immediately produced his fielder's mitt and sponge baseball and cried out, "Ready, Dad?" Stan's deliberate face looked puzzled. "Uh, not today, Jon." "But, Dad, you promised!" "I know, but look, Jon," and he quickly shifted to glee as he raised Jon off the ground and swung him in the air, away from promises, "I have something special for you instead!" His anger rerouted, his arousement sneaked up upon, Jonathan, against his will, asked, "What is it?" Stan winked, having him. *"That's* the surprise part." And Miriam, dressing Rosie there, knew that her son had been cheated again, not only out of his game but out of his anger.

When Jon went off to get his jacket, Miriam said coolly, "I'm very curious myself to see that special surprise. When you think of it, let me know." Stan's face tightened and he said, "Are you trying to say I'm *lying*

27

to him, Miriam?" He took a threatening step forward. "Trying to poison my children against me?" "Oh, why don't you come off it, Stan," she said, *not* saying, "Why can't you at least be a man about it and let the kid have his anger out at you!" Not saying it because Jonathan would, today or the next day, bear the brunt of Stan's vengeance. Blackmail, divorce-style. When the boy came in, Miriam noted that he was thinking baseball again. "Now, don't look so glum, you are getting a surprise, you know." "Yeah, I know," he muttered, tugging his jacket onto his shoulders adultlike, the sort of competent gesture at his diminutive height that never failed to surprise Miriam. She finished the job for him and, on her knees, worked on Rosie.

Through contact lenses, Stan eyed Miriam the way he did sometimes, as if examining a guinea pig or pigeon, while she dressed Rosie. He took Jon's hand firmly, and Jon, resentful, knew better than to resist here, in front of Momma, with a whole weekend with Dad just beginning. But as Miriam worked on Rose's zipper, she was transported back to Ann Arbor days and Stan, with his wild hair, talking excitedly, and *Forgive me, Dr. L., I'm not supposed to . . .* When she looked up, there was Professor Stanley Brown, stockier, medium height, looking *official* in jacket and tie, masked neatly in trim beard that looked like you could detach it at one sideburn and remove it like releasing the strap on a police helmet. Feeling suddenly self-conscious of her blue jeans and raggedy sweater, her stomach tingling with unreasonable fright, she longed to rip it off. She controlled herself, rose, and released Rosie. "Have you been well?" he asked then, as if the conversation were being taped. "Yes, thank you," she replied evenly, wondering what was up his polite sleeve. She countered, "How's Röchel?" restraining her wish for a cigarette or drink. He nodded, approving the question too. He still had his way of summoning up in her the most primitive emotions, from helplessness to murderous impulse. She took a mental grip of her weakened body. And as if by osmosis of intimacy, he sensed this between them and stared at her, holding Jonathan's hand, punishing her. The awful moment of power was finally dissolved when she reached over and put Rosie into his arms. Useful daughter. "And how's my little sweetheart been this week?" Stan asked. "Have a big hug for Daddy?" Her small arms crept around his neck, pleasing him, and she giggled over the beard itch.

Miriam turned aside, knowing he'd be better away from her, and the kids yelled goodbye with gusto as the door closed. Somewhat shaken, she went to the pantry and poured herself bourbon, adding water. Leaning against the kitchen cabinet, she drank the warming potion, feeling heavy, impotent, alone. She had failed him by not civilizing his emotions, though she knew she couldn't have done that alone, without the help of a doctor, which he wouldn't hear of. Her eyes welled up. Should she call Harry and ask if he was free that evening instead of the next? She was tempted, as she cleared up the batch of assorted shopping notes on the countertop.

A name and phone number on a pad caught her eye: Bruce Thorndike, with a Newton exchange (332). A psychologist who had heard about her from a mutual friend at the institute and who had phoned her three to four weeks ago, with a request. Miriam had never called back, not really interested, though the money he offered had tempted her. (She still had to put in those occasional hours editing texts for the Smithsonian and M.I.T. scientists, to supplement the child support, Radcliffe money, and little bit of inheritance savings that remained.) Now, the bourbon mingling with her sense of separation and loneliness, she felt the need for something to happen, an immediate action to fill the sudden awful space. (So different from other spaces, which were fulfilling and necessary.) She decided to make the call to see if they were free. Dialing, she considered that her place would be easier than lugging equipment to Newton, not to mention the safe familiarity here.

Mrs. Thorndike ("Oh, do call me Mary Ann, please!") was cheerful and accommodating, checked with Bruce and a live-in sitter, and said they'd be there in an hour.

These people mean business, Miriam thought, pouring more bourbon to get through it. She got out her floodlights and two spots and her camera, looked about, and understood with some amusement that her bedroom was really the only place to shoot. So she brought all the stuff in, set up the spots, and put the television on for company. She sat on the bed, nervous, helped by Wild Turkey (for special occasions), watching a melodrama about the police. She thought of something else and dialed Harry. No answer. Tried Jamie, no answer. Finally, she reached friend Nathalie and told her she wanted to grab a nap but had no alarm clock, could she call her at ten to make sure she was up? Nathalie said sure, and Miriam felt better. Protected, without alarming anyone.

The next half hour of waiting was tense, though the liquor helped. She checked her camera and film, tried out the lighting, returned to the tube, put Mozart on for extra company in the living room. Flute concerto. She had never done anything like this before and felt nervous, uptight. Stanley and superego still had their influences.

Bruce Thorndike was tall, slender, blondish, with a thin head and goatee, while Mary Ann was round and sensual and brown-haired (flip), a fifties-cheerleader type. When they introduced themselves, Miriam asked Mary Ann if she was from Indiana. "No," she laughed, excited, "from Wisconsin. But I went to school in Indiana, Ball State—know it? And Bruce is from Muncie, how'd you know? Did you live there or go to school there too?" "I thought you looked like someone I once knew," Miriam said, liking the girl and thinking of the place where all her Midwesterners came from, Winesburg, Ohio. Bruce had with him a Gladstone overnight bag and asked, after a few minutes of polite chatter, where they might change. Miriam directed them to the bedroom and said they would shoot there, too.

Waiting for them, she finished her drink and allowed herself a little more. The door opened and Mary Ann Thorndike, in a dressing gown, said they were ready. No cutesy stuff, which Miriam appreciated.

Walking into her bedroom, her stomach went weak. She had done much riskier work this past year with her camera, but none this bizarre, somehow.

The Thorndikes had laid out a navy bath towel on the blanket and set their clothes neatly on the chair. Thoughtful. Miriam felt badly for a second or two that she hadn't offered them a drink, at least, but who cared?

"Shall we start?" Bruce inquired politely.

Miriam flicked on one spot, and Bruce did the other, at the bureau. The yellow light poured down on center stage, the double bed. She kept waiting for one of them to say, "By the way, would you like to take off your clothes and join us?"

They were half-smiling, calm, Mary Ann sitting on Bruce's lap.

Miriam, mildly astonished by it all, realized there was no sound, the television having been turned down. "Mind if I put a record on? It relaxes me when I work." She went into the living room and put on a familiar one, a Rasoumovsky Quartet, Op. 59, no. 3, and returned. The opening strings calmed her, and she got her camera from the table, saying, "Okay."

Smiling politely, the Thorndikes removed their robes and, naked, lay down on the bed.

"One second." She suddenly remembered the *reason* for the whole scene. One of the reasons, anyway. "I'm sorry, but I forgot—"

"My check's on your desk there," said Bruce Thorndike, sitting up nonchalantly, "in an envelope."

Miriam, embarrassed about the request, thanked him. She wanted to confirm it, but didn't have the nerve. She took a breath, perspired, and said, "Well, whenever you . . ."

For a moment Mary Ann nearly blushed, but it turned into a large smile, and she lay back, teasing Bruce's chest with her hand. Like two white animals lit up in yellow, they moved in and upon each other, as if they were in a forest, not a stranger's bedroom. This fascinated Miriam so much that they were fucking before she realized she had a task to perform.

She started snapping pictures from different angles, not really knowing the point of it. From the sides and back, she snapped shots, anchoring her concentration to the Lenox String Quartet in the background. It was like being a portrait photographer, only in a pornography shop. Not for her. Surprisingly enough, while she had witnessed this sort of scene before this past year, in much wilder circumstances, she was more shocked and shamed here in her room. Burning, she tried to remember the hundred-dollar reason, and that awful feeling of Stan's spite in her chest.

Five minutes or so of picture taking went by before she got a certain angle, looking down over Bruce's back and to the side, where she could hardly tell which body was which, or what exactly they were doing. Intrigued, she held this pose and snapped one, two, three, four pictures. They had become less of a recognizable couple performing a sex act and much more a frame of abstract curves in motion. The fleshy movement was transmuted into something more purely aesthetic. Or so she and her shutter conceived it. This new perception gave her something to shoot for, and she searched for that same point of transformation at different angles. Shyness, embarrassment, shame, and fears receded, and she snapped pictures. If it was nowhere near the excitement of her other sex photographs, neither perhaps, she rationalized, was it a totally commercial and pornographic night.

It all took about fifteen minutes' time (including a shift in the love-making methods), and she shot two rolls' worth. When they were done, she moved out of the room immediately, and remembered the envelope. She removed the check, got out her Suburban West phone book, and corroborated the name and address. They were legit. Then there was Shelly at the institute, just in case.

They were as fresh as daisies when they reappeared in five minutes' time, beaming as if they had just been married. Mary Ann had added an orange ribbon to her hair.

"How do you think it went?" asked Bruce.

"Can't tell till I'm in the darkroom and see them."

"Do you know when we might get them?"

Miriam, smoking, said, "I'll give you a call first part of the week, how's that?"

"Swell," Mary Ann said.

Miriam couldn't resist asking, "By the way, what do you hope to use them for?"

"Frame the best ones and hang them all around the house," Bruce said, holding his wife. And then, in reflection, added, "And maybe, just maybe, use them in co-counseling or encounter sessions, somehow."

In a lighter tone, Miriam said, "Well, I hope they're what you're looking for."

"Oh, they will be," affirmed Mary Ann Thorndike,

bobbing her pretty head. "I'm sure of that. We've heard so much about your work from Shelly, it's really our pleasure!"

Shelly Ascherman at the institute had seen some of her old Cambridge shots, but how did she get from gabled houses or the Charles River frozen over to intercourse pictures?

Miriam smiled.

They backed to the door. "I hope we didn't disturb your . . . routine or work too much?" Bruce offered.

"No, not at all. Good night."

"It was *really* nice meeting you," said Mary Ann. "I can just tell from the way you *concentrate* that you're someone special. Thank you."

Miriam waved and they departed. They left her with the sound of the TV on again, and she went in the bedroom and lay down on the bed. Exhausted, feeling odd, she found herself dozing, the television lullabying her.

The phone ringing and Nathalie asking if she was awake roused her at 10 p.m., right on time. "Thanks, dear, I'm awake now."

She meant safe, of course; managed to get up and turn off the set, do her evening ablutions in the bathroom, undress and fall back into bed and asleep.

On Saturday she worked most of the day in the darkroom, making the contact sheets. Some shots were okay, she thought, observing them through a magnifying glass. But she was relieved it was over, and glad, too, to have discovered so painlessly that that sort of thing was not for her. She looked upon it as warming up, doing calisthenics for the real thing, her own pictures. There was something too safe and clean about last night, something too detached. Porn. And uninteresting. Or that's the way it seemed now, one day later.

It was lovely being without the kids for an entire day,

34

working well for herself, knowing that they'd be back tomorrow night. A solitary feast of work, privacy, and space in a cluttered life. With Harry coming around later tonight, it struck her as all she'd ever want. She took a long, lazy, hot bath and, after an omelette dinner, sat in a living-room chair, waiting for him.

At one point she remembered some old photos she had taken of Harry, at play in his loft. In the file under H she found them and took them back to her armchair, Harry Baumrin, thirty-five, was a bit different from Jamie Cagney: hazel eyes and wire-rim glasses, casual sloppy dresser, scraggly salt-and-pepper beard. The shell ordinary, the interior interesting. There in those 5 by 8's, he was grandstanding for her, by his paintings. In one photo he was on his knees in solemn prayer before a painting of a thirteen-year-old model rock dancing ("À la Balthus," he called the series), and in the second he was preparing buckets of whitewash for a reclining nude. Miriam laughed aloud now, recalling the performance. After two more pictures—Harry making like Adam and covering his genitals after emerging from a shower—she came across two 3 by 5 index cards that he had typed out for her. A passage from E. M. Forster's "The Raison d'Être of Criticism in the Arts," which he had read to her first over the telephone, a day after returning from New York and his own highly charged and mixed one-man opening of a year ago. Keep it for future reference, he had told her. Literate and literature-loving Harry, using Forster as much as Rosenberg, or Strindberg as much as Pollock, as his points of reference. The passage expressed Forster's pessimism about the aid that criticism could give the artist, the key lines being, "The only activity which can establish such a *raison d'être* is love . . . That alone raises us to the cooperation with the artist which is the sole reason for our esthetic pilgrimage. That alone promises spiritual parity." High talk. And she remembered Harry's excited comment, "Now I think if you substitute arrogance, ideology, or envy for 'love' you'd have the *raison d'être* of most critics besides Mr. Forster." Right on, my angry babe. Miriam had smiled.

Yes, her nervous, driven boy-man had been out of his mind with confusion and helpless fury in those days, from some of the reviews. Snatches of conversation stayed with her, especially those after the *Times* art critic had panned the show, accusing Harry of being a cheap opportunist. "You can't believe it's the same man who can write so well about Cézanne or Matisse! Instead of accusing me of being vulgar, why doesn't he deal with the *subject of vulgarity* in the paintings? . . . Why didn't someone tell him that I took two paintings down, against the advice of Kahn, just because they might lend themselves to the charge of 'sensational'? . . . And did I create the publicity surrounding the show? . . . And what about the last five years of living and working on fifty-five hundred a year? . . . Well, at least I'm free of my last illusion, that you could at least depend on certain critics to tell the difference between a serious attempt at something original and pure fraud. Hopeless!" And so on, her friend had raged. Actually, it was painful and moving seeing that other vulnerable side of her usually indomitable strongman. "No, it's not hopeless," she had settled him down a bit, "you now have some dough and a reputation, and if the cost of that is some silly name-calling, so what? Besides, it's not as if you didn't have your backers in all this, is it?" And in a few weeks, after remembering all the artists "treated" to criticism—Keats, Woolf, Rembrandt, Pollock—he was working again, driven and peaceful (at the same time). Saying to her, "Wanna come over, kid, and see my cheap and vulgar new painting?" And, from that work, his ego and confidence were returning to their natural giant size, though she knew too, then, that the hurt lingered below, where he'd keep it for a while. The boy of unspoken need beneath the large and tumultuous artist ego.

She leafed through more photos and found his brief letter from then, telling how much he enjoyed the photos she had shown him, but reminding her that you couldn't keep doing what you did well but had to move on to other, tougher challenges. "And who knows when you get there, or who can tell what tougher is?" This note came the morning after a bouquet of white chrysanthemums had arrived by messenger. Another post-Show habit, sending notes of congratulations to friends who were having successes, and small presents to friends who were down. (A mutual friend told her about *that*.) She admired enormously the way he took her work seriously, surprising her with brief letters several days later. Two more photographs of play alongside his paintings, with the same dark-haired teenager sprawled on a sofa, feet over the arm, reading and eating an apple, and in the other, two friends bending over pop record albums, in indiscreet and suggestive positions. The combination of young girlish beauty and preconscious sexuality, in conjunction with the trivial, vulgar culture of their lives, was striking to him, and formed the subject of his recent work. It had helped Miriam to her own pursuit of the erotic, amid the routine, with her own camera. Here was another note, on Harvard stationery, elaborating his theme;

Look, America will take these terrific girls and do the same things to them that she does to the natural environment, ruin them. You've met Toni; can you imagine her as a tract girl of hairdos and pants suits when she's twenty-five? And what about when she learns to cash in on her twat, one way or another? It's all over, Baby Pink, right? Madison Ave. has won her real virginity, her spirit.

Well, not exactly right, Miriam smiled now, but she got the idea and agreed—that the erotic in its pure form was *against* or *outside of* business and money and piety, the country's religions.

She got up, took a cigarette, looked at the clock, and saw that he was already twenty minutes late; another fifteen or so and he'd be on time, his. She sat back down. Too bad her other friends didn't write her notes or were shy about being photographed, so she could have files on them too. Send them to the government, perhaps. A motor roared downstairs, she listened . . . no, not Harry's pickup.

In real-life erotic, her baby was another matter. He had his own interesting style, Miriam assessed, which more than made up for the lack of sheer production next to Jamie and Ad, say. Bed was complicated, naturally. She had thought it was complicated enough during the thirteen-year lease Stan had on her body—she remembered crying during those excruciating discussions with Dr. Levanda about sex—but it had gotten richly more complicated now that she was out and truly experiencing it. If there was nothing so enlightening as variety and difference, as she was coming to believe, there was also no education at times more painful. For during those various encounters and performances she knew for sure, she knew it in the muscles of her body as well as her brain, how limited and ignorant she had been of the sexual life. She hardly even knew how much she had *hated* it then. How awful to herself she had been, and, by being so, how awful to everyone else. How awful to her her husband of all those years had been too. How damaging, deadening, near-lethal he had been to her psyche and spirit by the way he treated her body. Only she didn't know it then, she wouldn't have believed it then; *words alone* wouldn't and couldn't have convinced her. *Only other bodies did.* And in a certain way it wasn't even poor Stan's fault. Wasn't it hers nearly as much? The nature of the beast, after all, was a labyrinth of family culture and upbringing. It took a fisherwoman like Levanda to pull her up to some clarity.

Bed, of course, was complicated, she repeated, but perhaps especially so for smart people whose energies went elsewhere. After all, her Billy Budd Jamie, if not a Mayflower truck driver, was also not exactly an intellectual. Yet consider Harry in bed, in her. The body was not terrific, but it was not bad; it could play basketball well and jog smoothly, and he had incredible stamina for painting; yet look how at times he didn't really work well with another body. She thought she sensed the answer. He had been spoiled, in a different way from Jamie-boy, and the act of coupling with another body was, in a certain way, beneath him. The act of intercourse was ordinary, and confirmed for him no special power or attribute *extra*ordinary. Besides his superiority, however, there must have been fear. The fear of not being at the top of the game, as he was at practically everything else—pictures, talk, understanding. The desire not to share himself with anyone else, the knowledge that the act itself was a common one, the fear of not being the best, kept him from administering serious love as well as constant good fucking. With Jamie the narcissism was fed by his ability to fuck women, and by his own stunning image; with Harry, the narcissism, if it could be called that, was fed by work, and he seemed then to reward himself with the attention of women. One tended to be extremely active in bed, the other could be exquisitely acted upon; both were sensual to Miriam. Anyway, her two friends of supreme self-confidence got along well with each other the several times they had met; like a couple of three-year-old thoroughbreds who admire each other precisely because of their different styles of winning.

She was on the point of anger over his lateness when the familiar hoarseness and croup of the old Chevy engine announced her friend. And in a minute, upstairs (he had his own key), he said before she could open her mouth, "I know, I know, I'm a fuckup—but look, let's not be boring. Especially before you've opened these—ready?" And right there at the living-room entrance, looking half Russian revolutionary (beard and wire-rims), half cowboy painter like Pollock (in dungaree jacket, Levi's, and turtleneck), he tossed, underhand, a parcel across to her, which she caught. "Buying me off, huh?" she said, opening the pink wrapper and discovering a pint of Baskin-Robbins ice cream. She shook her head. "I *hope* this wasn't for Prince Jonathan? He's a Brigham's man, down the line, except maybe for Häagen-Dazs raisin rum." "Yeah, I know, but I couldn't take the Square on Saturday night. We'll eat it. All right, kid, ready?" and this time he wound up overhand, with a large kick like a regular pitcher, which frightened Miriam just enough so that she muffed the catch, although it was an easy one. "Just a change-up, you know I'm not going to fire a fast ball in a living room." "Get me a catcher's mask, and I won't turn away," she retorted, picking up this stiffer package from the floor. As she got the parcel open, he said, arms folded, "The remainders at Harvard Book Store are better than their currents. I couldn't resist. I've put markers at the points of interest. Here, I'll put the ice cream away and get us a drink." He departed for the kitchen with the ice cream, and she flipped through her three books. An envelope in the hard-backed *Eros in La Belle Époque* marked a section entitled "Claudine and Lolita," with photographs of Pierre Bonnard's "Little Girl" and of one "Dodo at Thirteen" from a Paris brothel supplementing the text. She read a bit, and when he returned she said, good-naturedly, "Why don't you marry one of these Cambridge teenyboppers and then you can have one of your very own?" "Now, don't go sounding like a wife," he replied, pulling her ear and handing her a drink, moving back across the room to his mound position. Watching her squeal in delight at the next book. "Hey, you remembered!" seeing a favorite photograph, Martha Graham dancing, taken by Barbara Morgan. She threw him a kiss for that. "If you'll look a little further, you'll see more." She did, and found two Mexican portraits by Weston and then a picture of another heroine of hers, Dorothea Lange. A profile of that moving woman in her beret, the sun on her face, the woman whose own "spiritual experience" at age thirty-six caused her to turn from commercial portraitist to great photographer, to take her camera out from the studio and into the streets. She had meant a lot to Miriam. If Lange at thirty-six and Ruth Benedict at thirty-three could begin their serious work, there was hope for Miriam at thirty-four.

Women in Your Thirties, Emerge! If not then, when?

He said, in mock annoyance, "Do I have to wait all night?" No one ever gave her presents that *fit* this way, fit her small wants and likes. "Come on, huh?" The third book was a blue paperback entitled *French Utopias*. She looked at him, puzzled. "Look at the marker." She did, and it was at a section called "The System of Passionate Attraction," with a reproduced lithograph of Charles Fourier, with a cane and a finger to one ear, dandylike. Like her own Adrien. "Not a bad title for my next show, huh?" he queried. "Not bad," she agreed, smiling. "It's a fine humorous section, too; read it. You can't beat the French for humorous treatises, can you?" "I feel honored," she said. "But you're not through, yet. Okay, kid, heads up!" and there it was, another packet floating through the air. Caught this one, lighter. "Oh God, not again." "Last one, I promise." Opening it, she asked, "Why're you doing this? What'd I do?" "You? *You* did nothing. It's *me. I finished a painting*," he said slowly. She lit up, got up, and moved quickly to him, and kissed him before he could ward her off, embarrassed. She knew that it meant, during this period, several months' work for him. "Now go ahead back over there, so I can watch." She bowed before him dutifully, and returned to her chair. Only this present stunned her—an elegant silk scarf from Paris filled with peacocks and Chinese dragons and luxuriant foliage. She sat still, shocked. "Aren't you going to model it?" "Sure, sure," and she did, finally, around her neck and on her head. "Looks good," he said, "good for you." She smiled. "Good for you too." First Jamie, now Harry. Flowers, books, silks.

"I'll put some music on and you can tell me about *your* work," he decided now. "How's it been going?" Referring to the Show photographs, she knew. She drank Scotch and draped her scarf on a table, while he selected a stack of records. He had gotten her a supply of those too, educating her to folk, rock, jazz, after her marriage of Classical Only. He sat on the floor, on a cushion; the sounds of jazz swung into the room, and he said, "So how's it going?"

She joined him there, on another cushion.

"Oh, I had an attack of Stanleyitis yesterday, after he picked up the kids, and I'm still recovering. I didn't get too much done." She'd keep the Thorndike dirty laundry to herself.

"That show's not that far off, you know."

"I know," she said. "Don't worry, I'm in good shape for it."

He drank and said that he had seen Stan in the Square the other day and he looked good. "His new wife must be agreeing with him," Harry said.

"She does, I'm sure. She seems nice, and proper. And obeys orders."

"Now come on, Ms. Bitchiness." Her guardian against negativism.

She raised her glass. "Sorry. Actually, she is nice. Röchel Lichtheim, from an old rabbinical family, I think."

Harry sipped his drink and queried, "How's Stan take not having the kids full-time? Think he misses them, or would ever try to get custody for himself?"

She shook her head. "I doubt it. This way it's perfect; he gets to see them weekends, or lets Röchel take care of them. He doesn't really like them, you know. Never spent more than a few hours a week with them."

"From the outside," put in Harry, "he always looked like a . . . dutiful father."

Dutiful. "Oh, he was that all right, on the outside. Fronts are important to him. If I looked like I was heading for the loony bin or was known for hustling the streets of Cambridge, yes, he'd be horrified that I had the kids. And properly so, I suppose, but this way, he's a 'responsible father' without any serious responsibilities."

Harry nodded reflectively and said, "He tells me he's just finishing a big paper too. He looks in better shape than ever. Losing you was not a bad thing for him at all."

She smiled, nodded herself, and replied, "And vice versa, pal. They ought to put a ten-year ban on marriage, an experimental moratorium just to try sanity out. N-o-w," she intervened, the subject dulling her delight, "tell me about the painting. Was it that last one I saw, with Toni the model?"

And as he began to talk, the record changing to a Dylan tune, she suddenly asked, "Do you fuck those little girls? Honest."

"Now come on, don't ask me—"

"Don't 'come on' me, just tell me. Or if you don't want to, then don't and say so."

He finished his drink, poured more, removed his dungaree jacket, and said, finally, "I'm not crazy, you know. Or *that* crazy. When they're under eighteen, I leave them for the Cambridge Latin boys. Pleasure's one thing, Miry, the law's another. Besides, the picture's what counts. I mean . . . in a way I prefer them as models. Cracking their gum, wearing their gym suits, and telling me about night gym basketball, and using that lingo of theirs. I asked Toni if she could work this Sunday and she said, 'Oh, Mr. Baumrin, I'm *demolished* this weekend.' Meaning homework and social commitments, like shopping at Slak Shak. Or when I asked her about Steve, her new boy friend, she said, shaking her hands, '*In-ten-so.* Really heavy up here, ya know?' " Harry put on Toni's face of awe. "But it's that energy in them that gets to me. It's terrific. In the language, the makeshift clothing, the music and the dancing. Especially when they're dancing to that music." He jumped up then and, screwing his face up and shaking his hips in exaggeration, sang along with Dylan: "I want you, I want you, I want you, *so bad.*" Dancing around for another minute to the electric guitar, making her laugh aloud with his face of mock hardness and his exaggerated awkwardness. Then he was down again, breathing hard. "See what I mean? Can you imagine when they're fifteen and rock-dancing to this stuff? Do you know they can't fuck *half* as well as they dance? Or talk a *tenth* as well? But when they're up there, dancing, with their little tushies bouncing or bellybuttons showing and moving"—he put his hands out—"what more do I want in the world?"

Enjoying, and loving him just then, wondering quickly how he knew they couldn't "fuck half as well," slightly jealous but not minding it too much, she pointed her thumb at her own chest and said, "Me."

Dylan harmonized the room, Harry thought about her suggestion, then he nodded, accepting it. "Sure."

She ran a finger along his waist and belly, exposed by the turtleneck moving upward. He said, "Just don't goof off. Get that pretty behind of yours moving on that show. It'll mean a lot to you. Maybe a teaching job next year."

She smiled and kissed his forehead. "Thanks. I think you look after me, and I appreciate it. More than you know. Fortunately, I'm not the goof-off type, although at times I wish I was. No, I'll just work twice as hard tomorrow. I really think if it goes well I'll have a shot at something at M.I.T. Maybe even old Harvard will leave the Middle Ages and do something about twentieth-century arts."

Playfully, he put his finger to her nose and chin and replied, "Well, you just go into that Visual Arts Center and let them know that Miss Miriam Superiority has arrived, and ask them what they're prepared to give you. Show 'em your letters from Cartier-Bresson and Walker Evans, tell them that you're a descendant of Mathew Brady—"

"Hey, how'd you know—"

He put his finger over her mouth. "And they'll put you right on. Meanwhile, before all that happens, you just settle down and put the best Scheinman punch forward in that show, and if it's really good, Superiority, then," he paused, considering that, "don't forget to duck."

She had started slowly, slowly, working him (and her) up by degrees of touch. The slowness of controlled sensuality. Of confidence in bodies. Of familiarity with a particular skin and its sensitivities. Of lust laid on ever so exquisitely. A teasing slowness perfected through practice and delicious routine. By this time her finger had reached idly around and down, along his backside, where he was weak, vulnerable, excitable. A child at bottom.

And as she fiddled there, she began to feel herself go

weak too. They had gotten each other into this curious ritual, a tight lock and key of dreamlike sensuality. It had gotten so obsessive, so rich, that it frequently was hotter than intercourse between them. She felt his strength to resist leave him and his eyes go slowly blank with a cat's pleasure; she, too, felt urges compelling her that were new and deep. These urges drove her hands now, her own crotch itching from the flight beginning, like going down a chute. Soon enough she had his dungarees down, and inside his shorts she ran her hand up and down, around, knowing and skillful at it now, starting to tease the ass that she loved with her middle finger. He squirmed, she grew hot; she stayed in control and tortured him. Armstrong was going to sweet town about the summer and the river, and she had to restrain herself for some minutes before putting her face down there.

She managed to lower his shorts some more—he frequently kept them on, forcing her to work through the fly opening, or with them lowered—and go into her passion, her new need. With this man, and this man alone. She had never, in her narrow sexual experience, had so much gratification from touching a man as she had with Harry, or from nurturing a physical desire. Starting with his penis, she worked her tongue downward to his scrotum area, and there proceeded to adore his testicles for long, exquisite minutes. Kissing, sucking, nuzzling them until he was squirming above her, a baby whose feet are tickled; finally sweetening the kitty even more by dropping those sweet, sweet orbs into her mouth—and enjoying them like her own private "bunch of grapes" (her phrase). A careful, careful succoring. The two of them, Miriam and Harry, were like some high-wire balancing act at that excruciating point where one false move from either and pleasure would turn to awkward pain. After fifteen or twenty minutes there, she came up and continued her moist adoration, and he was on the verge of coming, and he begged her to stop, just hold up and do nothing, and she did, maybe offering one extra teasing or reflexive lick; and then, in a minute, they were ready to go at it again, he by now curled into a semi-fetal position and she diving aggressively back into her trap of lust. Here was sweet mystery, miracle, and authority; here was dark need, ritual, myth; here existed early religion, spirit, species' instinct. After a half hour to forty-five minutes of this obsessive play, he gave in and said he couldn't take any more, and she wanted to feel him strong and powerful, and he jackknifed her head, and they became these two strange, crazy animals, she taking, he releasing.

Then they lay there, limp, for about ten minutes, the record long gone off, leaving only an occasional foreign voice drifting mysteriously from an FM frequency, slipping through the speakers. He got up, went to the stereo, and put on another stack of records. Miriam closed her eyes, heard music and a refrigerator close and a faucet, and then he was back by her.

And then, just as she was about to dive down to another, darker licking need, he went to work on her, after telling her to close her eyes, then returning and taking his position—he threatened to get them a priedieu for their special prayers to each other—started to spread something cool and sticky on her pubic area, and lower. And before she could look down—he had pushed up her skirt and pulled down her underpants—he was licking at the coolness (*her* now), in his own slippery orgy of finger, tongue, and nose. Greedily he searched out areas where his nails could tease, or he could urge sudden sliding openings. The cold sticky substance was then tongued up and down inside her, and she felt incredible flashes of sensation which made her heart pound. And in a matter of minutes—five,

47

ten, forty?—she was calling out loud her breathtaking gratification (the way he had urged her to), and pulling at his hair with helpless baby joy.

She took a few moments to focus on the months of frustration, the years of feeling dried up, useless.

When she finally opened her eyes, she saw, at their side, a jar of orange marmalade with the lid off; it struck her, on the plain maroon rug, as a perfect still life.

He lay by her vagina—he had taught her about delighting in genital odor, which at first had embarrassed her greatly—and she felt easy, lucid. The ceiling was ivory and needed a painting, but its stillness and regularity were appealing. She could think deeply later, in private. For now, she knew she felt good, and looked forward to this . . . playful sex as much as regular fucking. It was like having a backhand as well as a forehand in tennis. ("Oh really," she could hear Harry say, "then where's your serve?") Anyway, her lust for it had been cultivated, and it was addictive. Further, it encouraged her *aggressive* side, a therapy in itself. Lute music of Francis Cutting and Robert Johnson had soothed the room, and now the lyrics of "Greensleeves" sailed by,

Alas, my love, you do me wrong
To cast me out discourteously,
For I have loved you so long,
Delighting in your company.

Greensleeves was all my joy,
Greensleeves was my delight,
Greensleeves was my heart of gold,
And who but my Lady Greensleeves?

Nice. She lit up a cigarette. No, she wasn't getting decadent, she wasn't confusing lovers or mixing desires; didn't expect or want Jamie to get involved with Cooper's marmalade. He did his fucking with no odd or exotic frills, it needed or wanted none. It was Jamie straight and fine, the way he lived. While Harry-boy here, slightly jaded, more restless and inventive, perhaps less skilled (though at times he could fuck with great competence), administered to her with these special sexual asides. It had taken her several long months (and her regular sessions with Dr. Levanda) before she could take lovers in the first place. And a much longer time before she could accept the full flavor of *difference* in men, like tonight, and not recoil in fear and confusion. A bohemian at heart from way back, she found the process of de-bourgeoisification in sex more difficult than the same loosening up in morals and manners. Or was she kidding herself? Didn't the one delousing have to do with the other, the break in her marriage?

Now there was another kind of music, starting out with a kind of heavenly choir and moving into a powerful familiar rhythm. She recognized the Stones; Harry had bought her this record too. She got up now and went to the record player and put it back to the beginning of the song, which she had heard before but had never really listened to. If "Greensleeves," why not this? At the rug, Harry said, "You're beginning to round out your education. Good for you. I'll—" She put her finger over his mouth. The group was now whipping out the words; Harry stood up and left the room. She lay back and listened. After that curious choir had come a half minute of quiet, and now there was the sexy voice of Jagger, taking it up. The song pounded on and on and on; she got the chorus, she missed the next few verses pretty much, and then she picked it up:

*I saw her today at the reception
In her glass . . .*

49

She was practiced in the art of deception
Well I could tell . . .

You can't always get what you want
You can't always get what you want
You can't always get what you want
But if you try sometimes, well you just might find
You get what you need.

Returning, Harry handed her a cognac, and she asked, "How many times do you have to listen to that stuff to get the words?" He sipped and asked, "Did you get the main ones?" She nodded. "Do you really need the rest?" He had a point. Want and need stayed in her head. And the way they drove that message into the room, fresh, strong, rude. Yes, the rudeness attracted her now. "Well, I got what I need," she said, and reached over for him, "but now I want some more." He took her face in his hands, kissed her on the cheek, and said, "Don't take those songs *too* seriously or you'll miss the point. Besides, it's time for your beauty rest. It's not everyone who gets to get up at nine or nine-thirty and read the papers before he goes to work." Still thinking of her, or himself now?

He got his jacket, and she walked him to the door. He gave her an affectionate jab and hug, and departed.

It was almost eleven-thirty when she looked at the clock. Taking her notebook, she went down to the basement, turned on the radio, tucked herself into her chair, a blanket around her legs, and began an entry. One of those floating pages that she could shift around? No, not this one.

Why these strange doings with this man? Is this "pornographic"?

Somehow I sense the same delish. need and pleasure with H.'s testicles that I get when I play with Jon, tickling or wrestling him. Bizarre, Doc-

tor, yes? No, no, not at all. Too obviously incestuous. Okay, admitted. We've talked about this,
haven't we? Jon grew too close to me during the
last few years of the breakup, for protection, and
it's my job to make sure he sees his own peers and
society. Doc, I'm trying. But I guess I can't quite
help it if an impression or sensation jumps up at
me, from one area of life to another, concerning
my feelings.

Maybe I love doing things to him too bec. the
other men do things to me?

Or maybe I'm more jealous than I know abt his
other girls? Certnly the two I've met, the 17-year-
old and the 40-yr-old models, have stayed in my
head.

Except that I get as much or more pleasure out
of it all than H. I asked him if the others do that to
him, and he said something like, "Nothing like
you." Ha. What's the truth? I wonder. Can I hide
in his closet & peek in?

What abt the sex itself—pornographic? Could
be, to some eyes. But then, what's *that* mean? For
ex., if he were a stranger, I couldn't do *those*
things. With *other* men, I'm not interested, no desire. If it's pornographic to love a particular part
of the anatomy *of a man you care for,* then call me
Miriam O. Actually, I don't think it is.

On the other hand, Dr. Kinsey, where wld you
fit me?

Some time I shld comment on H.'s women, what
I know of them. And on that frantic neurotic private part of his life that he likes to keep to himself—the cheat!—while he's out there with me, calm
and even fatherly at times. A reaction to compulsive days of work and discipline.

Oh Harry, you are like a little boy of mine as
much as a lover and a father.

She sat back and listened to lucid Bach and observed
the basement she, with the help of her men, had fixed

51

up: Ping-pong table, concrete walls painted cobalt blue, old couch and chair, baskets with toys, one square wall devoted to her photos. Old pictures of Cambridge houses, New Hampshire mountains, Cape Ann rocks, Vermont meadows. Two prize winners: a study of the ancient stone slabs leading down to the ocean at Pigeon Cove (*Photography* magazine), and a geometric picture of the long, oblong Town Commons in Lyme, N.H. (M.I.T. contest, 1971). She sat in the worn upholstered chair, battered by children and ripped underneath by Merlin the cat, who now climbed onto her lap. She had another glass of cognac before bed. What interested her now in the pictures on the wall was the detached feeling she felt for them; the detachment and the boredom. They were too perfect, too impersonal, too easy. Geometric and *pretty*. God, how that bored her now. The flotsam and jetsam of a Nice Girl. Good enough to win prizes, make friends; a version of Dale Carnegie applied to art. Oh, she was hard on herself, agreed. They were good enough pictures; for her apprenticeship, especially. They just seemed to jar so sharply with what she knew and felt now. But did the pictures have to conform with feelings? Beauty to knowledge? And how did you manipulate visual beauty to conform to life experience? A dilemma that her most recent pictures tried to come to terms with. Did they resolve anything? She didn't know. She didn't care, though. They were risky and disturbed her feelings; hence, they approximated her new life. Good then.

Divorced and semi-free (did you ever get further as an adult?). Three men, a studio to work in, and streets to roam through; no great debt, financial or otherwise, hanging over her head. Still in her thirties, health intact, and the energy to do the work she liked. Was this the emancipation business? Okay. No, not for her Virginia Woolf tortures just now, or Doris Lessing lessons in solemnity (or lately, futuristic mysticism). Neurotic temperaments, as the good Dr. Levanda had told her, didn't have to be emulated simply because they were female. Miriam stroked Merlin and listened to a classical clarinet. Mozart? Opening her life had meant, in significant part, opening her body, putting it to use. Easier said than done, she reminded herself. Remember Ralph somebody, that first fellow? How many hours did I torture him, and myself, with discussions about sex? Going at it from every angle, except the physical. Adolescent defenses, at thirty-four. And then finally, talked out, trying it—what an incredible botch-up of awkwardness and ignorance—Jesus I never hated my body or sex more than in those sessions! ("Well, let's not forget your conjugal bed," as Dr. L. would say.) Miriam held up her cat's face, to see if Merlin was taking all these thoughts in; but all the cat did was complain loudly at having been disturbed. "Okay, okay," and Miriam let him go back to luxury. No, Ralph's night at Miriam's was about as interesting as a night at Maud's, phony to the last word. This new exchange in her life, between experience and biology, actually startled her; her body was no longer a stone but animate, with messages. She felt like a young animal just learning to amble and stretch and run, a doe or foal, say. "Are you trying to say something about your newfound innocence?" put in Dr. L., who reminded her of her old U. of C. humanities teacher. "Perhaps you should use those terms, then?" To mock herself, Miriam pulled at Merlin's whiskers, and the cat jumped down, having had enough.

From M.I.T. Ralph, straight and sincere—God, was he sincere, with those Magical Encounter Words, "commitment," "meaningful relationship"; the Beatles were better, with their Magical Mystery Tour—to her current variety of fellows was a long, long way. A melting pot of America come to roost at Hancock Street. She remembered a line from a Graham Greene short story, something like, "Yet to know a country must one know every region sexually?" Like Mary Watson, the thirty-nine-year-old English heroine of "Cheap in August," having her first affair after a long faithful marriage with an American academic, and through it learning about the taut parochialism of her life in America, Miriam wondered too, more than half seriously, about that question. Of course, she knew her three lovers in different ways, on different levels. Her Wisconsin Cagney, her intense Jew, her Harvard dandy—she had run into a lot of *difference* there. She fantasized that it was sort of like seeing a different movie a few times a week, her native country coming to life not in celluloid but in person; its habits and words entering her brain, its erections and sperms her vagina, its feelings her spirit. A fantasy which she quickly enough gave up, for the much surer fact of knowing three men (two, well), and experiencing the culture that much closer. She was getting to know men a little more, and *liking them more* after more than a decade with one man in which such friendships were prohibited. After all, if she couldn't mix with high society—not born to it or wanting it—why not use her femaleness to mix with male society? Democracy had its place in human relations, at times. How different all that fluid variety from her marriage. (*There I go again. But I'm allowed to think this way, in terms of contrast, aren't I?*) There, it had been different routines that had filled her, different roles—grad student, mother, wife. Escape from those routines was impossible, photography as a hobby notwithstanding, unless she were to become another woman, or Stan another man. And how did you do that, while you were locked into each other as man and wife? as perennial partners in small repetitions? Sure, her roles had their positive side: a secure ground to stand and walk on; no anxiety about a place to live, a man to take meals and bed with, knowing where your responsibilities were, who you were (or were supposed to be). All this was provided for you, on the marriage ticket, and it was not so easy to turn back from, or sneer at. It was only when your life was driven up against the wall, for one reason or another, that you began to sense the high cost of family routine and comfort; and only when you walked the streets, met people, began to have a life of your own apart from your husband that you began to sense how puny and narrow your life was when with him. How society, for example, in his company, was intolerable, whereas outside of him, on her own, it could be interesting. She was not determined by his taste, dominated by his tongue; she spoke for herself and created herself in her own way. All of this she had sensed without the foggiest notion of sexual openness, or the incredible constrictions imposed by her conjugal bed-life.

The question arose: couldn't civilized life be richer and more spacious, less repressive and less subservient, more powerful and more pleasurable? Were the limitations necessarily those of the species under Family Rule? those imposed by knowing someone intimately for too long? those created by Stan Brown in particular? And what about her "last ripe years," as Harry had so accurately called them, how many of those did she have left, four, five? (Harry, who loved to draw women of that "ripeness," along with his teenage models.)

She stood, and walked to the wall where, among the photos, was an old one of herself. She was about nineteen, on a friend's porch. Short messy hair, good smile, college sweatshirt and shorts, tennis sneakers. Every inch a coed. Confident. Young. The skin sunburned, smooth. Going to be what she wanted to be, a writer / painter / anthropologist, whatever. Upstairs, however, there were other photos of more recent vintage; she felt pulled there now. She closed down the basement, lights and radio, and went up there, the cat accompanying her, heading for Rosie's bed. In the darkroom, on the wall, she saw a series of portraits, nudes of herself. Taken with a timer and tripod, a little over a year ago when she first was alone. Not of any technical interest, they served a different purpose: honesty, brutal honesty. (Called masochism?) What hurt most, she remembered, was printing the pictures and seeing the sag in the breasts and the loss of tension in the body. Giving birth had enlarged her breasts; the lactation and nursing had taken their toll. It had been easy in a way to forget about that while married; but afterward, when she had to face herself again for the first time in a decade, it had depressed her enormously. Thus, she couldn't get over when Jamie had touched them, and her own feeling there. It was like resurrecting a dead city, covered over with dirt and time. Then Harry, who had drawn and painted her, loved to kiss and suck them, more pleasure-shock to her system. Or the coming to life of the bushy mound below, which she had thought of as an old fireplace boarded up and closed over for good. No, the woman in those 5¾ by 8 photos had no idea that she or her body could excite a man again. Her look showed it too, assessed Miriam. Determinedly hopeless, resigned; as if she had come from the holocaust. All six pictures showing that awful, brutal resignation in the face.

From the file drawer she got out a manila folder and removed yet another series of portraits, which she hadn't looked at in a long while. Taken during her year of hell, divorce year, these concentrated more on the face than the body. If anything, she saw immediately, they were harder to take than the body series. What these revealed, almost shamefully, was a woman on the edge, the thin edge of breakdown and madness. The eyes were dilated wildly; the lips were separated, almost paralyzed, in a space of helplessness; the hair was an overgrown bush of frizzy snakes; and the flesh on the face looked about ready to tear apart from the pressure within. Had she been that close to going down, to falling into the pit? There it was, laid out, in black and white. She found her arms hugging herself, shivering. Every one of those five pictures was the photo of a madwoman—for sure. Thank God for Dr. Levanda, who had pulled her up. She returned her photos to the folder and put the folder back in the file, out of sight. And left the room.

She undressed, and in the bathroom she soaped her face and brushed her teeth. And gazed at herself, nude. She no longer despised this torso, or considered it with indifference. After years of deep freeze, it was alive again, the holes functioning with pleasurable secretions, the fleshy parts with motion and new use. She cupped her breasts; they were no longer appendages, mocking her. And she had worked hard, steadily, doing Maggie Letvin's stretching exercises and yoga, to flatten the bulges, especially at the abdomen. It was better now, though a pouch of belly remained. But the major transformation, which had turned around her faith and psyche, had been engineered by the men; they had given substance to Dr. L.'s words. Was there anything more gratifying for a woman than getting a second life for a body at nearly thirty-five? Harry's comments after she had modeled for him one day returned: "You're better now than when you were twenty-two, for me, anyway. Your body is all woman now, ripe with experience and sexy as hell." Even if it was only Harry's view, or obsession, it was good enough for her. The face now clear, the skin smooth again, the hair shorter and in place, the eyes smallish and brown, and the look steady, calm. Oh, it was fine, fine.

She turned the lights out and got into bed. Yes, she'd include those self-portraits in the Show. *All* of them, she knew now. She saw clearly the *real* title of her show—Miriam at Thirty-four. The coolness of clean sheets swept her, and she arched her legs like a compass to sense the crispness. She was riding . . . level now, and she wanted to stay there. The curriculum for the next few years read: to work regularly, to have sex regularly, to give and get affection (one or both), to make good pictures, to have an interesting show. She had wrangled free in her thirties, stamina, sanity, and affections intact; that was a lot. She was not ugly or undesirable; that was revelation. Her face was back to normal, and even not bad-looking. She was still struggling with herself, with her past, and it would go on and on; okay. (A year from now, in the second year of her Radcliffe stay, she'd have to face seriously the dilemma of money.) Others were ahead of her, in this new bold era, sure. But meanwhile, she had Rosie and Jonathan thrown in, a sweet bargain. Not hostages but bonuses of fortune. (Essential bonuses, to be exact.) She lay on her back, one hand behind her head, the other over her forehead and eyes, without the sleeping pills and tranquillizers of a few years before—ready for sleep.

But then, were those nude self-portraits fair to her feelings now?

Determined, excited, she got out of bed, switching on her lamp. From her darkroom she removed her standing tripod, setting it up in the bedroom. Smoking, she looked around at the room. For a moment, the Thorndikes' ghosts appeared, but she smiled them away. Everyone had his Banquos. She set up her floodlamps, directed the spotlight toward her upholstered chair, and mounted the camera. Using a wide-angle lens, she checked the lighting with her exposure meter, focused, figured out her depth of field (two feet), and set shutter speed (1/15). Pulling her nightgown over her head, she remembered a favorite painting, Rembrandt's nude of Bathsheba, and spent a minute arranging the full-length mirror by the low bookcase so that she could observe herself. Satisfied now, she set the ten-second timer and moved quickly to the chair, facing the camera and also glancing at the mirror. The shutter clicked; she stood and returned to the camera, advanced the film for the next frame, reset the timer, and got back to her position. She proceeded to take a dozen pictures that way, possessed by her new sense of self and hoping that the Leica eye would catch it too, on celluloid. Stronger now, no longer ashamed, a surer Miriam, perhaps even a model for some photographer, who for the moment happened to be herself.

At the end of the sequence, exhausted with the voluptuousness of solitary work completed, she practically fell into bed, and nestled to sleep like a great bird after some long journey.

The fine feeling lasted through the next day, when she worked hard at printing negatives at the institute. It prompted her to try the women's group that Wednesday night. First she promised Jonathan to go through an issue of *National Geographic*, with a feature on frogs in Costa Rica. He had seen a yellow *Geographic* in the Cambridge Library and was glued to the vivid pictures of volcanoes and snakes, so she took out a subscription. As her own father had, when she was little. Now, early Wednesday evening, she opened the glossy pages with glorious pictures of "Nature's Living Jumping Jewels." The pictures divided the frogs into two classes, the real ones and the replicas carved in precious stones by Costa Rican artists through the centuries. The leading two-page spread showed a two-inch replica of a frog, with bulging rubies for eyes in an emerald-green setting. "But what's the name?" Jonathan asked. "Well, he's called *Agalychnis callidryas*." Try that, kid. "Agilkniss Calleydris*s*," he repeated, awed. "Can he poison you?" he immediately asked, his

59

favorite question that year. "I don't think so," she answered, and turned the page. Figurines of golden frogs, which didn't interest him. Rosie, meanwhile, was crayoning and chattering away to her creations at the end of the bed. On the next page tiny bushwhackers and croakers and screechers on close-up leaves, with Jon repeating names. "Gosh, Mom, look at those!" "Look," Mom said, "this one's called the 'frog without trousers,' " pointing to a yellow frog with a Halloween cat on its back but no pattern on its thighs. Jonathan roared and tumbled over in bed, saying over and over, "The frog without trousers, the frog without trousers!" knocking Rosie over in sly accident, forcing Miriam to pacify her and set him straight. Then back to the bulging, orangy Ecuadorian mother-to-be, carrying her eggs in a fold of skin on her back. "Looks like a bank president to me," she observed. He looked at her, getting it, "Oh, yeah, I betcha!" Picking up her cue, he pointed to a group of yellow-and-orange-tinted harlequins upon leaves, "Look, scuba divers!" A page later, she admitted to Jon, "This one *is* poisonous." He studied it with rapt excitement. "Really," she emphasized. "A poisonous Peruvian frog. And know what those are on her back?" He shook his head, not daring to be foolish or stupid about a poisonous case. "Her tadpoles. She backpacks them for protection, until they're big enough to fend for themselves in the water." "What's backpack?" "You remember what we did with Jamie last fall, when we went to Maine and stayed overnight in the woods and carried packs on our backs?" "Oh yeah, I remember. Why don't we do that again? And find this frog to take along with us!" "Smart aleck!" She pushed his nose and then tossed him on his back. "See, Momma," said Rosie, getting into the act, "see my frog?" Miriam attended very seriously to her daughter's green and red scribblings.

After the baby-sitter arrived, she gave him the phone

number where she'd be and drove off to the women's meeting. While she was driving, Jon stayed in her head, with his wise-guy commentaries. How supercilious she had been the other night (and pretentious?), when she called those children the "bonuses of fortune." Glib and silly. In point of fact, she wouldn't have survived without them. Without Jonathan looking up from the Peruvian frog to say, "Can he poison you?" she'd have poisoned herself, for real. Could anyone who didn't have children understand this? Could fathers feel what mothers did? Stan hadn't. What counted, she knew, was that boy and girl, and the photography. That was the combination that kept her in one piece, when she was near coming apart. A point confirmed by the doctor. No, it was only later that she received her bonuses, the men with their adult penises and interesting courtships. The cream on top of the cake. She smiled at her slip and searched for the street signs, half of them missing on this seedy side of town.

Though she was too old for crowds, too bored by slogans, too arrogant for conformism, still, there had been moments of real interest and surprise. And a woman here and there whom she'd like to know. So she'd try again. She parked, crossed over past a small group of teenagers who half-eyed her, and moved up the rickety stairway of number 24. The flat itself was an odd assortment of 1930's nostalgia. In the living-room area, a barber's chair in one corner with a beaten-up chaise longue on the other side; in the adjoining space, created by a wall knocked down, a ceiling-to-floor wooden bookcase, housing a small Wurlitzer jukebox and reissue albums of the twenties and thirties. Posters of modern girls in knickers, blue stockings, and parasols adorned the walls, camp-style. Miriam, about twenty minutes late, stepped through a maze of girls seated on the floor to a space in the corner, a window seat. She sat and listened.

The girl talking to the group of a dozen or so women was dark-haired and prematurely graying (not unhandsomely), slender in man-tailored shirt and jeans, and smoking rapidly. A self-proclaimed veteran at thirty-three, she was recognizable to Miriam from other meetings. They had been discussing the variety of men's vulgar passes at work and on the streets, whereupon the speaker took off.

"At this stage of movement consciousness, I don't see how we can help but have a certain anti-male base, in all honesty. I don't mean on a personal level, of course, but in a general way. In order to raise ourselves up to positions of equality, we have to do two things, develop ourselves naturally but also lean on somebody. It's only natural and inevitable that we lean on our old oppressors. After all, how do you think they got up there in the first place?" She gazed about, for emphasis. "On our bodies and on our heads, sisters. That's how." She inhaled with satisfaction.

A young blonde, named Dody, sitting squawlike on the floor, asked gently, "But weren't there sort of . . . matriarchies first, and all that? In some societies, at least?"

As Lena Bernstein, the speaker, began to make a case for re-establishing matriarchies—a quaint idea, thought Miriam, requiring only a few thousand years to fulfill—Miriam tried to fathom the other lines, about anti-male, but in a general way only. *Now come on, Mir, either speak your mind or shove off.*

At the next hiatus several minutes later, Miriam spoke her mind. She asked from across the room, "Could you make it a little clearer how you mean anti-male on a general but not a personal level? I mean," she shrugged casually, "in your own relations with a man, do you treat him as the Oppressor?"

Lena eyed Miriam skeptically. Then, her face relaxing in a show of magnanimity, she nodded, approaching the question boldly. "Look, I make it clear from the outset to any dude that I'm not his *plaything*," she began, rattling off the words with New York accent and old minstrel's fondness for ready formula, "that I have a mind and feelings, *as well as a body*." (Where was that? Miriam wondered immediately, noting the determinedly anti-female costume. How could men go for that body if she didn't? Come on, Lena, tell us what it's like to be a woman without hips or tits, *the hurt involved*.) "And you can tell soon enough whether a man's a pig or not, or what kind he is. The games he plays are not hard to detect. And look, I'm the first to recognize that some men are victims as much as oppressors, that they're unconscious of the piggish attitudes which have been heaped upon them. It's just that I'm not interested in having them unload the shit that society gives them onto *my* head, and I let them know it right off." She lit another cigarette and added, "Look, a woman has to get her own shit together, and that's hard enough. With men around, and family, let's face it, it's simply four hundred times as hard."

A pragmatist, huh? mused Miriam, smoking herself, and using her cigarette holder. The statement, wrapped in lingo that Miriam despised, had its element of truth; but it also had something curious about it, the way it was uttered. Lena had already turned away, the question settled, when Miriam recalled it. "But could you try to be specific about 'men as oppressors'?"

Lena turned, and sighed perceptibly. Several girls picked up the signal and glanced around at the intrusive latecomer.

"Yeah," said a pretty redhead in the other corner, "could you be specific?"

Miriam felt cheered. Lena was surprised.

Another dramatic pause, then Lena said, "Look, my ex-husband wasn't that bad, he didn't even know half the time when he was fucking me over. We were as unconscious as any other academic couple where the husband has his degree and the wife is still on her dissertation. Oh, later on he knew, all right, but not at the beginning. But once I got into my own feelings and started sorting the shit in my head, well, I let him know about it, all right. And one thing for sure," she added, with her eye for subtlety, "*my* liberation wasn't exactly easy for *him* to take."

Miriam would be a pain, wouldn't she? "But what sorts of things did you let him know about, specifically?"

"Everything." Lena smiled slowly. "You name it, I let him know about it. From cooking and cleaning up to watching the kids and sex."

Miriam smiled back and said, almost cheerfully, "Did you manage to liberate him in terms of watching the kids? Or sex?"

Lena eyed her narrowly, cat and mouse. "Well, he has the kids now, but I don't think he looks upon it as being liberated." That odd (to Miriam) statement was accompanied by a look of victory. "I thought it would be an interesting way of educating him, as well as of freeing myself more. Believe me, he's *learning*."

Miriam eyed the ideologue, this Lena Lenin who could give up her kids for educational purposes. She suddenly was a little frightened of her.

"And did you liberate him sexually?" The words trailed across the room like a slow torpedo following a moving destroyer. "Or yourself?"

"You can only liberate an oppressor of long standing so much in one lifetime." She wasn't liking this, and didn't make any bones about Miriam's naïveté. "A pig is a pig, Miriam. He's the product of a *long* history, no matter how nice he may be individually." A bourgeois is a bourgeois, thought Miriam, remembering other slogans from another political past, or even, a Jew is a Jew. The lecture continued, however. "If his breed is used to treating a woman's body as something merely to get off on, like some sheep or goat, you're not going to change that too quickly. And I think we all know that it's not too much fun being treated as sex objects."

"But the trouble with my ex," retorted Miriam evenly, "is that he *didn't* treat me like a sex object often enough." *Yes, Mir, and tell her about the current pleasures of being treated as that "object" by the boys. For example, Jamie and . . .*

"Are you trying to come on strong for some reason, Miriam? Make this a *personal* thing? Two can play that game, baby. You've built up a little reputation yourself, you know." She paused momentarily, and added, "Which is your business, of course."

For a moment Miriam was too startled to speak. She desperately wanted to ask about that reputation, stunned as she was. Her intimate life known publicly? She restrained her fury, her curiosity. "A personal thing," she said, responding to the initial question, "only in the sense of trying to be specific about these things and get at the truth." She shook her head slightly. "Maybe it's just my truth that I'm getting at."

An opening which Lena didn't miss. "I think that's a serious problem, here. Not relating one's personal experience to the larger issues, the political sphere that's common to us all. What the movement is all about really, Miriam, is exactly that—relating the individual instance to the larger political issues at hand. Otherwise," she concluded, with palms outstretched for understanding, "we're back at a pre-movement level of consciousness."

Like reverting to God's mysterious ways when you brought up the holocaust. "Fine," responded Miriam. "I'm trying to get at the individual instance now. Like 'sex object,' a phrase we're always using. I've found," she said deliberately, "that I actually kind of enjoy that role these days. It's new for me, and it gives me great pleasure." Her reputation up front now, she added, "And you?"

Lena smoked, and looked around in an actressy manner. But the girls were waiting now as spectators, not students, the classroom a small theater. "Oh well, look," Lena said, trying a new tack, "of course, we all like to be objects of sexual attention, if *that's* what you mean." She blew some smoke out of the corner of her mouth, making a child's point out of the apparent paradox. "You know what I mean when I use the phrase. When a body is simply a body, not part of a person, *a whole individual human being.* And besides, you know as well as I do"—a start that always made Miriam skeptical—"that women are so different from men here. That it takes them much longer to turn on to sex than men, that there's much more to sexuality than *simple attraction.* That a woman wants to get to know a man first, while the man right off wants to get into your pants and *not* know you."

Hopeless. Okay, Mir, you keep it honest. Was that categorically true what she had just claimed? If it was, wasn't that a product of crippling habit too? Don't I love my new habit of feeling up Harry's prick or ass immediately upon seeing him now? Something you couldn't have paid me to do with Stan. And wouldn't it be nice to be able to pick up a stranger who appealed to you, and to go to bed WITHOUT THE EXCRUCIATING TANGLE OF KNOWING?

How odd, though, to hear that curious language that, she, Miriam, probably used when she was twenty-one. And probably believed in some way up till not too long ago. The language of Clichétown and Pietyville.

"But haven't you described another female hang-up, really—sexual shyness and timidity?" pursued Miriam. "Shouldn't we try to liberate ourselves from that too?"

"You do have your way of interpreting things, don't you? But that's all right, that's what we're here for." Lena the liberal schoolmarm, recognizing the demo-

66

cratic right of any silly child to give her stupid opinion. "But to answer your question, no, I never did liberate my ex, though God knows, I tried. As for my liberation, I like to think that there's nothing like a moratorium on sex with men, to learn about yourself and straighten yourself out. Now when I meet them I can handle them, and myself, much better. Play fewer and fewer games. And that's where it's at, isn't it?"

At such moratoriums? Not for this baby. I had one, roughly speaking, for nearly thirteen years. I handled nothing better from it, men, work, myself. The curious thing, actually, was that her own emancipation had led her to a *pro-*male feeling, if anything. Miriam eyed her adversary up there and felt a certain sympathy for the girl, despite herself. Despite the cartoonish aspects Lena showed. Disguising her pain through slogans, abstractions. Somewhere it had to hurt, and that hurt was now getting buried deeper. A road that led away from men, away from children, seemed not like independence but like flight. Flight from the real. With that rigid short haircut and male-like costume, a flight from the feminine too. Putting the pretty Lena in a mummy's wrapping of ideology. Not a flexible try at redefinition, thought Miriam. For a moment, Lena Lenin looked like Sue Bridehead, a girl terribly vulnerable at her toughest. But without Hardy, she quickly faded back into someone less interesting.

When a girl asked Lena about work conditions at B.C. and Lena rattled off more certainties, Miriam tuned out. Is that what opening yourself up meant, turning Lenin enemies into Bridehead human beings by a willed compassion? You didn't win many battles out there that way, did you?

During the coffee break, just as Miriam was about to leave quietly, a girl tapped her shoulder. "Just wanted you to know," she said with a bit of Boston accent, wearing a dungaree shirt, "that I dug what you were saying and asking about. I'm Kelly Monaghan. I rapped a few weeks back, remember? Anyway, what you were saying was interesting. Maybe we can rap sometime? Chicks like Lena may mean well, but cheesus—they're so moralistic and one-tracked about things. When she takes over, it's like being back home in Newton."

Miriam laughed, but was flattered. The big, good-looking teenage girl had indeed spoken, an hour and a half of freewheeling honesty that Miriam thought was the best session she had heard. Not ideology, paranoia, or formula from this Kelly, but personal experience and serious self-questioning. "Here's my number during the day," Miriam said. "Just ask for me, okay, and we'll arrange to get together. I'd like to." Kelly took the slip of paper, and Miriam added, "I better duck out while I can." As she departed down the rickety steps, she thought how this meeting suffered from the drawback of most meetings, a surplus of uninteresting minds. Something you had either to forgive, forget, or else split from.

Well, splitting now out into the cool, dark, loose street was a blessing. It was like emerging from a wind tunnel of rhetoric. Kids hanging out by a souped-up Chevy, that row of sagging wooden houses, the trees beginning to leaf out—they were an antibiotic against pretentiousness and bad talk. Which was worse, Stan bullying in front of the kids (and at dinners) or Lena patronizing in front of the girls? As she made for her station wagon, one of the local boys eyed her up and down, and Miriam almost laughed out loud, wanting him to get the pass out. But he didn't, turning back to his friends with a brazen hitching of his jeans. She smiled to herself in the car at the shy little toughie. And cheered up immeasurably when she thought about home and her own shy baby-sitter.

The baby-sitter was reading *Victorian Studies* in the worn armchair when she entered.

"Hi," he greeted her, looking up.

"Hi."

In the circle of lamplight he looked like an odd antique object, designed by an American pop artist. A handsome maroon sweater with burgundy velveteen bell-bottoms, plus leather cowboy boots complete with small golden buckle. Oscar Wilde named Adrien Weatherspoon III from Cuthbert, Georgia ("On the road to Eufaula, Alabama," he had explained casually, when asked the geography). With rings on his fingers, a single earring, Victorian sideburns and mustache, and a formal manner of wit and understatement that shielded all emotion or fear. What better lover for an older, growing Jewish girl than this strange young Southern peacock?

"Anything wrong?" Ad asked, at her long gaze.

Her spell broken, she replied, "Nope. Anything wrong here?"

"Not that I've been able to surmise."

Good for your verbs, honeychile. She lit a cigarette and said, "Why don't you fuck me?"

An involuntary smile and pink color crossed his usually imperturbable face. He still couldn't get over their affair. Neither could she.

She asked, why didn't they adjourn to the bedroom, at least he, and she'd join him in a minute? Lit a cigarette. Made herself a Scotch and water—a great open freedom now that Stan was gone; he had always claimed that she would wind up a *shicker* like her father, that gaunt, sober man who had a nightly drink—and then checked the kids. Rosie was lying that odd way of hers in her crib, behind propped in the air and small body diagonal on stomach, face pushed against the crib's bars. Miriam pulled her back, though she

69

knew Rosie would get to those slats again. The incredible habits of these tiny creatures! In the other room, Jonathan slept with his hands at his cheeks, having his "night dreams." She left the room, leaving the door ajar and the hall light on.

When she came into her bedroom, Adrien was sitting on the bed, the hurricane lamp throwing light on his candy-cane shorts. He was puffing on a cigarette. Except that his had a sweet, drifting odor.

He smiled his slow smile. "Here," he drawled, "leave off yours, try mine." He set her Scotch (and cigarette) down on the night table and put into her mouth a thin brown reefer. Her casual re-entry into youthland, looseness. Oh, it was different this kid drug; it hit you more suddenly than the gradualness of liquor and transported you elsewhere in a more magical way. Also, for Miriam, pot seemed to add a touch of aphrodisiac to her inclinations. A nice touch, that.

She inhaled deeply, the way he had instructed her. The drift tickled her throat, somewhat irritatingly, but she didn't cough like the first times. In all her years with Stan, they had never smoked; nor had she been permitted cigarettes in his presence, without a fight. At first, when Adrien had offered her the stuff, she had said no casually, much too self-conscious to perpetrate yet another cliché (after "the younger lover"). But as she was drinking her next Scotch, she gazed suddenly at it and smiled. One cliché for another, she thought, and dropped her piety. Just now she returned the stick to him. She was growing smaller, the sweet smoke taking her for a quick spin around the room, like a copter hopping around the jungle. His striped shorts were silk, and now she could sense what he meant about his liking the feel against his skin. After his drag, he smiled at her and got to his knees, the action slow motion now; he proceeded to unbuckle her belt and rummage at her blue jeans. He was really so curious-looking, the muttonchop whiskers and handlebar mustache, and the long dirty-blond hair, parted in the center and hanging shoulder length. A good boy for Dody or Kelly, perhaps. "What are you smiling at?" he asked, holding her bare knees fondly. "Just thinking about you with a pretty young girl I saw there tonight." He got the rest of her pants down. "Oh, I forgot my little surprise. Close your eyes until I say so." She did, and after BCN radio produced rock, he said, "Okay." She opened them. "Where'd you get that?" *"The Duchess of Malfi.* I'm in it, don't you remember? Like it?" "Well, it's different." She had never been in a room before with a man who wore a black eye mask. The bedroom she knew so well now drifted farther toward the unfamiliar. "Why don't you keep it on?" she suggested, as he reached to remove it. "You look . . . Lone Rangerish in it . . . I might like it."

And even if it was kinky, or kooky, that was all right too, so long as she had Dr. L. to talk to later on, in her diary, right? She touched the cloth mask to check out its reality, during her own sweet fading out, and ran her hand through his long soft hair. Like lying with a girl friend, perhaps. How odd. Would Jonathan turn into one of these androgynous creatures? She really couldn't tell how far Adrien's bent for esoterics traveled, or in what erotic direction. Masks, rings (black onyx on left hand, amethyst on right), single silver earring. Was he kooky, or just curious? Futuristic, or regressive? Where were the—and were there any— lines of demarcation? Or were they blurred by now, as in Rome, say? Sodom? His spoken voice, even in suggesting the bed, was half Georgia drawl, half English affectation, like nothing she had ever heard. It reeked of indolence and oddness, like a strange smell winding through an old house. Words and sentences became other than what they seemed, mysterious presences. Or was she getting very high?

71

Too high now, into the second weed, to want to control things. And besides, she liked the way he did things, changed pace imperceptibly on whim. On the queen-sized bed, wearing their undergarments (new bikinis for her, Jamie's embarrassing present), he began to run his nails up and down her body. Startling, those long nails he kept; and startling when he excited her this way, delight bordering on hurt. As she returned those sharp favors, the sound of rock music pounded at her, some simple, repeated rhythm signaling animal-time. Scratching at each other in this warm-up game, she began to whisper the obscenities that Harry had elicited from her, those incredibly embarrassing vulgarities from some other self ("Come on, let's see you shove me that *big thing* of yours"), which truly spurred both of them and spun them somehow. Oh, it was strange indeed to see her young lover back there, looking like her old favorite radio cowboy, and she was sorry to see his high leather boots on the floor. "Maybe you ought to wear a costume sometime too," he drawled, adjusting their bodies, and in her daze she thought it an intriguing notion. During these dreamy moments, he had turned her about, his favorite position. And for her to turn back and catch glimpses of this masked man behind her, driving her, was weirdly thrilling; it pushed their regular pleasure with unusual lust. Oh God, she wondered, were books ever so *adventurous* as this? Photographs? And slowly, steadily, as this mounted stranger worked upon her and she returned with her own learned variations, the smell of the boy distracted her crazily. How she had come to love that mixture of body smell and patchouli oil from her pretty dandy, and how she craved it! It seemed to her a sure sign of approaching, surging orgasm. In fact, the greater the smell, usually the stronger and fiercer that peak of pleasure, which now began to turn and lock her, and make her moan loudly and dearly love her young fucking studboy from Cuthbert, Ga., home of the man with the pickax and German shepherds!

It was a solid, drawn-out gratification, which soon led to another one, and she thought of Kemo Sabe and the white horse, and for a girl who for years had to labor for a struggling half hour, these newfound climaxes after ten or fifteen minutes made sex something that she hadn't ever imagined, just never dreamed of, for her. Was she a whore to want that pleasure all through her thirties at least?

She had taken him out of epicene timidity; he had taken her to richer, if more ambiguous, adulthood.

Down, after a few minutes, cigarettes again, the drift of odors and the intimacy of legs crossed upon each other. Miriam, an old-fashioned girl, had come a longer way than twelve months of calendar time would indicate. Driving her body to new desires made her feel larger, younger, less innocent, and, somehow, instructed her spirit. Made it sense the mysterious, perhaps. Was her spirit the whore then? So be it.

Adrien removed his mask momentarily and replaced the rock music with a baroque violin sonata on WCRB. As she saw once again the reality of his Roman nose and slender, honed body, she realized she had wanted to ask him something for a while now.

"What's it like, sleeping with boys?"

There was a brief minute or two in which the perfect calm of his face was disrupted, and the edges of the upper lip seemed to quiver. Slowly, that passed, and he was himself again, composed. "Well, I'm not sure I want to answer that." Not surly, just matter-of-fact.

She recalled the first time she had put the question to him, about whether he had men as lovers; that same flickering anxiety, his hesitating answer and her calm acceptance, and the look of relief, no, gratitude, in his face. Those were the only two occasions where vulnera-

73

bility and fear had broken through that mask of imperturbableness. It had moved her.

"Then don't," she replied.

He blinked, his green eyes staying on her, and for a second or two she thought about him, not with Dody, but with her Viking, Jamie. Or Jamie with the two of them, Adrien and Miriam. Or she, Miriam, with Adrien and a friend of his. The combinations were dazzling, like chess problems.

"It's different, I guess," he offered.

"Oh, come on, you can do better than that," she urged gently. Secretly wondering if it was the same Miriam Scheinman she used to know asking these questions. The leftovers of marijuana?

"Come on, one, two, three, how different?"

He laughed at her familiar fun with Weatherspoon III.

She reached across and lifted his Lone Ranger mask and tried it on. The rubber band squeezed her temples, and her eyelashes brushed the cloth. He stared at her, in surprise, and smiled slightly.

Shifting positions and raising his knees, he spoke, in a slow, reflective way. "I suppose I like bodies, and don't try to distinguish for gender . . . I feel comfortable with a body nearby."

She imagined Antony looked something like Adrien here, and she was Cleo, asking about the pleasure of battles, slaughter. "And the differences?"

"I'm not sure," he began, stroking his whiskers absentmindedly. "With Peter, one boy I see now, I'm much more in charge. More . . . aggressive than with you, generally. You dominate me, even though at times it may not look like it. Obviously, I . . . like that. With Ricky, my long-time lover, on the other hand—" He turned toward her, suddenly aware that he had an audience. "This must seem rather silly."

"No. Not at all."

She waited.

He stroked, and lay back languorously. "You're the first woman really whom I've sort of . . . had sex with *and* respected. Or stayed on with for longer than . . . a night or so. You're intelligent, and most girls . . ." He did something ordinary, a shrug. "Relations with boys seem to be . . . more real for me."

She felt maternal, protective. The music was Chopin, said the announcer. She didn't want to break the spell, this talk which slowly was seeping from him, almost furtively.

He was running his nail down the exposed part of his cheek, reflecting.

"Go on," she urged gently.

"With Peter, it's really almost a spiritual thing. I hold his penis and feel it getting larger and . . ." He smiled, bewildered. "It's as if I were holding his hand. It was that way when I first met him and did hold his hand. I mean, it's friendship as much as anything. And when I put my mouth to him, I get excited . . . in a spiritual way, if you can understand that. Can you?"

She didn't know if she could or not. "Where did you first meet him, by the way?"

"At a homophile dance in Boston." He laughed slightly. "Neither of us would go to our college coming-out dances, but there we were, at the general Boston one."

She smiled to herself, about the new proms. And getting back to his reasoning, she said, "And when you put your mouth to me, is it spiritual?"

He blinked and thought, a cherub speaking about earthly things.

"Well, it's so different, you get so wet down there, and when you wrap your legs around me, I suppose it's very womblike." He was blushing, and it looked lovely, it was so uncharacteristic. "I must sound awfully foolish and mechanical."

"Don't be so self-conscious." Self-deceptive, she meant.

He half-smiled, regained his poise and pallid color, and smoked a cigarette. "I suppose intercourse between Peter and myself is very different. You see, it's his first real affair and he fights the desire a lot, until we're . . . doing it. Then he can't help himself. It is exciting, I must admit, to see him want to keep back and then make love to me. First times are, well, unique." He smiled brightly.

She was seeing a new side to him, a rather uncontrollable one, she thought. She appreciated his particular homage.

With surprising tenderness he suddenly produced, "I wouldn't want you a virgin, honest. You're special this way. Do you believe me?"

She laughed aloud at his attempt at making it up to her. She reached over, took him in her arms, and said, "But I am a virgin, in ways you may not know about."

And then, in a moment, he was telling her about a very different sort of lover, Ricky. A much more compelling figure, one much more dominant, it seemed, than he, Adrien. And as the boy spoke, with a mixture of affection and awe and some fear, Miriam wondered how he'd handle it all, the confusions and complexities. He was twenty-one or so, and society had given him a *carte blanche* now to get in as much trouble as he wished. She caught up with her own puritanism then and realized that homophile dances were better than urinal meetings.

He was saying, "You mean a lot to me, in your way. It's good . . . to be able to talk freely with a woman this way." And then, in his formal politeness, "You must come to me too, if you ever need aid, or to talk, or whatever."

Another boy began to cry in a far-off room, and she sat up, saying, "I better see."

"Hey," he caught her, "the mask."

She removed it, eyeing it as if she had never seen it before, shivers striking her spine curiously. She threw on a robe and went in to see Jonathan. She picked him up, wondering about how much longer she could do this with his packed little weight. "What happened to my little boy, a bad dream?" The curly-headed boy brushed his face against hers in a sleepy nod, and with one hand she straightened out his blanket and pillow. "All right, you go back now and dream better. Okay?" She set him down, on his stomach, and he immediately got his thumb back into his mouth. The curls reaching down the back of his neck took her heart away, and she put her hand to them, instinctively. Finally he squirmed, and she stopped. Suddenly, for a second, she saw another boy lying there, with long muttonchop whiskers. It stunned her. She went out softly, leaving the door ajar, and returned to her bedroom.

"Something wrong?" said Adrien, pulling on his boots, looking up at her.

She had the power to shake her head no, that was all.

And when they kissed good night, she found herself hugging him to her tightly, almost crying. She turned and waved, in hiding.

The next day, at the institute, she plugged in her coffee pot and got our her diary, for an entry. A dramatic scenario for Dr. Levanda, starring Dr. L. and MS.

MS: Am I living over my head, Doctor? Are these good times for real? Am I covering up?

DR. L.: Obviously you have doubts. What are they?

77

MS: I'm not sure, exactly. Maybe I doubt my ability to have a good time.

DR. L.: Again. All right, why?

MS: Again, yes. Be quiet for a minute. Not enough love, or love lost too soon. Dad couldn't express it. Mother, who could, died too quickly. Stepmother practically drove me out of the house at age 13. Wld have been better for me if I had gone, too. But I was too young and, of crse, also too good. So I paid. Anyway, those years with Stan, when I thought *that* was a good time. Years of quiet subservience, trying to prop his ego up. Trying to be strong for *his* sake. And not being strong at all. But still trying to be good, as if somehow *that* would save me. But what that accomplished was to suppress my anger, my dissatisfaction, me. Doctor, can I be simple and say I despise trying to be a good girl? It's cost me so much.

DR. L.: Good for you. [*Smiling*] And those doubts?

MS: You don't shake your life or your shadow too easily. You don't wipe the slate clean of bad experience or lifelong habit by words or by piling new deeds over the old ones. The ghosts remain in the background. And they're admitted as evidence.

DR. L.: And the sex then? The good times? Are they for real?

MS: As real as the ghosts, I think. It's a contest, me versus old Ms. Superego herself.

DR. L.: What's the odds on the winner, would you say?

78

MS: That's what I like about you, Doctor, the
         way you've adapted to native ways, habits
         of thinking. How about fifty-fifty?

DR. L.: [*Laughing*] Now, who's playing the na-
         tive? Such optimism! Speaking realis-
         tically, how about the two-to-one, against
         this Miriam?

MS: [*Against her will*] Okay, accepted.
             One other thing. Are my new sex es-
         capades, or whims, dangerous? Habit-
         forming? Why, Doctor, do I do them?

DR. L.: You tell me.

MS: [*Pause*] In my attempt to beat the odds,
         which deep down I seem to know, I'm
         willing to try most anything, to take risks.
         Willing to extend the boundary of *what's
         possible*. And wanting very much to kick
         the Good Girl Habit, I may be especially
         inclined toward breaking my old taboos.
         Even risking a Bad Girl Habit. (Whatever
         that is.) Also, I'm willing to play it by ear,
         see what hurts or what pleases as it comes
         along. *Knowing, of course, that I can always
         come back here with you and talk about it.*

DR. L.: And your little play-acting? With your
         young man and his . . . props?

MS: My own nouns used against me, huh?
         Okay. What's wrong with props to add to
         one's enjoyment? Of course, the influ-
         ence of his medicine—his grass—helped
         my boldness. But isn't that good for me
         too?
             And remember one of your earliest
         questions, repeated again and again:
         "Are you hurting anyone by doing that?"
         So far as I know, I'm not. A prop is a
         prop is a prop, like you once said about

orgasm, when I tried to avoid *that* embarrassing item. If it's a crutch to sex, I'm against it, but if it's an aid, an impetus, why not?

By the way, a question for you: when do things get easier? So I can stop explaining myself here?

DR. L.:   How about next lifetime?

Miriam began then to sort out the contact sheets for the Show, with the help of her magnifying glass. Her mind drifted to the night before, the curiousness of that boy, her sudden mother's anxieties, the odd prop adding to her sensual pleasure, her orgasms. She drank coffee and looked at photos of merchants' faces and M.I.T. dormitories curving by the Charles. She recalled the first time she had ever heard that word used seriously, when Dr. Levanda asked, "And do you have orgasms?" Burning with embarrassment while the doctor looked at her evenly, matter-of-factly. Forcing her to think, and talk of that small, tucked-away secret, that taboo subject. Miriam was not one to parade her privacies in public, not one to consider herself *that* way. The patient but realistic doctor, dressed impeccably in a lovely skirt and blouse, helped change all that. Puncture her girlish piety.

Still, abstract talk was not quite as real as a young man with body control. After three meetings with Jamie, she was able to forget the earlier disastrous flops with two others; she marveled at that unlikely team of male Wisconsin body and female European mind, Jamie and Dr. Levanda. She had never thought it possible, never dreamed that those biological explosions, that sexual ease, could affect her consciousness so profoundly, could turn staid Miriam Scheinman into a version of sexhound, Lena's implied whore, a woman with a "reputation." Thirteen years with Stan, thirteen

80

long faithful years, had convinced her that, if not frigid, she was at least one dry fish in bed, unexcitable and unexciting, timid, near helpless with anxiety. It was an old story, really, those who don't have it, when they get it, value whatever it is much more than those who've had it all along—success, affection, sex, a house in the country.

She sipped more coffee. How nice to daydream in the midst of more practical work, with no telephones barging in, no domestic duties to fulfill. Her season of orgasms had indeed made her into a stronger, bigger woman. Selfless, martyred Miriam, the old Socialist, was learning about the benefits of selfishness. That stuff which she had taken for kid stuff, sex, was now reviving her adult life, giving her something to look forward to besides the work and the children. (And it had revived her photography too, hadn't it?) That rising orgasm of last night which had swept up her whole body and head. Orgasm, sexual gratification, was an Absolute. She smiled as that endless professorial refrain popped into her head about the "search for absolutes." For here it was, this cunt and brain connection, the only One going. But why didn't they inform undergraduates that orgasm was a real version of the Platonic Good? Wouldn't an old realist like Aristotle have described it that way, if he had written a *Poetics of Sex?*

Now, in room 416 of the institute, this memory sorting, with first Adrien and then Harry and Jamie dallying in her mind, provoked a certain rubbing pressure against her thigh, moving upward. The chair? Underpants trapped? Before she knew or could resist, however, she found her hand sliding down her jeans, to explore the pressure. Checking it out furtively, almost. She began to touch and rub there, opening the zipper and moving her fore- and middle fingers along the white cotton. (What was silk like?) Her eyes opened and closed slowly, and she seemed to breathe in more deeply, and somewhere in her head she took a perverse comfort in sitting there like that, deliberately going ahead with her grown-up naughtiness. All the years in which she had resisted stubbornly, dating back to adolescence, when she had sought to be "above" her common friends, and extending into her frustrated marriage, when she worked it out in work, or closed it off, now were being avenged with these rather regular masturbations. Thinking how this made thirty-something over the past year, and imagining Jamie beginning to move her and Harry's tongue and Adrien coming closer, she brought herself to a slow, deep pleasure, biting down on her lower lip and almost tasting blood. Near the end she thought of those women in Bergman films who masturbated, and how she had never felt or understood all that; and how she'd look in celluloid, sitting in her Radcliffe chair, surrounded by her work and gazing out toward Brattle Street and not bothering to lock the door and giving in to herself and massaging herself and fingering herself. Knowing, too, that later she'd feel no guilt about it. The pictures by Walker Evans on the wall wavered and expanded beautifully.

Afterward she got up, straightened her jeans, put certain contact sheets into manila folders and then into a ribbon-tied accordion portfolio, and departed from the office. In the elevator, Harriet Gershorn, a professor of classics, smiled. "Have a *productive* day?" The favorite institute adjective. "Not bad," replied Miriam, noting Harriet's briefcase and wanting to tell her how grandly she had wasted it and then culminated it. "You do look particularly serene, if I may say so," put in Harriet, smiling. "I'm slightly jealous." "Yes," agreed Miriam, "it had its productive side."

At four o'clock she took Jonathan to Hancock tot-

82

ground, where her friend Elizabeth Morrison had taken Rosie and where Jon's best pal, Margaret, six, would play with him. She loved it at that time of day, late crisp afternoon, sun slanting auburn, walking with her son, who was explaining very seriously about the first baseball game of the year that day in school. (She was sure he'd be a ballplayer of some sort.) In ten minutes they were at the playground, and Jon, in his little mac, immediately ran to his sister, almost knocked her over (purposely) with his hug, and then ran off with Margie (hard *g*), leaving Rosie trailing in tears before she returned to a newly made friend.

Elizabeth Morrison waved to her from the green wooden bench, and Miriam walked toward her, already feeling good from her friend's presence. Slender, in her thirties, freckled, with horn-rims, Elizabeth was for Miriam the Emily Dickinson of Cambridge. Plain on the outside, she emoted on the inside and wrote poetry which she showed to no one, with one exception: she had twice shown poems to Miriam. They were a surprise. It was the combination of logical mind and narrow but precise feeling that brought to mind Emily D.; it was a poetry of need, not custom, pruned of florid landscaping and new-fashioned "gut" displaying. Miriam had tried to get her to send the poems out, but she couldn't take the rejection slips; she had received two, several years back, and she had stopped writing for a whole year afterward. "I hear that Jonathan was a great star at Peabody today," Elizabeth announced, brown freckles letting in pink color, a trace of stammer in her voice. "Have you heard about it yet?" "My son inform me of his heroics? Never. His mother has to hear about the baseball season beginning." They sat down, and Elizabeth proceeded to tell the dramatic story—related secondhand, through daughter Margaret, Jonathan-adorer—of Jonathan's exploits in open classroom hour, turning Vietnam into an antiwar puppet show. ("Do you think that mime troupe could use him?")

Miriam looked up and found her little director arranging with Margie an obstacle course for the jungle gym. She viewed him with something deeper than pride: fear approaching fright. The boy was too closely tied to Miriam in blood and genes; at the age of six his instincts and imagination were developed to the point where *Miriam saw herself there*, in the small, well-built body; and the vision or clairvoyance known to mothers terrified her. For she saw there, already at that incredibly young age, the same proclivity for fits of deep introspection (or would those flights from reality eventually produce originality?); the sure uncanny feel for adults, knowing how they could and should be related to, on what level of trust, irony, dissembling, indifference; and the enormous amount of emotion and trust he invested, so that disappointment or betrayal crushed him for days.

Elizabeth touched Miriam's arm suddenly, indicating the sliding pond, and Miriam bounded up, calling out, "Jon, Jon!" She ran for him and the little redheaded boy he was bullying at the top of the ladder. When she got there, the boy was perched at the top in terror, and Miriam climbed the steps to retrieve him. Jonathan stood there too, possessed, staring directly at his mother, the old wildness and anger flaring in his eyes. The son who had suffered through his parents' battles, their furious chaos, and was now paying them and the world back for his fate. A stare of challenge and accusation: she had betrayed him with her attention elsewhere and her personal confusion! It all took fifteen or twenty seconds, and then, saying, "Are you crazy, Mom—I was just trying to teach him!" he was shooting down the slide, squealing as if nothing had happened. Miriam, in a daze, lifted the other boy in her arms, saying something or other to him, thinking, *He knows what he's doing, he consciously wants to be better, he simply can't control these outbursts.* Would he ever? she wondered, near tears herself, remembering those other symptoms of regression and withdrawal at age five. Knowing again that if it hadn't been for the children's increasing pain and disturbance, she never would have mustered the courage to split from Stan. Slowly she carried the freckle-faced boy down the steps, soothing him, the scars of Jonathan seizing her.

She sat the boy down at the merry-go-round and returned to Elizabeth on the bench. Getting a grip on herself, she said, "My little Napoleon on the march again, I'll brain him one day. Thank God for your daughter, my dear, she civilizes the little monster. Now, where were we? How's teaching, by the way?"

At Miriam's strategy, Elizabeth began to talk about her teaching, at the Commonwealth School in Boston. The talk, boring as it was, calmed her, as it always did, here in the small park in the late afternoon, with amber light falling through the trees and the smells of ice cream and early lilac scenting the air. With her friend, a thrush, turning up to sing for her. In a few minutes Miriam was able to concentrate on the present again. Several mothers were about, at the new iron swings, the sandbox, and the wooden merry-go-round. It reminded Miriam of the subtle change shown toward her by several of these women since her divorce. She suddenly wasn't one of them; it was not 1972 but 1843 and she had donned a scarlet *A*. She had tested her perception, to see if it was paranoia, by asking Elizabeth, who, after stammering around, confirmed the new coolness. She no longer wore the team uniform, CAMBRIDGE MARRIEDS, that was all. It was enough, however. Oh well, respectability had prisoners on both sides of the gender. Still, being here at the old familiar post of the past four or five years filled Miriam

85

with a sense of yearning as well as of freedom. And even her friend's singing, her current talking high, the reddening spirit in her pallid face, had an edge of sadness to them, because Miriam also knew that in the presence of her stolid, dull, lawyer husband, Elizabeth was no longer a thrush but a stuffed owl, a frustrated and spiritless mute. But that was another story. At least, unlike the other ladies guarding the park, Elizabeth was beyond the prison of social custom and the cell of woman jealousy. In fact, after the breakup, Elizabeth had become, if anything, more kindly, more sensitive. It gave the present routine its old full flavor and soothing power, to remember that. "Uh oh, I think negotiations have fallen through with your other child," Elizabeth interrupted her own story and Miriam's musing. "Thank you, my dear, I'll lock her up for this, I promise. Hey, Rosie, hey, toughie!" And she ran to her, grateful for the more ordinary child she was.

At 9 p.m. that evening, the last Thursday in March, Julia Havens, the high-school girl from around the corner, came to baby-sit for a few hours while Miriam went to visit Kelly Monaghan, who had called earlier. Walking over there, Miriam realized that visiting alone at night, with women or men, was itself almost worth the price of separation.

To Miriam's surprise, that sloppy, denim-shirted girl of the women's group lived in a lovely house in a fashionable section of town, off Irving Street. "How do you manage this?" Miriam asked, upon being shown into the large, well-furnished living room and comparing it with her own graduate-student-type flat (at thirty-four).

"Oh, the pad? It's my old man's. We've been here just a little more than a coupla months. You'll meet him later on, maybe. He's out giving a seminar now."

86

Miriam continued to be surprised. "I don't quite get it . . . How old are you, anyway?" "Nineteen. Well, in two weeks to be exact." No, she hadn't been mistaken, Kelly was a kid. Miriam sat down and back in a modern black-leather chair. "What's he teach? And where?" Her guess was the Adult Education Center, where the main credential was desire. "Philosophy," Kelly said. "He's doing a seminar on Ayer and the logical positivists. Want something to drink?" She looked back, through her long red hair. "Or would you rather smoke?" "Some Scotch might be nice. With water." Still taken aback by the girl's poise and the facts. Going into the kitchen, Kelly called out for Miriam to put on the stereo if she wished.

Miriam stood and slowly walked around the room. Expensive, modern, tasteful. A working fireplace, a fire-red Scandinavian rug, good Danish couch and deep leather chairs, a Bentwood rocker, several filled bookcases, a fine component system. Miriam took the drink from Kelly's hand, saying, "Looks like someone's been shopping." "Yeah, we just went out one day and bought out the Workbench, DR, and Upper Story— bang, just like that!" A low light voice, not much of an accent, fine fair skin, and that red hair. "Like rock?" "Don't really know it." "Here, try this. Steve Miller Band. They're pretty heavy." She put the record on. Miriam sipped and asked, "Where's he teach, did you say? And what's all this . . ." "All this *about*?" Kelly laughed, her large bosom shaking in the denim shirt tied-up, showing midriff, her green eyes animated. She towered above Miriam, at five foot ten or more, a large Irish Rita Hayworth. Before sitting, Miriam lowered Steve Miller. "Oh yeah, my old man," the girl began, seating herself and throwing her legs over the arms of the chair. "Teaches philosophy over at B.U. In fact, he holds some sort of important chair, in 'moral philosophy,' if you can believe *that*." She drank easily. "His name is Tyson Rawlingson, heard of him?" Miriam shook her head, intrigued. "He's kinda well-known, I think. Here." From the white bookshelf she pulled out two books and gave them to Miriam. *The Evolution of Moral Philosophy* and *Three Greek Philosophers*. "Impressive," commented Miriam, looking at the Oxford University Press books. She asked, "Read them?" Kelly smiled. "I read the section on Hume, yeah. He's a ball, my favorite philosopher. Now old Immanuel K., that's a whole other bag." Miriam drank now. Kelly returned the books to the shelf and said, "We started seeing each other in the fall, and landed here about February or so, after Ty split from the family." "Whose family?" "His. It was a real hassle there for a while."

"What do you mean?" Kelly drank. "Oh, I left out a step. *Mrs.* Rawlingson. *Evelyn*. You know, I actually got to dig her. She's *okay,* I've come to see. Just didn't want to give up Ty too easily." She paused. "I guess I don't blame her. If I were her, I mean. With four kids and all." "Oh," observed Miriam, "four kids?" "Yeah, it was a regular nuclear family, kids and all. Just like old times. Don't worry, I don't take the credit for breaking them up. Ty's assured me on that point. The marriage was on the rocks before this Kelly came along." "Where *did she* come along?" "Oh, I had Philosophy I with him at B.U. It was the only hour I could sit still without going crazy. You know what most classes are like—they suck. But Ty's a great teacher, even when he's putting on a show. He relates the stuff to *real life,* and boy"— she tapped her temple—"he's got the marbles." She turned sideways and shifted her feet the other way. She asked, "Ever live with a philosophy prof?" Miriam smiled and shook her head. "It's a trip, believe me." Miriam believed her. "How old is your friend, by the way?" "Forty-seven or forty-nine, I forget. Right around the old half-century mark!" She brandished her glass, in a toast to age. *See, Mir, everyone has their younger playmates.* "I kid him about it too.

"Anyway," she went on, "I dug what you were saying the other night. I'm going to tell you something, but keep it under your hat. Lena has her other side, though she's careful about letting on. Actually . . ." She put her forefinger to her lips, and with her legs tossed over the chair that way, she looked two years younger than her almost-nineteen. "Actually, she's *not* so careful about letting on. It turns out she's a les, or bi anyway, and she put the make on me the night after I gave my own little spiel. Told me what a great talk it was, how the movement really depended on kids my age, how my 'consciousness' was *really* way out front—oh, she laid a whole flattery rap on me. Then, before I knew it—we were in her living room, see?—she had her hand on my leg and was asking if I had ever made it with a chick. I said yeah, I had, so what? So she'd like to make it with me. Bam! I said, No dice, madam, *not at home.*" Kelly shook her head in disbelief. "Know what she did? Started telling me how my 'consciousness' was still 'arrested' in certain areas! Oh, that went over big, I can tell you. I told her I didn't give a *fuck* about my consciousness, it was my body that was at stake! And I wasn't interested in putting that body, sweetheart, into her hands, or hers into mine. She said I didn't understand, and all the time sort of breathing into my ear, or tit. Finally I told her to fuck off, and if she didn't, I'd belt her one. Well, you shoulda seen the next number she pulled—moved away and started spieling me about how I wasn't really the proper one after all to start up the campus movement in the Northeast. Didn't have the right 'attitudes,' yet. Cheesus, what a hypocrite! That's why when you challenged her the other night, I kept saying, Right on, baby, right on! To myself, that is. With chicks like that around, the movement is going to get a bad name. And some of those girls are really just the opposite, the best around. Like old Dody there, she's o-n-e f-i-n-e chick. Know her?" Miriam shook her head and finished her drink.

As the girl went on to talk about the changes in her life since she had become "Ty's roomie," Miriam was impressed with the mixture of poise and girlish ways in Kelly; by the 180-degree shifts in her life (her last boy friend was a rock musician) and her casual and willing acceptance of such changes; by the startling fact of this teenage girl living with this eminent man and father of four! What was interesting, also, was that Kelly's attractiveness grew rather than diminished as the hour and a half passed; in spite of the actressy gestures she put on as she talked. She would rock her shoulders sexylike and quote a line from a Bette Midler song; or wink and sing from Janis's "Mercedes-Benz" (in relation to *why* she decided to move in with Ty); of course, all this done with a sense of mockery, at the material and at her own participation in it, or aspiration toward it ("I'd give anything to be a rock singer!"), that was totally captivating to Miriam. Tyson had himself a real package here; the only question was how long the package would hang around a comfortable Cambridge apartment. And whether it was worth giving up the continuity for four to six months of that package. Maybe it was. And maybe four months could stretch to four years.

What she talked about—hands gesturing, body moving—was how different it was being a mistress or wife. "Not that I'm forced to do anything I don't want to. Cooking, for example. I couldn't cook a bean when I started out, but Ty is super at it. I sort of just hung around the kitchen with him, out of boredom and maybe embarrassment, and picked up things here and there. And as for cleaning, he has a woman come in and do it. He hates the cocktail circuit, there's no sweat about that. So it's not any of the routine gigs of a

90

housewife that I'm involved with. It's just the fact of living with one dude all the time that I'm not quite used to. I'm used to my freedom, baby, dig?" Roll of the shoulder. "Once I asked him if I could go out with an old friend, would he mind? He said no, he wouldn't, but if I slept over with him, he would mind, yes. Jealous. You know, *I dug that.* Yeah, I liked that note, to tell you the truth. Knew where he stood, without moralizing bullshit or big sells . . ." She shrugged. "But most of my friends bore him silly. They don't dig books, really. And he's not interested in the 'kid scene,' as he calls it. Just this kid." Her thumb in her full chest. "So I don't see them too often." She paused, and said in a new tone, "I thought me and you might be friends."

"I'm flattered," Miriam said. And, "Why's he with you, if I can ask that?" Adding, "Or you with him?"

Kelly smoked, reflected, looked prettier than ever with that ebullient face and wild red hair. Already Miriam had a partial answer, before the words came. "We get along, I think. I like to play, feel loose, have a good time, and so does he, once I get him going. I make him feel young, he says." She shrugged. "But he gets me going too. He has all this extra energy, once he's in a good mood. It's my job to get him there. Especially when he's down from Evelyn and the kids' pressure." She paused and thought. "It's so different for both of us. I've never been with a man with real work to do every day, with an orderly routine. It's cool not to have to wonder what you're going to do this weekend, next summer, what you're going to 'major' in, or read, or be. Cheesus. Get what I mean? Ty has his own questions, he's anything but dogmatic, but they're different sorts. And I dig it. I been on the loose for almost two years now, and I guess I'm kinda tired. I been truckin' a lot, you know."

No, Miriam didn't know. And so Kelly told her

about Kabul, London, Vancouver, San Francisco, Baja. Miriam now saw where the poise came from, why it was authentic. Teenagers were a different sort, these days. The Female of the species anyway. And where would Jon and Rosie visit as teenagers—Venus, Mars?

"Hey, what about men?" Kelly asked suddenly. "Have things really changed that much between us and them since your time?"

"My dear, please, I'm not an octogenarian yet." Miriam raised her eyes in mock seriousness. She considered, and replied, "Yes, relations have changed, sure. But not because of *them*—because of *us*. We're the ones who are going through the changes; look at yourself. Especially in contrast to my friends when I was eighteen or twenty. It's you, really, who have forced women like me into changing . . . you who are pushing all of us up against the wall . . . you who are the new species, kid. Making us all come out of our closets, or caskets, with your new . . . boldness." She winked, though she was serious. "Especially sexual boldness."

Kelly stood and did a whirl, turning it into a quick, exaggerated, grind-and-rock step—breasts jiggling, bare belly moving, the edge of her ass line slipping into view. Thank God, she, Miriam, wasn't a man, facing all that. Kelly ceased and asked seriously, "And how does this 'new species' affect the men?"

Miriam smiled. "Oh, it depends on the man, I think. Though for sure one type of man will be clearly threatened by it—the more settled-in creature, the Victorian-Puritan, the less secure, whatever his age. Aren't there already, just recently, many more cases of impotence and homosexuality at the shrinks? The negative-fallout side."

Kelly raised her forefingers like a cowgirl pointing a pair of six-shooters. "Hey, I know where you're coming from. About a month or so ago I was with a young dude—let's keep this between us—and did he ever have a bad sex trip. Not only couldn't he get it up, but he thought that it was probably a permanent affliction and that he might be gay. He started crying, right there in my arms! Yeah, I see what you mean about *power. Ours.* In the midst of trying to break out of prison—how odd, I never thought of it that way!" She stopped in her excited tracks and asked, "And what else are we besides more powerful?"

"Oh, freer women, better women, maybe. Those that survive and make it through with their good feelings intact. Those who keep their . . . sense of delicacy about the whole matter. The delicacy to realize how potent, or destructive, the boldness can be, as well as liberating."

"Responsibility along with the liberation, huh?"

"Something like that, yes."

She paused. "Yeah, I'll buy that. Sure. Tell me more about that plus side."

"Well, it's sort of nice to be sexual, as well as frilly, maternal, teasing, moral, spiritual, and whatever else we're supposed to be. I'm sure that we've helped to make them, the men, into hunters with one purpose in mind as much as they've made us into the prey, the willing prey. No, it's great, lovely, to be able to make the pass for a change, or to look men over the way they do us. Makes it more interesting all the way round. Of course, I haven't *quite* gotten to that stage, yet."

Kelly laughed. "Well, I have, Octo-G, I can tell you that. But I'm a little kooky, you know that."

"Oh, not kooky. Just way out front, that's all. Ahead of the herd—but don't worry, they'll follow along soon enough if they're not there yet, I know I'm in line myself."

Kelly, sitting, asked, "What about you—what do you want?"

She shrugged. "I don't quite know. It's like being nineteen again, I'm a *child* in terms of my emotions. I

93

want everything I see, and I'm curious about everything. Everything has suddenly become *possible*, and that's been so new for me. Thank God for the kids and the photography, otherwise whoosh!" She gestured upward as if to fly away. "But you know what?" She stood up and pointed her finger at Kelly. *"You* ought to lead that campus movement, Lena or no Lena. You've got a lot on the ball, Kelly, why not spread it around? And here we are, both complaining about Lena's way of doing things; well, why don't we—or you—do something about it? Think about it. If I didn't have some children and photography on my mind, maybe I'd be out there with you. As it is, you do it. Besides, I've got too much trouble just figuring out my good times myself—you can't expect me to go public about them."

Kelly laughed, jumped up, did another little rock movement, thought, said, "That's a nice number, thanks. Yeah, I'll buzz it around my bonnet some. Even talk to little old sugar daddy about it. He's very cool about getting me to do things on my own. And you know something? I kinda figured you were digging your life, having good times, from the way you were talking the other night. Nice and easy like, no defense razzmatazz." She buzz-sawed her hands. "Yeah, that's a *boss idea*, Miriam, thanks. Get me active again." Roll of shoulders.

Miriam got a kick out of the phrase, and in a few moments got a chance to see the other boss, in person. Only Tyson Rawlingson, when he arrived, was very unlike the mental image (tall, lean, athletic, smooth, one of the Olympian middle-aged) Miriam had formed of him.

Tyson was a short, nervous man, dressed neutrally (a dull striped tie, corduroy jacket), a cigarette smoker; the face was oval and rather plain, tending toward the puffy side in the chin and cheeks; his sandy hair was thinning perceptibly. "Tyson Rawlingson," he said, nodding, pleasant, somewhat harried, in fatigue an old man indeed. "Hi, love," said Kelly, greeting him with a warm kiss on the cheek. "I'll get you a drink—vodka tonic?" "Thanks," he said, loosening his tie and dropping into the chair. As soon as he did, he seemed to hear the music, rock, and jumped back up. "Godawful sound for more than two minutes, isn't it? Mind if I change it?" Miriam shook her head. He moved spryly to the record collection and chose one. Bach? His trousers, Miriam noted, were cuffed and wide-bottomed in the old fashion; Kelly had herself a Prufrock. Sitting again, fighting his distraction, Tyson said to Miriam, "You're the photographer, aren't you? Kelly came back the other night raving about you. And she's not one to rave, really." Kelly returned now, handed the drink to Tyson, brushed his forehead as if it were filled with a mop of hair, sat on the arm of his chair, and slid her arm tenderly around his neck. "How'd it go, love?" After his long sip he half-shrugged, saying, "Not bad, I guess. These evening things are getting a bit beyond me, though." The voice was low, and the accent slightly English. Miriam, seeing his semi-exhaustion, stood. "I better go." "Oh? Sorry about that," he said politely. "I looked forward to meeting you. Why don't you come to dinner sometime? Kelly, why don't you fix it up with Miriam?"

"That would be nice. Don't stand, no need."

Kelly walked her to the door. "Too bad, poor Daddy is really pooped, isn't he?" "That's all right. I like him. Invite me to dinner. I'll come." "Good, I'll call you. I should study myself now—probably won't, though." She winked at Miriam. "I have too much fun cheering up my sweet daddy." She kissed Miriam on the cheek. "Thanks for coming. Peace."

Walking home in the evening air, Miriam thought about how the times had changed; about education provided by great difference (youth and age, here); about the show of mature warmth suddenly revealed by Kelly, there at the end. A surprise. The girl was all right. Better than that, even. Imagine having all that coolness—along with the warmth and humor and looks—going for you at nineteen! Two weeks short, yet. Yes, girls were getting bolder, and the results were interesting. Miriam smiled, jealous. The walk from the girl's house was ten minutes, and Miriam felt uplifted from the visit. A visit impossible in the old days. Too informal and easy. She paid Julia for the two and a half hours ($3.75), thanked her, and was glad that she lived only around the corner and could walk home alone. For a moment, standing alone in the living room, Miriam was culture-shocked by the return to secondhand sofa and odd old chairs, bedraggled rugs, smallish rooms. Could she get her own sugar daddy to chic things up? When Stan had left, she had given him gratis his "adult" furniture to take with him, and turned her living room back to a version of grad-student shabbiness, in homage to unbourgeois youth and romantic bohemianism. Stubborn and childish, she knew, but she couldn't help starting over that way. Couldn't help loving her secondhand mess and tat-tered chaos as if it were an orphaned childhood. It was time to change, no?

Miriam drew herself a hot bath and lingered in it for twenty delicious minutes. Except for one dark memory which flashed across her mind. *She was running a hot bath for herself, with Jon sleeping over at a friend's and Rosie, two, trailing about after her. The telephone in her bedroom rang and she went for it. A friend making arrangements for the day-care center. Suddenly, a barely audible splash . . . a thought . . . Miriam jumped up and dashed. Her worst fear confirmed . . . Rosie face down in the steaming bath . . . Grabbing her up without thinking or feeling, turn-ing her upside down and slapping her back over and over*

96

until Rosie began to cough up water and vomit. Then she was breathing in and out again, and crying. Miriam carried her into her double bed . . . patted down her warm red body with a thick towel . . . found her favorite blanket . . . got rid of her phone call, and lay down alongside her tiny mortal daughter . . . For a half hour she lay there, saying over and over, "It's all right now, pumpkin. Momma's here and everything's all right." Feeling the little girl touch her sweater and cuddle, and seeing pink color return to her face. Finally, Rosie raised herself and, brushing hair from her forehead, asked, "Can we do a color book now, Momma?" Miriam nodded and hugged her, her own heart beginning to beat more regularly at last.

Out of the bath now, she got into bed with her favorite book, *A Vision of Paris.* A large square book of the photographs of Eugène Atget, another photographer she loved. (With fragments of prose from *Remembrance of Things Past.*) These photographs of Paris around the turn of the century and in the twenties had so taken Miriam that she had done a terrible thing. She took the book out of the Cambridge Public Library, and told them, after three weeks, that she had lost it. They assessed it at twenty dollars, and she wrote the check out at the wooden desk, hot with guilt. That copy, and the one in Widener, were the only ones she had ever seen; a standing order with the Strand Book Store in New York had gone unanswered for nearly eighteen months before the drastic action had been taken. The book still contained the check-out card on the inside back cover (f.914.436 At29v/Atget/A Vision of Paris, with the due date, May 7, 1972) and the library's cellophane jacket cover. Just in case Strand's ever came through.

Now, in bed, she turned those intimate pages, starting with the picture of Atget at the beginning, taken by Berenice Abbott. That legendary picture, taken nine days before Atget died; when the American lady came to show it to him, it was too late. She did manage, however, to save his mostly unknown plates and thus rescue from the ashcans great photography. The frontispiece picture of Atget was one of the three or four most moving pictures she had ever seen, not because of the legend but because of the pose, the face, the color. All you had to do was to look at the stooped old man sitting on the high stool, the body wrapped in a wool overcoat that came straight from Gogol's clerk, the profiled face weathered ghostly, the forehead furrowed, and the thin hair trailing like wings on the back of his head, the whole effect—face, coat, bent pose—of simplicity, poverty, unashamed defeat and unabashed mortality, shown in various shades of brown—all conspired to move you as much as any picture or art work you'd ever see.

In a moment she cleared her eyes, and went on to the remaining variety in the book, pictures of the Paris he lived in all his life, photos of buildings, monuments, side streets, cafés, parks, flower sellers, shop fronts, doorways, rooftops, the river front, bridges, ladies shopping, newspaper readers, children playing, courtesans, voluptuous residences, stairways, bedrooms, sculptures, latticework, railroad tracks, five versions of water lilies, trees, roads, newspaper and flower stands, fresh-produce districts, trams pulled by horses, corset and wig shops, cobbled squares. No attempt to camouflage or euphemize any section or class of life. At the next-to-last picture, a 4 by 6 shot of a narrow canal lined with small sailboats tipping sideways on the muddy banks or in the water, she picked her head up, terribly moved.

What was unusual, even extraordinary, was the slow revelation of beauty emerging in all those pictures of ordinary things and ordinary people, objects that you've glanced at and passed by thousands of times daily. What stirred Miriam so was that beauty of spirit, that theme of underlying exaltation that traveled beneath and apart from the formal excellence and external harmonies. An underlying spirituality through all the ordinariness, caught by Atget's camera eye, that made Miriam cry. Or was it simply the evidence of things passing by, into extinction? (Her own extinction? The waste of thirteen years?)

She treasured this powerful feeling, hoarded it like a bird hoarding its nest; yet it hurt her too, embarrassed her, shamed her. Lying there, surrounded by her movable friends—old hurricane lamp, threadbare brown blanket, ragged bookshelves, and old paperbacks, novels, social philosophy, art books, books that had started out in Cleveland Heights childhood (Bronc Burnett sports stories by Wilfred McCormick, *Jo's Boys* by Louisa May Alcott, *All-Of-A-Kind Family*) traveled to Hyde Park and then to Ann Arbor, where they were added to, and continued to proliferate in Cambridge; paperback eyes and ears from four cities, witnesses to how many Miriam Scheinman moods or lives?—lying there, she tried to understand the curious waves of feeling sweeping her, started by this old man's pictures of Paris so many decades ago. She knew, to begin with, that not since the first year of knowing Stan, during those charmed months of her twenty-one-year-old innocence, naïveté, idealism, soaring spirits—framed by Ann Arbor elms and mountains in Aix-en-Provence and Montenegro—not since those months of light-years ago in her life had this feeling existed; this sense of enormous tenderness, spiritual affection, openness to life. Was it love? Did you have to be innocent to experience it? Did one feel it, in adult life, only through art or work? Was it pre-eminently a woman's feeling? or desire? or need? Was it that the men friends she had now were short of it, or without the desire? Was it that she, Miriam, would never possess it again in life? She looked again at the photos . . . but Atget could do only so much. He couldn't fill her heart's great need.

Was her mind too cluttered with everyday duties, with too much intellect and knowing? and her emotions too scarred by experience, for the sense of complete openness and acceptance of life—the way Jonathan could do it, say—to bloom once again? She didn't know. She absolutely didn't know. Nor did she know what the others felt. What she did know was that Atget produced, and what once, in her life, she had felt; and she knew that she missed having it in her life now, and blocked herself from thinking about it, too painful. Momentarily, Harry came to mind, because he stirred that impulse but never fulfilled it, and it made her angry, angry and frustrated. She realized through this half hour of reflection that she had been staring at the blue baseball cap hanging on the corner of a bureau mirror. The Indian cap of her tomboy youth, which she had promised Jonathan he could have, once it fit; however, he felt very ambivalent about betraying the Red Sox, and in the end had refused her. ("Nah, you can be an Indian, Mom.")

She got up, went to the bathroom and washed her face, drank a thimbleful of whiskey, and returned to bed. She mustn't lose anything, not her yearnings, not her memories (even of losses), not her new hopes. She must gain, build, add to; somehow connect the old Miriam to the new one. With her will, and with her camera. Even if it scared her, this trying to make a bridge in uncharted territory. After a while memory began to mingle with dream.

She was on her first two-wheeler, named Champion after Gene Autry's horse, pedaling slowly, with her father right there, to preserve her balance. It was a serene bicycle ride around the block of small private houses, back again to their place. And as a reward for completing the ride without once falling, Dad surprised her with her own baseball cap! The pigtailed girl jumped for joy at the blue cap with red C (and Indian face) on it, not allowing Dad to set it on her properly. Her cap! Too big for her just now, her vision blocked out, but that was okay. She hugged Dad tight, real tight, as he crouched for her (she couldn't get over how short he could get that way). She couldn't wait to get into the house to get the baseball bat and glove and maybe play on the vacant lot with Jason, her brother, and Dad. Amid the umbrellas and galoshes and shoes, she found the pair of bats, the pale-yellow Louisville Slugger and the handle-taped, light, softball bat. She had just managed to get the gloves when Jason appeared, two years older at fourteen, and they began their regular property battle. Dad settled matters by proposing a bat and glove each, and he'd carry the balls. "See?" she said to Jason, springing her cap on him, though she was careful about letting it drop over her eyes and shame her. While he drooled in surprise, she made for the door with Dad.

She never made it. A jerk of her shoulder, a familiar smell of onion or garlic, and her stepmother said, "Where do you think you're going, young lady? Are you still trying to be a boy? Put that down immediately! Lew, are you starting this all over again? Do you hear me, Lew; don't just stand there looking dumb!" And there was Dad, gaunt, shamed, betrayed, trapped on the porch he had built with his own hands. The loser of too many battles by then, he approached his daughter and whispered privately, "You listen to Helen now, okay? And we'll do something later, okay, Miry?" As he was forced outside by the woman's force, with the bats and gloves and Jason, she missed him terribly. *She kept her tears back as Helen turned her about with a sharp pinch on the shoulder. "Wanting to be a boy, shame on you. You can't, don't you understand that. Here, I'll teach you," and with that, she pulled the cap off, and put on over her head . . . a catcher's mask. "You go over there and keep that on now!" Miriam strained to see through the thick wires, the mask weighing heavier and heavier—* She woke in the darkness, her face pushed up against the intricate bamboo latticework of her headboard, shaking. She sat with her knees pulled up to her chin, a little girl again, in darkness, in grief, seeing the ghost of her father adjusting that cap as if he were real, right there, and missing him desperately, desperately.

The dreamlike details of adolescence had returned like a boomerang of pain, now, twenty years later. It wasn't fair!

Finally she got out of bed, shivering. She took two sleeping pills, knowing she couldn't afford just now to remember. But when could you? she wondered, slipping back into that dreadful bed. But she could record it later, in her journal. And that made things better, easier. Oh Esther, she wondered aloud to her doctor in Tel Aviv, now I'll have to explain catcher's masks to you, along with other kinds!

The dinner party that she attended with Harry on Saturday night, forty-eight hours after Atget, was pleasant, good fun in lots of ways. The guests were intellectuals, mostly from Harvard; the conversation okay, if predictable; the dinner itself superb, a homemade crab soup followed by marinated fresh fish and asparagus in hollandaise sauce, and then cold fruit dessert with thick cream. Nathalie Reibman was a first-rate cook, when she wanted to be. Harry, in Mexican floral shirt and suède bell-bottoms (given by Miriam, based upon Adrien's velveteens), stood out amid the standard formal uniforms of ties and shirts; he was also handsome and lively, not crazy the way he could get, just lively, funny. Miriam, in a yellow blouse and black skirt, liked the host Reibmans very much. Arthur was dark, handsome, with a hawk's nose and graying black hair, a full professor of politics (Harvard) at age thirty-three (now thirty-seven), with a saintly soul and a clean democratic socialist past (no sectarianist diseases, thought Miriam proudly). He cut bread gently, loved old maps (like Miriam's father), still preferred baseball to football, and offered his original opinions without jargon or machismo. He was a find. Nathalie, who had found him, had meanwhile emerged attractively from her own cocoon of Jewish family and Ph.D. mentality. Blooming in her mid-thirties, she had taken up writing, returned to the cello of childhood, and seemed to get better-looking every few months. She dressed half Old World (wool suits and skirts), half Harvard Square hip (bright sash belts, balloon cuffs and hip-hugger trousers), and she reminded Miriam and Harry of some Biblical girl. Though when Harry would compliment Nathalie this way, she protested vigorously, "Oh, here we go again, who am I supposed to be tonight? Esther by the well, maybe? When does Miriam get to play a part?" "My dear," said Miriam, "I'm straight New Testament. Sister Mary Magdalene, perhaps."

What Miriam felt during the evening, beneath the friendly times and easy cordiality, and taking in stride the usual two or three thorns that prick at such events, what she felt was a nagging sense of repetition, an unstimulating repeat performance. Miriam would have much preferred either dining alone with the Reibmans, where the chance for real talk was good, or else seeing slides of their last Israel trip or Scottish highlands walk. The conversation about McGovern's failures and the upcoming Watergate committee hearings was okay, and shrewd enough, though all from the relatively same liberal point of view, and it was as if the scene were a still photograph of a not very interesting event taken years ago, a daguerreotype pulled out of the drawer, musty, shown before, in need of replacement. True, the talk was different, some of the people were new, but the photo really was the same. Immediately she daydreamed of an alternate evening, looking once again at favorite photographs (of Dorothea Lange, Margaret Bourke-White, Barbara Morgan), developing her own prints, touching up pictures, letting images and ideas flow into her head while doing the boring, lonely, evening darkroom work. But she had warned herself against this dreaming habit of hers, and put away her present fantasy for real life. She tried her best to animate the photograph and turned to the nice lawyer with the fine long face who worked at City Hall. He was pleasant and, in his way, informative; a good citizen. Okay, she listened.

She did do one thing to amuse herself at the affair—was it to amuse? she wondered—committed a small naughtiness that was new for her. She had worn an old skirt she had shortened, and at one point, she tested her lure power. The fish was a tall intellectual pickerel, the distinguished husband of a fortyish, book-reviewing lady who laid down the law on books the way a henpecked judge ruled over separating couples, say, or a schoolmistress taught arithmetic to a slow third-grade class. So Miriam, sitting next to the smart owlish fellow, who was talking about Hannah Arendt's theory of evil in relation to the Nixon bunch, held her re-filled cup and allowed her short skirt to hike itself upward a few inches. She was sure that from his angle a bit of red underpants flashed, surrounded by lots of white thigh. He talked on, seemingly oblivious. "Could you hand me that ashtray?" she pursued, getting him to turn away momentarily, which gave her time to slide one leg away from the other, and angle her pelvis back and toward his eye. He smiled at her politely, "As I was saying," he continued, spinning on, "it does seem to me that Arendt's position here in regard to the banality of evil is now beginning to be seen in better perspective . . ." It struck Miriam for a split second that she might just try to put her fingers down there, to see if that would get his attention where she wanted it, for spite. Cerebral, smart, henpecked Sid Klein had long, long ago traded in the public interest for the public. Was it all silly baby wickedness? *Épater le bourgeois?* Or did girls like Miriam expect more from people some five thousand years after it all began? The way she was no longer content with just a history, just a cultural theory, if it didn't take into account eighty-seven different fields of insight? She smiled at her own serious thought, plus her child's desire to be naughty. (Would Lena add this to "reputation"?)

She suddenly felt badly and wanted to apologize to Sid Klein.

But it was too late, he was gone for a drink with his wife, and in his place now was one Sonny Goodson, alert to that red bait, she knew. Embarrassed, she crossed her legs casually and listened, confused. In his thirties, trimmed beard on angular face, wearing a fashionable leather jacket and a medallion on his chest, Goodson was talking about what it was like being a serious writer in Hollywood. She caught only bits and pieces of it, however, her mind elsewhere. On her adolescent provocation, and the reasons for it. As Sonny talked about Nathanael West, she wondered again, was it just childish? Was the question of her own attractiveness the issue? Was she still angry, more upset than she liked to admit? She didn't know, realizing only that she had done something totally out of character. Perhaps injuring Sid Klein, insulting herself. Where would it end, this sudden delinquent behavior? How? Where? Resolve itself in diary entries, not in real behavior? "Why don't I call you and we can get together sometime?" Goodson was asking. Miriam gave him her number, realizing she had missed his story too, and excused herself.

In the bathroom she peed and splashed cold water on her brow and face. She looked in the mirror, to see, to understand. Were they fooled by the still smooth cheeks, the full lips, the men friends on her arm? What did they mean—the crow's-feet under the eyes, those increasing gray hairs? Age only? Voices in the background, she saw faces in front of her. Not a double exposure of Miriams, but multiple—Miriam the mother, Miry the daughter (yearning still), Miriam the photographer, Miriam the ex-wife, Miriam the mistress, Miriam of New Pleasure and Miriam of Old Hurt and Resentment, Miriam the little girl, Miriam growing old, Miriam in doubt—could they come together? Or stay apart, imposed and superimposed upon each other, in reasonable health? Which face did people go for? Or she, Miriam? Someone was knocking at the door, and she dried her face and departed.

Outside afterward, in the pickup, Harry took note of Sonny Goodson's interest. "Though he couldn't help it, could he?" She observed her favorite friend and said, "How nice to see you jealous. I hadn't thought you were that healthy, actually." "Jealous?" he protested, offended. "*Jealous,* sweetheart." She leaned to kiss him for it. "It's a nice change." The pickup bumped along, and she loved the musty smell of the 1959 Chevy and the insane collage of small reproductions—Matisse, Cézanne, Pollock, Piero della Francesca—with which he had decorated the cab ceiling. "Will you see him?" "I'll see how I feel when he calls. Depends on my mood. If I can meet Jack Nicholson, sure. In any case, I can learn all about 'American-success' from the inside, if you know what I mean. Or *he* means." "Yeah, from the inside," Harry observed. "And now that you're fully liberated, why don't you work on me in public places? I never get such . . . open invitations, do I?" She smoked, adoring his trying time. "If you're good, maybe I can fix you up with . . . Tuesday Weld." Which brought a smile, at last.

"Let's go to your place for a while," she thought aloud. "What about your baby-sitter?" "Oh, on Saturday nights Julia has her boy friend over. They won't miss us." "Maybe they know a few new tricks, should we join them?" "You mean swap, huh? Is she your type?" He reflected. "She does have that great teenage butt, doesn't she?" "Oh, it's all right." "Jealousy, sweetheart, is beneath you." She smiled. "No, it's not. It's new for me and I rather enjoy it."

She liked the loft over the small hi-fi company down Pearl Street, off Central Square. She felt at home in that working-and-living loft, at home in her adolescent fantasy from years past. Casual, messy, books and clothes everywhere, old chairs and a double bed in the far end, a wide area for painting with canvases on walls and easels, paints, spotlights, cot, even a rolltop desk (with top gone). A studio to paint and her freedom; a bohemian setting for living in which work was at hand, and the work dictated the space and design. Here was open space, paintings, colors. Even her own photos on the wall. Romantic about this imagery, but so what? This sloppy, carefree loft was the dream of that fifteen-year-old Miriam—who would take the bus to the Cleveland Museum and wander amid Rembrandts and Ingres's drawings, after her own easel attempts at the Cleveland Institute of Art—and she clung to the loft, the dream, with wonderful, admissible yearning. (Other yearnings she marked "Inadmissible" and wrote off.) At that moment she resented her children, those hostages that kept her, now that she was free from Stan, from realizing the dream.

"Cognac?"

"Sure," she said, sitting on a velvet Victorian platform rocker.

He brought it to her, from a liquor shelf of bricks, and sat opposite, in a director's chair.

She sipped it from the cognac glass and felt it singe her system with smooth perfection. She concentrated on a favorite small painting on the white wall behind him, which she had forced him to put up; a cityscape drawing that moved her strongly. Most of his work did, actually; it was, in the midst of skills with color and drawing, evocative, human, moving (her terms, which he smiled at). Qualities which one didn't see in him personally too much. No, her darling here had a fine time with his self-love and his sense of himself and his cool, almost professional concern for the girls he had affairs with.

"Contemplating me?" he wondered, knowing her. "No need. Did you have a good time?"

Was there anything better than retiring to this loft-retreat, without the kids, after a social evening? "It was all right. Pleasant." Too complicated to go into fully. "Good fish, wasn't it? And the Reibmans are the Reibmans, saints."

"Yeah. They shame the rest of us. Should we offer them a visa to get out of town? Or trap them somehow into fucking up and being bad?" He drank and smiled. "How was Sidney Klein?"

"Oh, he's a smart fellow. Something got into me, and I turned . . . perverse. And I never did get around to talking with him."

"So I noticed."

Was that, in part, why she did it? She smiled. "Odd, isn't it, that I don't like *not* being taken for a woman at the same time that I want that. Do you think he'd ever make a pass at me, or is that interest diverted permanently?"

Harry eyed her sideways. "Oh, I think that sex is not of paramount interest to him. He's got other things to think about. Besides, it's not simply sex as pleasure with him, or with his generation; it's more complicated than that. It's guilt and betrayal that it's involved with. Sex as sin."

"Very Jewish is what you're saying?"

"Or very Christian. Think of Liz Morrison's spouse

108

straying from the roost. Or look at the tortured adulterers in Greene and Updike."

"So the gentlemen need liberation too, the Jewish and the Gentile husbands."

Harry smoked and reflected. "If you call affairs 'liberation.' Actually, I don't think you do. Or, for that matter, is that little perverse number of yours supposed to be liberation?"

She hated the words, but took it.

He offered her more cognac, and she took that too.

"Can't I be naughty one night in my life?"

"Sure. But not arrogant too."

He looked at her, then got up and put on a record. Fats Waller piano and singing, light, easy, drifting from two corner speakers.

Chastised, but secretly liking him for it, she drank.

The new cognac was touched with orange sweetness, and edged her cozy, between desire and sleepiness.

"Come here, why don't you?"

His eyes blinked; he stood, balding slightly, thinner than six months ago.

A furry body with a large chest and those powerful legs and thighs that she loved. Maybe even, she wondered, she loved him?

He set his glass aside, and came to sit on the rocker's arm. She took his arm to her face and brushed it, and started rubbing the small of his back. He put his face down to her hair, smelling it, rubbing his own face in it, kissing her scalp. She massaged his back and waist with her fingers. He leaned down and across her, seeking a hunk of white flank, and almost threw them both over. Surprising her and scaring him. "I'm glad I can still make you laugh whenever I'm in trouble," he said. He said something about the bed being nearby, but she wanted his silence, his body, and the Oriental rug right there beside them.

So she got them there, half sliding, half moving with

awkwardness onto the rug. On their knees, facing each other, circled by soft yellow lamplight, they kissed, no hands, just mouths and lips and noses, a sort of courtesy opening. Their faces together, then, their hands roved upon each other softly, knowingly, his to her breasts (outside, then inside), and hers to his stomach, chest. She moved her hand in circles, using her nails too, and he delighted her by teasing her titties, then squeezing them more forcefully. Such sweet openers, she thought, for their curious upcoming roles. His dominating, his vulnerability, her willing submissiveness, her strength; all performed in a ritual of trusting, easy lust.

She got his dungarees and shorts down again, and got out of her skirt, underpants still on. Cognacced and stirred, she kissed his stomach, her hands reaching feathery across his penis, his testicles, beneath the scrotum. Another stage in her sexual biography, the way she loved to spoil this man and his body. What made her yearn to do these things to him, gestures so bizarre for her when translated into words? She was licking at his penis now, up and down and around; dipping any second down to those incredibly tender testicles; and also, her hand was right there now, at his long crack, fingering up and down, testing, probing, introducing. She knew she was headed for that underneath region now, it was the absolute destiny of the moment, and even when he tried to resist this special pampering—as he tried now—she wouldn't be daunted. It was her will versus his, and hers was stronger here, more purposeful, especially this night, it seemed. Her high cheek rubbed briefly against his lower cheeks, and she moved up some, feeling at home, *there*, where she wanted to be, felt like someone walking through unfamiliar territory toward a familiar clearing, where she could set to work; determined, pleasing, knowing, prolonged work.

That clearing was his rear triangle, a bottom of smells and vulnerables that she couldn't get enough of. Of course, on her way down, down, she stopped off at his testicles, not able to resist their sweetness, their exquisiteness, for a brief adoration. But her deeper destination now drew her, as the rhythms of jazz sweetened the background, as her Harry-boy began to squirm ever so slowly, not wanting it and wanting it at the same time. Like a long boot or sock, she slipped him over her and down, moving into better position. It was odd, humorous, humiliating, hot, very hot, that a clean and respectable girl like Miriam would get to love such a thing, to need such sex. But there she was, holding him around the front whenever she could, while getting high, getting herself wet, on the loving of a man's bottom. Only later, of course, did the whole escapade seem to break the respectable rules of sex. At present there was only the passion.

She lay beneath him in a comfortable position, a body mechanic or grease monkey lost in a labor of love. What had surprised her most was the way her pleasure had increased with time in relation to her skill and his wildness, his loss of control. Her passion was slowly, surely, becoming her power. When he had first suggested this, she was skeptical and openly sardonic, explaining it away as his narcissistic line. But now, she believed him. She had come to see how much she adored making him moan and plead and squirm with lust, this perfect self-lover who usually needed nothing or no one outside his sacred work.

But now he *needed* her all right, beneath there but in control, as she called the shots, now raising him slightly above her knees in order to brush-stroke up and down that long dark fault, or to shift inwardly, mine deeply, with more competence. The rug soft and hairy upon her neck and back, she spread him out more fully with her hands, poked, teased, and licked, let her head go

111

exotic with the strange smells and his occasional dropping down over her, viselike, in helpless pleasure. New and strange territory simply became, after a while, old homey grounds, as it was with this passion; grounds for her power and need, her ardor and desire.

She didn't know where she was, who she was, what she was, and it was a while before she realized he was begging for her own parts to hold and work upon, and against her will he was taking her mouth away from him. God. It took several moments to get acclimated here, to this reverse position. But he arched her, and began to make her cunt and ass (this last with his finger) a swamp of different desire and need, and the room was swirling gorgeously before she knew that now he was inside of her, moving around slowly, making it very hot down there and in her brain. How nice for conventional pleasure to be heightened by unconventional doings. And somewhere or other her ear was being bitten, her man was panting, and she was making her own lewd sounds; the upcoming rush reminded her of a partridge being flushed, its wings flapping loudly in terrified flight. The bird's sudden flapping and the semen filling her and the body falling into liquid all over everywhere made her momentarily wonder if there was anything anywhere as good or as gorgeous as this bliss of bodies.

He lay on her, a splendid form linked to her, and she felt weightless, clear, open-headed. He didn't speak, neither did she, the record had long gone off, and the cars whisked by in the distance below.

He said to her, low, "I'm sort of getting this quaint need for you, aren't I?"

And she, shielding her cockiness, replied, "Are you?"

They moved drunkenly onto the bed, and she watched him doze. She slipped off the bed, switched on the overhead fan, and watched it turn like a hovering helicopter. Purchased at a Wednesday morning auction at Hubley's on Broadway, it was one of those old black fans with great black bars or propellers, a relic from one of the big Newport hotels. Naked and odorous, and easy, she walked back to the bed, got in, and watched it spin, reminded of Hong Kong or Cuban hotel rooms with Bogart, Greenstreet, Peter Lorre; she was transported by it. Childhood flooded her: old movies, ballet lessons, rope skipping and hide-and-seek, kickball, and roller skating. She thought of her baseball cap, her Bronc Burnett sports books.

On the white wall opposite her, lit by a pole lamp, were her photographs, framed. Buildings, interiors, faces, cityscapes. Six pictures, 11 by 14. Joseph Goldman, the Cambridge tailor, wearing his tie and fedora and smiling with his perfect teeth and skin at age seventy-six, standing in the doorway of his shop. The beauty of the aged who like their work and still do it. Another doorway character study, on Tremont Street in Boston, three black prostitutes on a summer afternoon, with earrings, bracelets, white boots, miniskirts. Painted lips, African noses, two cheerful, innocent faces, one tough. Teenage theater of the damned. A third portrait, a distinguished Harvard professor of literature, with pencil mustache, narrow tie, briefcase; firm narrow face. Comic Upholder of the Past, out of August Sandor (she liked to think!). Next, a construction site, a skyscraper in the midst of going up, with its concrete guts and see-through spaces and rough industrial energy up front; an idea taken from Harry, and Hannah L. at the institute. Catching the building at its peak of power, before it got tamed by boring, mundane finish. A photograph at Harvard Square, in front of the Coop: hawkers of underground newspapers, well-dressed suburbanites, hairy students, tweedy scholars, a small band of Buddhists in orange saris and worn sneakers chanting their Hare Krishnas in a circle, a FABULOUS SHIRT SALE in the background windows of

113

the Coop. She had spent two whole weeks taking shots there before she got this mélange into one print: capitalism and pacifism and militancy, the Eastern Spirit proffered by shaved Midwestern boys and girls, the studious learners and the opulent buyers in Cambridge town. Who would recognize that melting pot? Finally, the photo that meant the most to her, that even won for her a prize at a Yale competition. Her father's small study in their Cleveland house, his cramped retreat, his one victory over his second wife, Helen—sagging bookshelves, a wall with maps and two old wooden globes, rolltop desk with small lamp (now hers, here), wooden armchair where he sat and read. The ten-by-twelve world of a dreamer, a would-be cartographer turned into a tormented husband; an escape hatch from silly furniture and domineering wife and the life of a traveling appliance salesman. The chair empty at the desk, the glaring absence, crushed her. She desperately wanted that tall, gentle man to be there again, to come and speak with her again, about the Indians or the Indian Ocean or the Second World War. Would she see him in afterlife?

She was sixteen, returning home from a movie date. Curiously, her father was waiting up for her, and they went to his study. Getting out his pipe, he fidgeted with his tobacco pouch, scratched at his scalp. Surprised, Miry sat down, smoothing her pleated dress carefully, and asked, "What is it, Dad?" He wore the long-sleeve khaki skirt that she adored, the open neck showing a bit of sleeveless undershirt; his lips moved awkwardly as he spoke. "Miry, your mother and I . . . that is, she's spoken to you before, in a way, and . . . and maybe it's time I said a word or two . . . There's no one I respect more than you, Miry, you know that, but you're still very young and you have a long, long time ahead of you . . ." (Fidgeting, scratching.) "You see, Miry, sex for a boy, especially a teenage boy, well, it's quite different than what it means for a young woman . . . it means less to him, you see

114

. . . it's a thing of the moment and . . . whereas, for a young lady, well, it, it can ruin her life, Miry . . ." And on he went—her daddy, her best friend, in the study they both loved—embarrassing and wounding both of them with his uneasy warnings, uncharacteristic fears. He did it wrong, said it wrong, treated her like some ordinary *girl. The trust in her judgment, in her as an adult, was suddenly crashing! And he too, she felt, sensed his indelicacy, his violation of their bond, his inaccurate reading of her capacities, his crude messenger work for his wife. But, she observed in his face and mannerism, he couldn't control himself. His mouth, usually peaceful, now grimaced at every other sentence; his wonderfully smooth face was tight; his ordinary casual manner was replaced by some unyielding force, a secret will in him moving against his normal grain. She wanted to say, "Daddy, please don't say these things, don't talk this way to me, please, Daddy, please don't." Not a word could she utter, however. Four or five tears ran down her cheeks, slowly. And later on, in her bed, she cried her heart out to her pillow, her room. Replaying the evening's date and the strict limits she had placed on kissing (no French) and petting (no breasts). Remembering all those dates of strict limits, where being good was so difficult—struggling against her own natural instinct at being touched, against her own early reputation as a cold, prissy bluestocking. And those nicknames: Miss Stuck-up, Miss Frigid, or that horror, Cocktease (for trying to give in a little). And now Daddy had betrayed her!*

She switched back to the pictures on the wall. How innocent those pictures seemed, next to her recent ones.

The hotel fan whirred and ticked; she remembered Bacall lighting a cigarette beneath one, she reflected on her odd obsession with this man and with herself. This long high loft, the fan, this Harry, the white walls with her photos and his paintings, for some reason they suddenly broke her heart and she clenched her teeth to suppress tears. Ridiculous. She sought to identify

this strange yearning, this slow sense of leavetaking, of
bodies turning to dust—she looked on the floor by the
bed, and ran her forefinger over the wood, picking up
particles—her—and she tried somehow to match this
ambiguous yearning with her earlier passion. That
graphic sexuality with this romanticism? They didn't
seem to fit. Sudden, deep feelings, about father, about
death, alongside that aberrant body loving.

Pieces of Miriam floating like separate little islands in
the same body of water. What was it? A sense of something absent in her life. A premonition of a future that
would remove her present pleasures? Or a buried
memory surfacing, of something lost and irretrievable?
She told herself that the mood would pass, that it
didn't count, like the moon going behind the clouds,
and concentrated on that turning fan.

Later, they were driving in the Chevy, back to her
place.

The 1 a.m. air drifted nicely into the cab of the
truck, and she asked, "Have you ever been in love?"

He wore a Levi's jacket over a T-shirt and suddenly
looked boyish. "Sure, dozens of times."

"No, come on now. Tell me the truth."

He drove, silent. "I don't know what you mean. Does
anyone? Do you?"

She reflected. "Probably . . . Maybe."

"Good for you, then."

She thought about that too. Was it good for her? Or
bad?

"What is it you're up to?" he asked. "Are you trying
to tell me something?"

"You love yourself, though, don't you?"

He fought the urge to joke it away. "Oh, I don't
know. Yes and no. Maybe not in the indulgent sense—
I demand as much or more from myself as from others. And it's tied up with work more than *self*." He

paused. "Or at least I'm as hard on myself as I am on others, or harder. Am I hard on you?"

The word hurt her. Her next sentence came to her, but she wanted to cry before she said it to him. She said, "I bet you fuck your work better than you fuck me."

He was quiet, hurt. The Chevy bumped and jostled loudly in their silence.

"I thought we sort of liked sex together."

"We do. *I* do. Honest. But I also know that you don't give me . . . yourself as much as . . . you might. Not emotionally, either."

He didn't answer.

He asked, "Wasn't it pretty good tonight?"

She nodded, truthfully. "Yes, it was grand." She kissed his arm. Words always came out too simple, too crude. "It's all right. I love you anyway. I feel closest to you of anyone."

He drove and didn't talk.

"It's funny," she began, "I mean, my friend Jamie does a lot of fucking, and I'm sure that you really like me better than he does." She tried to say it better. "The quality of your liking, or your affection, is finer, I think."

"But his prick goes deeper? Or more often?"

A good question. "Yes, more often."

"So it's not a question of emotions then?"

"Yes and no. With him, not; with you, yes. At least I feel it that way."

"Why don't you take his prick and my affection?" Said easily.

"That's not a bad idea." She shifted. "Of course, I'd have to have you to suck. I can't do without your prick. Or your balls. Or—as you once told me, you'd rather have me need your prick than you. I do, though sometimes it's a bit hard to separate the two."

117

He smiled. "You don't do that stuff to him?"

She shook her head and gave her own little laugh. "Are you kidding? I've never done that to anyone. Or wanted to."

He half-smiled. "Maybe that's love, then."

"Or sex," she said.

"We've reversed positions. Just in time too."

Onto Hancock Street, where she lived.

She kissed him good night and whispered, "Give yourself up, love me sometime, will you?"

He gazed at her, his light eyes through the glasses full of affection and curiosity. This boy who had his work, his loft, his bevy of girls hanging around, things his own way.

"I do, in my way," he said, and paused, his face tightening slightly, just slightly. "Besides, it's intelligence that's the gift, the important gift. Intelligence, and maybe talent, if that's included in the package. It's better than love, or whatever. It sticks around, it's with you all the time, it keeps things from going stale and impossibly boring. If you can get anything else, like affection along with the intelligence and work, great."

She saw for the first time in him some sort of male principle at work, though she hated the term. She saw something like maleness and male ambition and male reductiveness by means of that catchall word "intelligence," that word which enabled him to avoid direct flow of emotion for her, say. A narrowing clinical intelligence that had nothing to do with the sort of intelligence that is connected with emotion and intuition and experience, the creative sort. And yet she knew, too, that in his work it flowed, it was always there, better than the isolated cerebral intelligence he was now speaking of. A man's fear and simplicity. Oh dear.

She took his neck tenderly in her arm. "Good night, Intelligent Man."

He got it. "See you in the cave, under a full moon, huh?"

She slipped quickly out of the truck, jumping down, and walked upstairs without turning around.

But upstairs, in her nightgown, in bed, she felt restless, her mind jumping with thoughts about the evening with Harry. Why is it she always thought of things to say later on, *after* a conversation? She lay in bed, smoking, radio on. (Where would she be without FM?) Come on, Harry dear, what about all your ladies, what do they mean? Why are you so paternalistic and caring with me, and frantic elsewhere? And what was that directive really about, your wanting me to need and want your prick more than you? Why don't you see a therapist; it's about time, isn't it?

Now Ms. Big Talker, what about you? Let's start on you, Ms.

Notebook open, pencil out, she set to work.

Now we're going to be a good brave girl and dig down to talk straight about a real subject. No fooling around here, or playing it polite, okay? And no getting trapped behind the barrier of language. You musn't think me rude, lewd, disrespectful, or crass. Remember, I'm merely following orders from Dr. L. Shall we make an outline first, in preparation?

Subject: Harry's ass (or tushy), and Miriam's affection for it.

Circumference: ¼-inch-diameter orifice, once inside, with finger and tongue. Does seem to expand once there, but this may be my imagination, under the influence of lust. A territory the size of Estonia, say.

Length: nearly six half thumb's walk in crack between cheeks, from scrotum to tailbone. Tender tailbone, result of pilonidal-cyst operation. Poor tail.

119

Topography: peach fuzz and black hair, soft, curly. My nose loves that childish fuzz and the smooth, flat, hairless cheeks. Close-up, a curve in the cheeks, but mostly a man's flatness until you get him cozy and he scrunches up like a fetus.

Olfactory keys: varies richly. Mostly hardly at all; or if I'm worked up, I can hardly tell apart from body odor; occasionally a rich fecal smell which works me up sexier. The familiarity of recurrence too, like going to your favorite delicatessen and getting a whiff of the salami, tongue, corned beef. Something like a delicatessen?

Psychology of clothes: his shorts, esp. the brief red trunks with the thin white stripe down the side, are like erotic zones. My hand and face go there naturally, magnetically. Become my obsession. Was the great Carlyle too shy, or upper-Victorian literature too priggish to include a discussion of men's undershorts?

Scholarly authority: from *The Nude,* by K. Clark, "Looked at simply as form, as relationship of plane and protuberance, it might be argued that the back view of the female is more satisfactory than the front." Can't I make the same argument for the specialness of H.'s backside? Though I wouldn't want to go overboard, Sir Kenneth, and argue that it is more satisfactory than his front, with *those* pendulums and protuberances.

Examination

DR. L: Have you had your fun, my dear? Shall we talk now? What's a nice Jewish girl like you, a mature woman with children, doing down there?

MS: Difficult to answer, since I've never done this before. It gets me excited being down there, and especially so, getting him excited over it. Maybe I want to be special with him?

DR. L.: Good for Specials. Will you say something now about masochism, subservience, degradation?

MS: Okay, but what about them? Degradation, perhaps. To be rid of goodness once and for all? Possibly. But what about boldness and aggressiveness in pursuit of pleasure? new desires? Or pleasure in watching myself break new boundaries? Sure. The rise from repression has its costs, we both know.

DR. L.: Like showing off like a little girl?

MS: Maybe.

DR. L.: And getting frantic, more neurotic, out of control?

MS: Easy, easy. Yes and no, to what you say. Out of control *during lust,* yes. But I do try my best to discuss it here, Doctor. And why should a few more inches of anatomy call for such terms of censure? Could it be that you're just a bit prudish?

There are literary precedents, of course. Look at how Molly Bloom takes Leopold's obsession. And then there's Rabelais, who makes me look prudish when it comes to anal play and fondness for excrement. Not to mention Faulkner—

DR. L.: Thank you for your literary guide. Can we now get back to *your life?*

MS: Aggression. I'm learning to be bold, Doctor. To follow in the footsteps of teenage Kelly. To be a woman on the move, not a creature of inertia or passivity.

DR. L.: Will you next take up a gun in this pursuit?

121

MS: Bold in sex, Doctor. Where it harms no one, and pleases the two of us.

DR. L.: And your psyche?

MS: It's intact, I promise, so long as I have you here, to question me and remain skeptical.

Oh Diary, do you think I can write Ann Landers about this deep, no-good liking of mine?

No, sweetheart, just make sure that he's nice and clean for you. Or prep him yourself if you have to.

"Prep" him? Where'd you get that from?

Not from Ann or Abby, dear.

Will I ever be able to tell my friends about this new passion (fetish, dear?) or will it forever be confined to you, Diary? Am I the only woman with a passion for my lover's ass? I can't believe that. But I'm afraid I'm a little too shy to bring it up in public. Or at a women's meeting. Or in the *N.Y. Times Sunday Magazine*. ("Miriam Scheinman on Anal Fun"?)

Two days later. She was sitting with Nathalie and Kelly at the Orson Welles Cinema, for a special Film Society showing of *Deep Throat*. A deal had been made with Nathalie; Miriam would see *A Night at Maud's* if Nathalie would in turn see *Throat* with her. A deal had to be made, because Miriam felt about serious French films (or novels) the way Nathalie felt about pornography. Except that Nathalie would never see any. For the porn movie, she had invited Kelly to come along, when the girl had called to invite her to dinner.

"Oh, I don't think I'm going to be able to make it through this," Nathalie said, during the opening scene, with the delivery boy going right to work on the woman on the kitchen table, sprawled and open.

"Now come on, you know the contract."

"I know, but this is harder!" She half-laughed.

After a few minutes Kelly leaned over to Miriam, in the middle of the group, and whispered, "Cheesus, I wish he'd stop. I'm getting h-o-t from it! I should take my old man to see this. And it's just the beginning."

Catcalls and boos started almost right away, and after ten or fifteen minutes, the first spectators—two girls—got up and left.

About midway through, at the scene with the two female roommates having sex with eight men, two couples in two different parts of the theater stood up too. Making about a dozen who had had enough. "Can I go with them, please, Mir? I'll go see Garbo in the next theater and come out when this . . . this *thing* is over."

"*Maud* was *anguish,* believe me."

"I know, I know. But nothing like this." She laughed and prepared to leave. "I'll pay for the coffee later, okay?"

A group of three girls two rows down went out, and Nathalie joined them.

Kelly stayed cool, claiming early on, "With talent like Linda's, she could run the rest of us out of business." And during the gangbang: "Makes you want to try out one of those little parties, doesn't it?"

An interesting question. "I'm not sure I could handle one, to tell you the truth."

Kelly practically jumped. "Oh, I could handle it, if I could get high enough to do it in the first place! I'd be so *scared* before they arrived, or when I first met them. Maybe if we all could wear masks?" She giggled. Miriam smiled. "But just imagine, all those men—and women—*working you over from every single angle*—it'd be a groove! And a learning experience, too."

A groove, huh? wondered Miriam. Maybe it would be, indeed. And a learning experience, too. For credit? For a moment, maybe a minute, she thought of her three lovers in the room at once, "working" on her.

The focus disintegrated, however, from mutual embarrassment. She whispered, "Maybe it would be easier with strangers?"

Kelly looked at her anew. Then said thoughtfully, "I don't know. I've had two at once, and it was a ball. And they knew each other too." The big girl giggled and ate more popcorn. "It's just like more mileage per minute, or getting more gas in your tank, zoom!" Her face was glowing.

Afterward, they found Nathalie in the lobby, reading (*The Rise of David Levinsky*), and went for coffee at the Pamplona, on Bow Street. Miriam looked forward to talking about sex with these girls, with Kelly, anyway. Though there were lines of people waiting to talk politics, philosophy, identity, sex was another matter. One paid for that talk by the hour, right? The Pamplona was a basement room of white cement walls, where teachers and students sat at narrow marble tables, talking, playing chess, having rendezvous. Miriam felt good here, studenty.

"I really can't even talk about it too much," Nathalie quickly admitted, sipping a mocha chocolate. "I just found it so . . . repellent. Disgusting."

"Why?" Miriam asked.

"I'm not quite sure," Nathalie considered, her face fixed in a look of self-analysis that Miriam found appealing. "Maybe it's because I'm so used to . . . sex in private, in my bedroom, and not up there on the screen. Or watching it with friends! Or maybe *cocksucking*"—she used it like introducing Cartesian dualism into the discussion—"is just not my bag!" Her eyes danced with merriment; the others laughed. And seriously, "In terms of arousement, it turned me off *completely!*"

There was a brief pause, as the waiter set down two pastries.

"With me it was the opposite almost," asserted Kelly,

removing long red hair from her eyes and sipping a fruit drink through a straw. "A lot of those scenes got me *too* hot. If my old man were with me, cheesus—I don't know what I might have done!"

"Oh God," confessed Nathalie, "I'm afraid I can't even think *or imagine* that sort of scene."

"Are you taking your orange juice daily?" asked Miriam.

"I better start squeezing my own, and spicing it with something too." Nathalie laughed.

Miriam continued, "I thought it was mostly fun."

"Good sweet fun, huh?" Nathalie was cheerful.

"Actually, yes. Camouflaged by the overt sex. Didn't you think it was good-natured? The pornography sweet-natured? There really were few pretensions in it, and some of the jokes were cute. Not great, just sort of charming. And the sex was, well—" she looked for the appropriate words—"informative, say. Don't you think?" She answered herself. "It's like a trip to a different world, isn't it? Sort of like a travelogue movie, only instead of Iceland it's Sexland. What's wrong with that?"

"Plenty, if you don't want to go there!" said Nathalie.

"Sure, that's fair enough. And once there, you can find it boring, that's fair enough too." She took a piece of pastry and paused. "You know, I really couldn't have seen that movie if I were still with Stanley. He wouldn't have sat for it and would have *demanded* that I leave, too. And I'm not sure that I would have been able to watch it even if I were alone, had I been Stan's wife."

"How's that?"

"I just think I probably would have been . . . ashamed, embarrassed. You know? I'm sure of that, in fact. The sex on the screen would have *shamed* the sex in my bedroom. Isn't that one of the connections between . . . pornography and respectability? Which explains, too, the jealousy of one for the freedom and license of the other. At least, that's what I suspect, looking at myself." She noticed the words hit home with Nathalie, and she felt badly, wanting in a curious way to protect her friend. She was as vulnerable in this area as Stanley's Miriam would have been.

"I guess I'm doomed to respectability and jealousy," Nathalie said.

"Oh, we all are, in one way or another," Miriam quickly replied. "Playful pornography won't save me, I assure you," she half-joked. "If anything, the opposite."

"What fatalists you guys are!" cried out Kelly, amused. "But another thing," Kelly turned serious, hunching her big shoulders, "isn't a *Deep Throat* a response to an uptight culture, one extreme reaction for another?"

"Interesting point," said Miriam. "Linda Lovelace may after all be the fantasy figure of someone like Hester Prynne."

Nathalie rolled her eyes. "Isn't that going a little far?"

"Maybe, maybe not. But, as Kelly implies, pornography is one level of attack on an extremely repressive culture, with its puritanical heritage. Which Hester was too, wasn't she? And aren't the healthy consequences of pornography, hopefully, not to produce more of it but to open up the culture to more freedom? more eroticism? To more . . . serious erotic intimacies? It's really a very old fight."

They drank their cold drinks, Nathalie eyeing her old friend anew.

"And who will play Arthur Dimmesdale then?" asked Nathalie.

"My old man!" Kelly announced.

Miriam laughed, and Nathalie considered. Miriam asked, "How would Tyson take it, by the way?"

126

No, she wouldn't ask about Arthur Reibman.

The girl smiled widely. "Oh, he likes *trying* things. I kinda think he'd get a kick out of it. Maybe I can get him to see it later this week, if it's still playing. Is it? That'd actually be fun, with him—unless it got me thrown out of the Welles!"

Later on that night, Miriam reran the movie briefly in her head, and considered her friends' reactions. The glowing excitement of eighteen-year-old Kelly, ready for anything that came along. The dark thirty-six-year-old beauty of Nathalie Reibman, contemplating the unthinkable for a moment and then retreating to safe ground—because of family? background? psychic necessity?—by means of good humor. Leaving Miriam where? Between the Gulliver ropes binding Nathalie, and the freewheeling kite called Kelly, moving with the wind and her whim? Anyway, it was good seeing the flick with the two girls and talking about it afterward. That was refreshing. Not having men around for a time was fine; she now understood poolrooms or wars better, and why men at times preferred them. A change of pace, scenery. Absence of need to dominate, sexually conquer. No need to be Sexual Man, just a man. Couldn't they invent Wars for Girls Only? So much more interesting than women's libber politburo and encounter sessions! She smiled.

She loved being friends with these two very different girls and spending time with them. Why'd she and they ever have to die then? She'd want to live even if they took away pornography and doomed her to respectability!

Still, there was homework to do. Sorting out, down on paper, in the notebook.

It's not the lightweight movie that counts, but the impulse behind it. Rememb. Aristophanes, in the Greek, as an undergrad? (Those Superiority days of bearing my Liddell-Scott, Autenreith's *Homeric Dictionary*, Graves's *Myths*, Munro's *Iliad*, the way some others flashed new engagement rings. Or putting up over my desk those phrases—All in Moderation, Know Thyself—when I really wanted excess and actually knew everyone else better than I knew myself.) All that obscene language and sexual exploitiveness was more of a literary education abt the Greeks than reading the tragedy writers. No piety, Victorian expurgation, translator censorship, no rules (moral or aesthetic). Just imagination, playfulness, obscenity, chaos, humor; and *against all* the big shots of the day (Sophocles, Euripides, Aeschylus, Creon), and their schools (sophism, democracy, imperialism). Old Aristoph. wld have a picnic today, taking on Skinner, McLuhan, Dr. Kiss, the Encounterists, and pseudo-analysts.

Of crse he'd write a porno movie. An Aristophanic scenario: Zero Mostel and the Second City group (May, Nichols, Arkin, etc.,) starring with Sid Caesar doing an encore as Tricky perhaps. Procurers, impresarios, madams, whores, clients, operating out of the Wash. D.C. house, where everything goes—cursing, befouling, graffiting, shitting, fucking, offalmongering, satirizing, and offending everyone (from literary prudes to establishment officials to the pornographers). Now, with Aristophanes in perspective, Linda and her romps are seen more clearly as the amateurs of kidding around that they are.

The phone was ringing, and she got up for it.
"Hi. Is this Miriam Scheinman?"
"Speaking."
"You don't know me, see, but I'm an old friend of the Thorndikes, Bruce and Mary Ann. Ralph Eggleston is my name, and I live over here in Framingham. I'm calling because I happened to see the series of pho-

tographs that you took of them last month, and they're really *way out, a gas.* So I was wondering if I could make an appointment with you to do a similar series with me and a few friends? Bruce told me the fee, and it sounds fine."

At first she was bewildered, and then she grew angry. As if someone had passed the rumor around, in high school, that Miriam S. put out for all the boys.

"Are you there, hello?"

Controlling her temper, she replied, "What do you do, Mr. Eggleston?"

"Call me Ralph, why don't you? Actually, I lead two lives, you might say, a computer programmer in one and involvement in different forms of therapy and personal growth groups. Are you into it yourself?"

"No, I don't think I'd be interested, actually."

"Huh? Oh. Is it a question of money? I think we can negotiate that."

"No, it's not a question of that at all. Thanks for calling, though."

"Is it just a bad time now? Should I try you in a few weeks?"

"I don't think so, Mr. Eggleston. That sort of work doesn't interest me, I'm afraid. Why don't you try the Phoenix classified, I think you'll find a photographer there."

"A little high-handed, aren't you?"

That surprised her. "Good night now." And she hung up.

Taking her portable radio, she went into the darkroom for a night of printing and developing. Had she asked for that last accusation? Perhaps. She jotted down the Thorndike number, to tell them that she no longer was in that business.

Two

THE NEXT THREE DAYS were spent in wandering around picture-taking, alone with herself, her camera, and—increasingly she looked upon it this way—her city. She cherished enormously that sense of peripatetic privacy and anonymity; and she found it quietly exhilarating to probe anew those objects of everyday life that surrounded her. It was not the way she had always chosen her subjects. In the old days, more than two years ago perhaps, her subjects were like pretty decorations for coffee-table books—fine houses, stately trees, touching creatures (animal, vegetable), impressive twilights. An idea of subject matter derived essentially from college classes (in English Lit. and Classics especially) and centuries (her lifetime to be exact) of romantic perception. Looking for beauty in pretty things; associating art with elegance, somehow. What period bullshit, she thought now. And inevitably, in the process during those apprentice years—before M.I.T. and photography classes, say—she had eliminated most of the common life of the cities she had lived in. Including the Cambridge of the past ten years.

She drifted around the city nowadays like a fish swimming alone in gray-blue waters, surveying, feeling her way, looking for new meanings to old places. As well as searching for deeper waters and odd hideouts. She traveled in one set of clothes to do this: dungarees, a navy jersey beneath a denim shirt, a cap occasionally, and hiking boots, a red-and-black-checked hunting shirt jacket (if the weather warranted it). Her Leica around her neck on its strap and a shoulder bag containing a notebook and rolls of film and extra lenses. A Cambridge student-peasant perhaps, a war journalist, an anonymous eye; not a tourist, a woman, a photographer if she could help it. To get places, she either used public transportation or walked. Taking pictures all the way. In the subway, for example, going across to Boston, she snapped faces, advertisements, the cars, or the river from the Kendall Street stop. And on this particular sun-in, sun-out day, she photographed crooked, decaying tombstones in the graveyard by the Square and the arching concrete bridges across the Charles. She then walked across town, away from Harvard, and had a sausage sandwich, standing, in a Portuguese grocery. The huge gold-toothed proprietress was overjoyed to have her picture taken, along with the young Spanish teenager who helped her out. Miriam then went on a merchant-and-shop tear down the street, using up one roll of film on both sides of Broadway between Inman and Prospect. Next she turned down Prospect, and at Trout Fishing, that dropout haven, she used another whole roll, on a blond girl, about eighteen, with an Indian band, a black boy with a silver flute and a beret, an eighty-year-old lady who had wandered in, another young photographer from Montana, a cowgirl.

Walking home in the late-afternoon April breeze,

132

she figured out that she had taken five rolls, 180 potential negatives, in three or four different areas of the city. Enough to keep her going for several weeks at least, printing and developing, though she also knew that in the next day or two she'd go out and explore buildings, houses, skyscrapers, streets.

And yet all this served, strangely, as only an approximation of her real connection with the city, of the new feeling she had developed with it. This connection or bond had been established once she had left the old pretty decorations and got into looking at the daily and dirty habits of Cambridge. So, for example, the constant changes that the city underwent appealed to her rather than disgusted her; appealed to her like a woman trying on new clothes: tradition, vulgarity, seemliness, respectability, ardor (new construction), ugliness (municipal buildings), humor, playfulness (glass department stores springing up like geysers), sadness (decaying synagogues, churches, graveyards), academic power (Harvard and M.I.T. skyscrapers), lonely aristocratic houses (on Dana and Trowbridge), legal rape (the rising of a new Mass. Avenue between Central and Harvard Squares). Now she felt this connection as a communion, a Sunday morning at church, a private bond between her and the city. Furthermore, she began to experience the city as definitely *male*, a male with secrets. Cambridge was becoming like Jamie, Adrien, Harry, a boy friend, a different breed of lover, and one whom she could arouse by uncovering different parts of his anatomy and photographing them.

It was all very odd, she thought, how she took these things for granted, in stride.

It got to the point in fact where a kind of game went on, a serious game, in which Cambridge tried to hide his secrets and Miriam tried to find them out. On the surface even, there were surprises tucked away: an optometrist who had one eye and believed in the occult, a transvestite shop just off fashionable Brattle, a little train of locomotive and two-passenger cars which passed underground, unnoticed, between Concord and Boston. And beneath the surface, deeper secrets, which the city seemed to hold back out of ordinary human motives, perhaps—shame, pride, anguish, fear? Obscure activities that were guarded as if they were artifacts from a lost civilization: a Machu Picchu or Masada hiding out within the actual city. Mostly these activities were acts of indecency, or persons revealed in the midst of pain and imbalance (perhaps insanity); Cambridge did not discriminate as to where or when these activities should happen. But it permitted them, housed them, and even, to Miriam's mind, encouraged them; sort of like a perverse boy.

For example, there was the semidesolate strip out along the Charles, near the Institute of Contemporary Art. There, amid the giant outside structures of painted steel and iron and the grassy banks, there, during the months of October, November, and then March, Miriam had come upon three couples having intercourse. Two heterosexual, one homosexual. Hidden away, fascinated, she had snapped her photographs. Once a young girl spotted her, screamed out; Miriam, perplexed, emerged innocently from an arch of iron and apologized, whereupon the boy friend said he didn't care much, would she like to take more? The young girl at first refused, furious, then settled down, and Miriam took more pictures, walking off after a bit without ever saying another word. (Another incident was a little different. The male partner, in the middle of his act, caught her in hers, and got up and ran for her. Miriam, like a big-game hunter staying to the last split second before shooting, got a picture of him coming at her, in sweater only, then took off. She was fortunate that he had no trousers on, and also that she had only forty or fifty feet to run before she emerged

134

on the highway, safe. She ran for her life, listening to the man scream, "You cunt, you cunt voyeur!" and turned her ankle just after darting through an opening in the hedge. It had been a very close call, she knew, limping along the highway, breathless, excited, prideful. It was a picture she had *earned* all right.) Now, for herself, in her notebook, she ascribed to the couples numbers under a heading called Revelations.

Another revelation. One day in the late afternoon she had been wandering around in the area of Garden Street and the Hilles Library, when suddenly, from between the thick hedges, a man appeared. A good-looking man too, in his thirties, who looked at her like a dazed angel, or like her own Jamie. It must have been a good half minute, at 2 p.m., that ordinary March Wednesday, before she realized what his underlying purpose was, why his face was glazed and helpless. Her instincts faster than her brain, she lifted the camera and snapped the shutter one, two, three, four, five times—catching his dazed bliss, the exposed penis in his hand, the hedges framing him like some religious triptych. She didn't scream, her heart thumped, she photographed him as he played with himself. Against her will and reason, she stayed there, sweating, heart jumping in panic, but keeping herself planted there, snapping him until he did what he couldn't help doing. Bang! She sprang off, darting into the public street and across it, hurrying away—more with the cold sweat of a thief than that of a victim. In front of the Sheraton Commander, she jumped in a cab, afraid of the new booty that she had uncovered and stolen. A booty which she had pried from the city and which she was afraid of paying for, somehow, somewhere down the line, like any criminal.

She consoled herself in the prosaic rattling cab with the thought that these pictures were the booty of the past few years, a booty commensurate with the risks taken. Risks which toughened her hide enormously, she knew, when she stopped shaking.

When she first showed Harry the developed pictures of the couple and the male exhibitionist, he was stunned. For the first time ever with her pictures. Worried, he asked how she had gotten them, and she told him.

"Are you crazy? Do you want to get killed? One of these nuts is going to pull out a knife or gun and use it on you!" He shook his head. "Come on, Miriam, use your common sense."

She lit a cigarette with her lighter. "You know, that's the first time you've ever been so upset or surprised by a picture of mine. That's interesting, isn't it?"

"Now look—"

"And is that how you paint your pictures, by means of common sense?"

He frowned, said that was silly, and took her by the shoulders, outside the darkroom. Fatherly, brotherly. Her hands were covered with chemicals (Dektol, stop bath, hypo fixer) and their curious medicinal odors. In the kitchen, where she washed her hands—9 p.m., the kids asleep—he asked her, "What is it you're after? Why do you have to take chances like this?"

She pointed to more prints.

He took them up from the baking pan, and she made a drink for both of them.

"What do you think?" she wondered.

He shook his head, bewildered. He wore his denim jacket and dungarees; he had lost maybe ten pounds that winter, with the help of yogurt and jogging, and he was straight up and down, slim. "I don't know quite what to say. I've never seen anything like them. They're pretty . . . real. And scary. The pain on this guy's face. How can you ever exhibit them publicly, though, without getting sued?"

She drank and shrugged her shoulders. She knew

she had done her job, her side of the job, anyway. Strong, disconcerting photographs amid a life of dishes, clothes to wash, books to return to the library, food to put away.

He sort of half-nodded. "They're interesting, okay. Maybe too painful, if anything. Or too erotic, I'm not sure. Or this one, pornographic. I just don't know what to make of them. Except they're . . . stunning. Or arresting. Yes, arresting."

She hit him playfully on the arm, with gratitude. "Yes," she said, "that's what I thought. That they'll arrest me for them. But that they're worth . . . the trouble." She laughed at the word. "Stan always said that I lacked common sense, anyway."

She too wasn't sure what the pictures meant; she admired their composition, yes. Some of them were first-rate technically. But mostly they counted because they were a completely new experience. She knew, she knew for sure that never in a million years with Common-Sense Stan would she have taken them. Why? to put in the closet? The good girl's photos of her first show had proved that, in a way. And what Harry said was true enough, about showing these; she'd probably be called a pornographer, a peeping Tom posing as a photographer, and if any of the participants happened to see them—she could be involved in a law suit. These thoughts made her smile inwardly for some reason. Perverse purity? "Yes," she said aloud, "I may never be able to display them publicly, that's true. Unless I didn't care about myself at all"—she shrugged—"but just wanted to show the photographs."

The trouble was, however, that instead of making her more cautious and commonsensical, those pictures had invited her to move in the opposite direction. They seemed to draw her out to *get more* from Cambridge. They tempted her to seek out more secrets and pry them open. They showed her by means of *black-*

and-white proof that there was loot out there, and all she needed to get it were risks, reckless behavior, a will to discover. That was all, really. And when you put those deeds into words like that—risks, recklessness, will to discover—they weren't that bad, were they?

"Look," began Harry again, leaning against the Kenmore piled with dishes, "it can't be that the only sort of pictures that excite you are these erotic sort? The sort that you almost have to take your life in your hands to get."

She reflected, her refrigerator humming. "Am I getting to be a pornographer, is that what you're asking?" A smile. "Could be, perhaps." She beckoned him with her head, and he followed her to the bedroom, where she opened a green file cabinet. She removed several packets of pictures, and several scrapbooks. "Here're some others you might not have seen."

Harry opened one scrapbook and began to leaf through it. The pictures were taped at the edges onto thick loose-leaf pages. He turned one page, then another, and another.

"You do get around, don't you?" he exclaimed, low. "When the hell did you get these? And where?"

"This winter. In the good town of Lexington."

He stared at her. "What are you talking about? Where in Lexington? How'd you get permission? And where'd you get the idea? Look at this one—who is it, Havlicek?"

She sat on the arm of the couch and looked at the ballplayer in the midst of a driving shot, one hand clasping the basketball from underneath it, the left hand and the elbow (especially) between himself and the ballplayer guarding him, the face a mask of concentration and *strain*, the whole body rising off the ground, maybe three to four feet, and arching like some gravityless astronaut.

"Look, here's a whole series. What do you think?"

There were at least a dozen shots of a handsome black in gray sweatshirt and shorts, working out. Another side of a ballplayer known for his gentlemanly behavior: in pain from getting hit in the ankle; head flung back and sweat pouring down his neck and torso, in utter exhaustion; on the bench, in profile, watching the court intently, even angrily; leaping straight up like a jumping jack for a rebound, his elbow catching another's neck; bent over with four teammates around the coach, diagramming, looking totally indifferent; in a near-battle with a teammate; by the water cooler, drinking from a paper cup, body relaxed, foot up; crouching like a jaguar, hips and elbow blocking out another ballplayer ready to go up for the rebound.

"Who is it, anyway?"

"Paul Silas."

"Where've you been hiding all this stuff?"

"Oh, just around. In my files. Waiting for it to . . . mellow."

She went on to explain how she had gone to Lexington to walk around some of the old places, and happened to notice two very tall blacks walking along those manicured, lily-white streets. She found herself following them into a drugstore, and asked one of them if they were "ballplayers." One name turned out to be faintly recognizable, from Stan's days of watching the Celtics play the Knicks on television. She asked this goateed man, a Malcolm X in business suit, what they were doing in this town? Tom Sanders laughed and explained that they practiced in the local high-school gymnasium. Could she come along and watch? she wondered. Sanders was surprised, and just then the second player came up, introduced himself, and said sure, she could be their guest. So there she was, in a white Country Squire station wagon, driving with Sanders and Silas to practice.

On the way she explained that she was a photographer, and Sanders, saying "Oh oh," pulled up to let her out. Immediately she protested her innocence, saying not the journalist sort. Silas grew interested; he had fooled around with a camera himself in an amateur way. In ten minutes they were at the Lexington Christian Academy gym, and they got her through the stern and awed high-school guard. For Miriam, it was like entering a kind of sports greenhouse, with lacquered orange woods, streaming winter light through tall windows, see-through glass backboards; a place that cultivated Boys of All Ages. The actual practice, viewed from different places in the stands (with about twenty-five other spectators), enthralled her. Those mechanical-looking puppets from channel 4 were suddenly human beings with small humors, warts, angers, and imperfections; and the practice itself was infinitely more interesting, she thought, than the two actual games she had seen at the Boston Garden. Both kinds of practice were surprisingly exciting, the routine of foul shooting and practice shots, and the individual conditioning of friends going one-on-one to practice a particular shot; and then the scrimmage between the two squads, stopped frequently by the tall, emotive coach. Gradually she came to realize, as she never had before, the exquisite selective art of Degas, with his emphasis on ballet warm-ups and practice, in which what you got was life-roughness, rather than performance, the boring perfection of finished art.

Ballet movements indeed were suggested by the various body movements that the players performed that afternoon, either with or without that springy orange leather ball, which was dribbled by the guards as if they had rubber bands attached to it. Floating toward the basket for lay-ups from the foul line, staying suspended in the air for three seconds while twisting their bodies away from the elastic defenders; looking one way, passing the ball another, cutting immediately for the basket and jumping up blindly, only to receive the basketball at the last split second, swishing it down through the corded net; leaping up like a chocolate gazelle way beyond the basket, retrieving the ball in midair with one huge hand and, in the same motion as if underwater, spinning about to fling the ball like a grapefruit maybe one hundred feet down court to a sprinting guard. It was extraordinary, and she took no pictures during it, rather acquainted herself with the dazzling leaps and the greyhound speed, the athletic lyricism.

After the scrimmage, Silas walked over, a race horse cooling off, toweling his neck, forehead, face. "How's it going?" he asked. She took out her camera and began to focus him, saying, "I didn't know they still used the give-and-go." His dark face broke into a great white smile, and he looked like a young Clark Gable, with black mustache and mature firm features. As he pulled up his gray-and-red wool socks, she began to snap pictures. "I didn't know female art photographers knew about give-and-go's." "We also know about back-door plays," she answered, safe behind the camera. "No posing, huh?" "No posing," she said, snapping his muscled calves and thighs, the perspiration running down his neck and T-shirt. Where was Michelangelo? "Sometimes it's not so playful out there," she said, snapping. He ran his finger over the inside of his mouth, and it came out like an oil stick, with blood.

By the water cooler, to which she had walked alongside him, he introduced her to Heinsohn. A tough Irish teamster, good-looking. At first skeptical, he then said, "You sure she's not working for Shue or Holzman?" He drank and walked off, calling out to a player. Silas explained the reference to the other coaches.

In ensuing days she returned on a twice-a-week basis when they were in town. Besides her first two friends, she had gotten to know one Don Nelson, a tall Midwestern blond who was interested in English literature and once talked to her knowledgeably about *Tom Jones* and R. S. Crane's article on plot in it. She was very impressed. Out of it all she had gotten about five scrapbooks of pictures, with a series devoted to the four players, Silas, Sanders, Nelson, and an incredible man who played all scrimmages as if they were play-off games, Havlicek. A bit of Czechoslovakia added to Harlem slums, Iowa farms.

"You do get around, don't you?" Harry acknowledged in admiration.

"The world's a big and various place, Harry-o," she told this Horatio, tapping his prominent nose. "And if you no longer have to worry about lunch for kids, dinner for husband, and Radcliffe gives you freedom for four to five hours a day, and you're nosy enough, yes, you *can* get around. And see things you mightn't ordinarily see."

Harry stood up, stretching. "Don't I know. You're making me jealous. I used to get around myself, to airplane factories, computer plants on 128, the shipyards in Charlestown and Quincy—those were the best. Watching the big ship skeletons go up—I needed to show them some real canvases to prove I wasn't a spy of some sort. Anyway, I used to get around, when I was doing those city landscapes. Now I'm indoors and inert, either painting myself or teaching students inside the studio. Actually, I should take them out more, to see some *reality*. Or maybe give up my modeling harem and return to the Big American Erector Set. Well, I repeat, I'm jealous." He reached down and returned her affection-hit, on her chin. Down on his haunches, he said, "You just stick to the basketball courts and stay away from the alleyways. Besides, you've got enough material, all told, for *three* shows. And all you risk is getting thrown out of the gymnasiums, not life. Remember that, okay?"

Like the way he would tell her to stop smoking, an uncle tutoring a young child he loved. Unlike Stan's chastising, which always implied *moral* stain behind the nicotine.

"Okay, I'll try to remember, Dr. Harry."

"Now don't be cutesy, Superiority." Making her smile.

She had an urge to show him the series of nude self-portraits, but he had seen enough pictures for one night, she figured. Another time, maybe. Besides, would she really use them in the Show? She wasn't sure.

After he had left, however, his questioning and challenging hit home, and she got out her notebook, in the living room, to respond, to think a little, to talk to the real doctor.

Dear Dr. L.,

Start with the basketball pictures. Why? A release from adulthood, from duty and responsibility (esp. with children) and return to my own childhood associations, a few hours a week of innocence. Also, obviously, a great change of pace(!) from my other content, not so innocent.

I also have the illusion / belief that seeing Silas / Havlicek / Nelson unawares, catching their awkward & angry & imperfect sides, adds a touch of Degas to Americana. My hubris, along with high illusion and hope—but what better incentives are there in order to make things?

The erotic pics. First off, why do I squirm at the suggestion of doing more Thorndike couples in bedrooms for all that loot? Bec. that to me is real porn stuff, mechanical, *detached,* a bore. Whereas, with my own chosen material, I feel like a war

143

photographer at the front lines. It's real, dangerous, and *participatory*. I'm part of the action, or the
camera is. Only the combat here is city combat,
men-women, men-men wars called sex. Combat
within that explodes *without*, and there I am, on
hand to catch it. The sex of the beleaguered, the
frightened, the pushed—with a displaced enemy
called a lover / victim. Frustrated soldiers, making
city sex.

STOP. SHIFT.

Is it neurotic if the chances I take issue eventually in interesting photographs? I mean, is that the
emphasis you want to put there? Isn't that an anal-
ysis-reductive way of putting it? Sure, I'm still angry / guilty, what have you, but it's not as if I go to
be beaten with chains and whips when I go out
there, on the hunt. Dr. L., what wld you say? You
encouraged me to move outward, take some risks
even—are these the right ones? I quote my old
hero R. Benedict here: "I gambled on having the
strength to live two lives, one for myself and one
for the world." So here I am, chaining my social
self, the good citizen Scheinman, for the sake of
the renegade photographer. My gamble too, right?
As a woman and a photographer.

Why cldn't I show H. my self-portraits? Are they
really too personal? Do they shame me? Are they
self-pitying and vulgar in the service of honesty?
How does one ever know or draw the lines? Oh
Dr. L., if you were around this year, I'd like to
show them all to you.

Over and out.

Fatigued, she stopped. She often felt tired after an
entry.

Later on, she remembered Harry's words about "material for three shows" and agreed. The overabundance of material was always a problem for her recently, not the scarcity. Too curious, too compulsive,

she collected too much evidence, sought out too many crevices of interest, allowing too little time for making the necessary practical arrangements for shows. Hence she had had only the one real show so far, before the upcoming one. Okay, she thought, putting her chimney to rest for the night, she'd try to remember dear Uncle Harry's advice, to be thrown out of gymnasiums only, nothing larger.

But it was difficult sticking to her resolution the next night when Adrien was over, sipping tea and talking about Thomas Peacock's dialogue. As he spoke, *this* peacock of elusiveness and affectation and esoteric knowledge, she began to drift restlessly right there in her own living room; and she suddenly had this curious thought that Adrien was a messenger of sorts for the city. With his Lapsang souchong, his hash (in his pocket), his Eng. Lit. talk, his bisexual desires, he was a lure put out by Cambridge to attract her, Miriam. She had felt these odd lures or impulses before, but she had always put them out of her mind, or down and away, under the reasoning Silly, Neurotic, Mystical. But just now she let the impulse go and gather and flood her, while Adrien went on speaking about his recent novelist discovery.

"Would you mind very much," she interrupted at an appropriate moment, "if I went out for a short while?"

He looked puzzled and, in puzzlement, oddly ordinary.

How nice, she thought. "Actually, I'd like to see if I can find this book I've been meaning to get hold of. I never seem to get a chance to search for it during the day."

"It's pretty late, for a book. Almost eleven." Worried husbandly?—how grand!

"I know, but the night air will do me good. Besides, the Paperback Booksmith is open all night, isn't it?"

145

He said sure, he didn't mind, and she kissed him goodbye, turning him back into a baby-sitter. Where, she found, she liked him.

Outside, the night air was cool and sensible, and the branching elm leaves were bathed in subtle mauve by the mercury lamps. A stranger to her own street in the late evening, she felt slightly afraid as she walked down Hancock toward Harvard Street. In sneakers, she moved silently upon the wavering old red bricks, the sounds of car whisperings and loud televisions and records creating the city night. Turning up Harvard, she was about to snap that eerie synthetic night-violet, but was mildly startled to discover the camera wasn't there, she hadn't brought it. And felt naked without it, defenseless. Utterly vulnerable. She walked on, turning up Trowbridge, her old street, full of big old lazy clapboard houses and stucco apartment boxes, ugly and new. And realized too, in this first solitary night walk in years, what everyone knew—how the city had changed in the last five years. Grown legendary with licentious menace. Everyone knew someone who had been burgled. Ripped off. That lingo fitted the times and the methods better. From the nice quiet Midwesterny atmosphere, Cambridge had become like New York or Bogotá, you were knocked down and kicked, stabbed and robbed, violated and vilified, spit at and cursed. (Just as the shopkeeper by day blew up at you suddenly?) Criminal and lewd, this atmosphere was good for movies or plays, not for life, not for strolling. Yes, she admitted, it had its thrilling side. Like walking around in a Jacobean play directed by a Genet, with its doped-up Manhattan Indians, old-fashioned teenage gangsters, paroled psychotics, television-watching gunslingers, expensive dangerous cowboys, blue-uniformed avengers. Not poetry but the gun and the knife ruled this night play.

As she approached the corner of Broadway, opposite

146

Cambridge and Latin High, she saw several kids by the darkened houses, this side of the corner luncheonette. Slowly, three teenagers came into focus, hanging about and joking with each other. Her heart began to beat fast as those legends looked as if they were coming to life, here and now; she felt Harry's advice—to cross over to the opposite sidewalk or else walk in the center of the street—shoot up and down her spine. She walked straight on, however, strangely animated, having a private stake here in her city this way. As she came closer, she felt their conversation stop, their eyes look her over.

"Hey, baby," said one short black boy, wearing mirror glasses and a cap, and speaking half humorously for his friends, "whatcha out lookin' for?"

"Can I be of service, ma'am?" mocked the second boy, maybe seventeen; eyes bright, maybe too bright.

With a subconscious common will, the three moved from the wooden stoop and car fender to narrow the passageway severely, and Miriam, her spine firing with fear, hoped her knees wouldn't fail her.

Just as they edged about her, like those menacing shadows becoming too real, Miriam stopped short and turned to the short fellow, as if he were her walking partner. "Yes, you could help me. Would you have the correct time? My watch seems to have had a breakdown." She held up her watch to her ear.

The boy was as surprised as Miriam. "Neahly a qwatah to midnight," he murmured like a good fellow, gazing at one of those huge, surreal, leather-strap contraptions. For a split second they both seemed beautifully relieved of their street roles and happy to help each other out, like neighbors.

Without moving, she adjusted her watch. Then saying thanks, she half-smiled and walked on, stifling her impulse to run.

When she was ten feet off, the boy called out sportingly again, "It's the bee-witchin' hour, babe, if ya gallup back this way!"

She waved her hand in casual acknowledgment without looking back. God. Heart pumping as if someone were winding it, she crossed Broadway and walked along the small park surrounding the Public Library. The breeze was a relief. The little confrontation seemed unbelievable to her, even though it had just happened; if they had jumped and raped her, for example, would her heart have beat any more rapidly? Was this the script for night walking in cities now—trembling fear when you didn't get raped? And what then if you did—shame, pride? Was her sudden pause and question with the boys risky and self-destructive, or shrewd, practical? (She was free and clear now, wasn't she?) She really didn't know.

Nor did she quite know or remember having walked all the way to the Square, or into the Paperback Booksmith on Brattle, until she was inside the store, where KLH speakers, fixed like Big Brother, blared and customers browsed. Had paperback stores replaced bars for night trysts for the lonely? Surrounded by paperbacks, smarting from sudden fluorescence, she saw that she and circumstances had made a truth of her fib to Adrien.

She started out in Photography and Art, but it quickly bored her and she moved over two aisles, to Fiction. A floor-to-ceiling bookcase running the length of the shop, maybe the pitcher-to-batter distance. The thousands of fictions stopped her momentarily, as she thought, All these make-believes in the service of how many truths? She decided to shop for the Japanese fiction that Harry had been telling her about, and began reciting names privately. Dazai, Akutagawa, Tanizaki, Oe.

She moved among the shelves, the titles and jacket designs all competing for attention.

"Have you read any of his work before?" someone mumbled, referring to the Mishima short-story collection she held.

"No, no, I haven't." She looked up to see a tall gaunt man in corduroy, his high voice and English or Irish accent emerging from a handsome, ruddy face.

"He's really quite interesting, especially these stories." He nodded, his smile revealing imperfect teeth but an attractive man, the hair on his head thick and untidy. In his worn corduroy jacket and shirt opened at the neck, half the collar in, half over the lapel, with his reddish complexion, he looked like a Hardy character come straight from the woodlands or the heath to the paperbacks.

He mentioned his favorite stories in the collection, "Patriotism," "Death in Midsummer," "Onnagata"; then asked her if she'd like to walk and perhaps get a drink.

She bought the book at the counter, and they walked along Brattle, past the Brattle Cinema and toward the Loeb Theater.

"It's prettier at night than by day, when the people are around," she said, feeling comforted by the size of this man. "The shops and stores look so much . . . less harried, don't they? As if they didn't want them around, either. Do you walk around here much at night? In Cambridge, I mean?"

He spoke in his mumble and she had to reach for his words. "Actually, I do a bit. I quite like it at night. I've just moved into town after decades in the suburbs. It's like being released from jail." "With the family or without, you moved here?" "With," he replied casually. They passed Design Research, a glass container of sparkling lights and vivid colors, a four-story toy. "And are they all home asleep now?" "The children are, yes." "And your wife?" "Well, she's a bit sick at the moment, actually." He paused and lit up a pipe. "How many

149

children?" Resuming walking, he said, "Four, actually." She looked up at him, this big, bearded Beckett-type who had appeared out of the night, out of the paperback section, with his family brood in the background. "How ill is she?" she asked. He blinked his eyes and walked on, the air humid, heavy. She felt bad for appearing to force him into a corner: confession for companionship. But it was too complicated to withdraw it. "Pretty ill at the moment. A kidney infection." "How old is she?" "Full of questions, aren't you?" he finally said. "Forty." Miriam concentrated on the man again.

Presently they were drinking in the dark bar of the Sheraton Commander Hotel. An exiled couple seated amid the respectable suit-and-tie citizens: the dark girlish woman in her jeans and black turtleneck and the tall bony Irishman in his sloppy academic corduroys. But he was all ease and competence, and his laugh was fine and infectious. A buxom woman sang at a bar piano. He had three straight Scotches to her single dry vermouth, and they discussed living in town rather than the suburbs and his classes at Boston College, where he taught modern literature and some Irish history. At one point he said casually, "Do you think we might take a room for a bit?" She sipped her drink and said, "Yes, that would be nice." The singer had moved from "Laura" to "Ain't Misbehavin'."

In the elevator going up, they discussed Joyce, and in the room he talked about Ireland and the civil war. A good friend of his was Conor Cruise O'Brien and he spoke about O'Brien's "quite remarkable life," from the Congo to literature to Irish civilian. Then Miriam was on the bed, propped with a second drink (brought in), observing the wing chairs, the anonymous landscapes on the wall, the thick rug. "Do you mind this?" "I like it," she said in reference to the classical music on the radio. He took his jacket off, dropped it on a chair in a bundle, and moved toward her. She saw how milk white and virginal his long neck looked in his open shirt, and when he reached for her waist, she raised her head to receive that neck upon hers. She considered the neck and lengthy, slim body as he caressed her, as they undressed. He handled her with an orderly tenderness that reminded her of Harry bathing her once and drying her down as if she were his daughter. Several seconds later she caught his mumbled words: "Ah, you smell nice . . . Am I hurting you? . . . That's quite nice, right there . . ." He made love to her twice. The first time was hampered by his desire to be on his good behavior, taking too much care that his large, bony body wouldn't burden her. The second time, a piano concerto later, was much more satisfying, as he let himself go more freely and worried more about his own pleasure. He stayed harder longer, and was wilder and slower too. All the time that he pleased her, she thought of his wife sick with her bad kidneys, and she loved him for that hour for *her* sake as well. Or that's what it seemed like to her.

Something else surprised her too. The way she took all the new matters—the pickup in the bookstore, the drink in the bar, the undressing and intercourse in the hotel room—in stride, matter-of-factly. There was no sense of embarrassment, shock, or shame on her part; there was simply the flow of the late evening and the ease between the two of them. Here in the Sheraton Commander, with this curious, kindly stranger; before with the three boys on dark Trowbridge Street; earlier, sitting with her baby-sitter, tempted out into the evening. It was a kind of late-night drama, with three acts, say, Miriam Scheinman holding it all together. But who was this woman—an actress hired to play Miriam or the old, real Miriam playing the part of a new woman? This interesting stranger look-alike, was she a shadow self as in literature, acting on commission or secret orders from the other Miriam? a woman who possessed the other's body, her books and clothes and un-beknownst desires? Or a whole other woman being evolved and formed slowly, anew. Or all of these, in one multiple image?

She lay looking at the light-gray walls and blue land-scapes beyond the fair and ruddy-skinned body of this displaced Irishman and thought she had a clue, per-haps. Did this other—present—Miriam work in some ways for the city itself, for Cambridge? In charge of the Bureau of . . . Making Contact in the City . . . an agent, a special hostess of the spirit? who introduced persons like this Colin—and Miriam—to each other, and to the secrets of the city, like showing them this Marabar Cave, the Sheraton Commander? Of course, this other lady, who worked at night casually, on her own, seemed totally at odds with the photographer by day, who had to struggle in every way to find and cap-ture furtive realities of the city. It was a kind of split that she felt, rather than understood, when she thought about it. But just now all she felt was a small real pride in her body, the way it had come through and behaved so well for this lonely, somewhat shy man.

"Will I see you again?" he asked. "Next week at the same time? Or maybe a little earlier—eleven in the bar downstairs?"

There were so many different kinds of hand-someness in men, weren't there? This ruddy face and swan-white neck and mop of red-brown hair; the high forehead that contained what sort of stories and pres-sures? The long-stemmed body trained so well in gen-tleness and giving. Whose hard-angled frame could bring her such pleasure.

And so many different kinds of penises too—Colin's uncircumcised one had taught her emphatically—though the laws about them were relatively simple. The great and simple lesson, she recalled fondly now after her early fumblings, was that the so-called fearful penis was actually an incredibly moody, frightened, and sensitive creature acting on orders from organs above. A fleshy barometer that rose and fell according to the level of trust in the psyche. So she'd put a little trust in the air, playing slow, easy, and patient with the shy beggar (and his two sacks of salty goods), and before you knew it, he'd be as big and bold as nature permitted. The truth for Miriam had not been men's power in the world but women's power in bed; a little deviousness, artlessly applied (or unconsciously perpetrated), and you could cause havoc with a man's mind and confidence, not to mention member (a word which always made her smile). Making penises hard or soft was a female power more intriguing than nature's, a responsibility more direct. And keeping them firm, nurturing their stamina, was as much due to a woman's talent as a man's. (Look at how she had proceeded with Harry.) And oh yes, they—the penises—were like little boys in their humorous and helpless extremes of behavior.

"You're smiling so oddly. It's no, then?"

She touched his hand. "No, it's yes, actually."

His face lost its hesitancy and flushed brightly. Delight was simple.

She liked the ride home in the cab too, as he told her about growing up in Dublin and then going to the University of London, all the while holding her hand in the dark. She said at the end, "You remind me of people like Diggory Venn or Angel Clare. Is that awful?"

"No, not at all."

"I'll call you Angel, then."

"And who are you, Eustacia or Tess?"

She thought, and shook her head. "I better stay Miriam."

He smiled. "Good."

She nodded and kissed him good night and got out of the cab.

Adrien was asleep in that same chair, thick anthology opened on his lap, happy in sleep. It was ten minutes after two. She hadn't been out alone that late at night since she was a single girl in Ann Arbor, almost half her life ago. She woke him up and he looked at her momentarily as if she were a total stranger, in disbelief. Actually, he was more right than he suspected.

After he had left, she tried to cool the humming in her circuitry by putting the still-hot experience into words:

> Excited, maybe terrified. Borderline between the two. I've never "done" a pickup before. And yet, if it had been filmed, it would have looked like I knew what I was doing and did it smoothly. The deceptiveness of action.
>
> Fucking a stranger, nice and casual, no moralizing, no pressuring, little knowing, makes sex easier, if anything.
>
> Did danger enter into the desire at all? Maybe, tho doubtful.
>
> The experience was something like going out for a reward—ice-cream sundae?—late at night, after homework, during high school.
>
> There is something v. v. nice about lying with a *strange body* that fits you well.
>
> It's such a tiny incident, infinitesimal in the world's scheme, and yet for me it's a major experience. To show you my true innocence, Dr. L.
>
> I feel loose and easy, not adulterous, and yet— did I commit a crime against his wife? Was that part of the excitement, once he told me about it on the street, beforehand.

That last line reminded her for some reason of a brief essay she had read recently, and she went to the bookshelf, got the paperback, and sat down with it. It took ten minutes to go through it again. Then she got back to her thinking gear:

WILL I ALWAYS be watching myself this way? ALWAYS live by and through Collier, Vintage, Doubleday Anchor?

Dr. Siggy gets an awful lot packed into those 2 pgs. "Criminality from a Sense of Guilt" (from "Some Character-Types met with in Psycho-analytic Work")—he can make up my titles any time! Do I take these risks and those pictures, "precisely *because* they are forbidden," as Freud suggests, and because carrying them out affords me a "sense of mental relief"? Interesting and scary, isn't it? Look at MS. Guilt stemming from early frustrated love for Dad, incestuous jealousy. But can it really linger on that long in one's life, deep down there through all the years, buried alive? Yes. And then overlaid, 2 decades later, with new guilt (incurred from possible damage to Jon and Rosie during the last bad years)? But *have I sought to become criminal because* of that reservoir of guilt? What a thought. Is there any end to the twisted routes and unforeseen detours of the instincts?

STOP. RETURN. Can that guilt really linger on? Again, as much as I admire you, Dr. L. and Siggy, I can't believe one's O. Complex completely determines the future of one's adult life. For hysterics, psychotics, and deep neurotics, okay, it's crucial. But for ordinary neurotic types like myself, there are too many other elements at work for one to be wholly stained by original OC sin. You may think I'm defensing again, Dr. L.—and you may not, since you're smart—but isn't it true too that there is a distinction to be made between us ordinary folk and them sicker folk? And that family, work, and adult successes may modify considerably earlier defeats? In other words, I just don't buy determinism-for-all, Doc. (Unless of course it's cultural determinism—Zuñi or North American—and even there, there are holdouts.) I buy instead the healthy individual spirit, running behind tested honesty and continuously sharpened under-

155

standing, even though Siggy might think me very
naïve, and the Zuñis would punish me severely.
(Of course, if the opposition out there—practical
circumstance and other wills—gets too tough, then
sure, one can go under.)

And maybe most imptant, if those photos are
good, as I think they are, then maybe MS will have
manipulated her neurosis to useful ends. Surely,
dear doctors, those pictures are to be looked at in
artistic terms as well as analyzed. Whether they're
good pictures or simply the hieroglyphics of a
driven woman, "M–34" will help to decide.

Meanwhile, it was like going out for a sundae, or
for a good conversation, Dr. L., Dr. Siggy—good
night, sweet shrinks, parting is such a pleasure, on
certain occasions.

And she headed for bed, less buzz sawing, more content.

Three

![decorative divider]

GRADUALLY OVER THE NEXT TWO DAYS she climbed to a new plateau of ease and confidence about her new ways, and a sense of deliverance from her stern conscience. This solid confidence, ironically enough, arrived at the same time as a letter from Larry Jacobson, Stan's lawyer, Friday morning, which announced that Dr. Stanley Brown had filed in Third District Court of Middlesex County, Cambridge, for custody of their two children on the grounds of Miriam's "moral turpitude and incompetence." She read the letter at the wheel of the station wagon, with Jonathan chattering away to Rosie (in her car seat), and she felt her breath come fast, in gulps. For a moment at first she thought it was some late April Fools' joke, but the letter was too palpable, the cruelty of the joke too sharp. She read the lines over again and again, trying to see if she had missed some crucial key which would discount the rest, until Jon was tugging at her sleeve. "Come on, Mom, we're gonna be late!" A message repeated immediately by Rosie. "C'mon, Momma, we're late!" So she turned

157

the wheel and pulled out, narrowly missing getting smashed by an oncoming car, her eyes wet from fury and shock, the children beginning to complain again. She forced herself back into functioning control, and looked this time before pulling out.

At the intersection of Mass. and Chauncy she shot the light by mistake, just missing a blue sedan that screeched to a halt, the driver cursing her; she waited for a siren, but it didn't come. The thought that kept hitting her as she crisscrossed Cambridge to the Peabody School was how just a half hour ago she was still basking in the glow of the past two days, warm and resplendent.

For in those two days, thinking intermittently about her night before, her changing-lover life, she had for the first time come to the conclusion—or was it the sensation?—that life was better and richer now, and that she had crossed over some barrier. She likened it to her experience of the past summer, in New Hampshire, when she had finally, after thirty-three years, learned to swim, learned to be easy and comfortable in water. It dated back to her early water fears. She had tried in vain for years to attain that blue ease; but without regular water and trusting teacher—Stan, yes, dear old Stan, who swam well and who could teach others well, was the worst one for her to learn from—it was hopeless. Water meant thrashing about in fear and panic. And then, last summer, Jamie had accompanied her into the lake every single day of their two-week vacation, showing her the rhythm of breathing, the sense of gliding through the water with her head in it like a fish, the way to duck herself and come up again until she got the idea that it wouldn't kill her down there. And like clockwork she had practiced every day, rain, cold, or cloudy, and suddenly there it was: one July afternoon she went back and forth in that demarcated swimming area, without fear about the water (above her momentarily), as if she were out for a walk. The steady practice and routine, the accumulation of technical know-how, the unconscious confidence developed by being in the water every day, suddenly clicked, as she swam back and forth that July 8.

Okay, now, back in life, after years of being a daughter, a student, a wife, a mother, a woman whose duty and responsibility were primarily to others, she had suddenly realized that what she had been pushing herself for, for the past year directly and the past five years indirectly, had been *realized: herself alone considered.* Not friends, not children, not a movement, not an ideology, not a husband. For herself. It was like a crystal formed at an exact moment out of chemicals and conditions working over a period of time. This bolder woman out of a host of good, proper, timid, frightened, respectable girls.

That is why the lawyer's letter so stunned her. It was not only a surprise in itself—though Stan had threatened such action in the past, from the start when they were breaking up, still it had been a threat only—but it undermined this newfound self, as if the ground she had built up to stand on was dissolving and she was dropping. Was Miriam Scheinman going to be returned to Miriam Brown, Miriam the Frustrated, Miriam the Pleasureless? It seemed to her particularly cruel, cosmically cruel perhaps, and ludicrous even, that such news—whether it had serious substance behind it or not—should reach her just then.

To top matters off, when she called her own lawyer and asked him about it—he had received a copy—he put to her a question which made her hate him fiercely, though of course he was only doing his duty: "Well, Miriam, what's your love life been like recently?" She hated him just then because he was the Law, and supposedly on her side, and yet here he was, a snake in the guise of a pink Princess telephone, intruding upon

159

her private life. And when she went over there to his Chestnut Hill office, it was worse. The made-up secretaries, the orange orlon rug, the hip striped paintings on the wall, struck her now as enemy territory. Then, Sandy's office, Sandy Fried behind the big glass-top mahogany desk that you could fit two corpses in, Sandy with his red B.U. Law School ring and his diplomas on the wall (next to a picture of Einstein), Sandy in his two-toned shirt and flare trousers asking her about matters that had no relation whatsoever to him, to the commonwealth, to her capability as a mother. She kept from crying by cultivating her hatred; she hated him for the questions and for her dependency on him. Of course, all the time she knew that he was only doing his job and trying to help her, in his odious way. "All right, lay it all out," he said, unfurling cellophane from a cigar. "Let's hope it's not as bad as I think it is."

She composed herself. She knew she shouldn't have worn jeans here; she thought about getting a female lawyer. She fought down the hatred, rational and irrational, and effaced the memory of her pleasures. She tried to erase the emotions that had been pressuring her chest in the past several hours (he had made her wait thirty-five minutes in the outer foyer, amid the secretaries, *Fortune* and *Forbes* magazines, the telephone calls and local chatter). The joys of the past few days, which she had announced and reaffirmed to herself aloud, were forbidden here. SMOKING IS PERMITTED, HONESTY FORBIDDEN. She had to remember to forget everything that she had worked to build up for the past twelve months plus.

She tried to be cold and objective and useful, speaking about Miriam Scheinman. Sandy Fried, whom she had nicknamed Jew Fried in deference to the way he spread grease upon the race, listened with his cunning, his crudeness, his cockiness, his "told-you-so" glee. It was *his ego* that was at stake, being gratified. She was at his mercy, dating back to the original divorce proceedings; unfortunately, he had no mercy. The inquisition lasted an hour and a half. She responded to all his questions, breaking down not at all as she revealed the facts of her life as if putting her cards out on the table in casino; the more she laid down, the more she saw, with his help, that she did not exactly have a winning hand. At one point, near the finish, he said, "You've really gotten yourself into a little mess here, sweetheart. And if the other side knows the size of the mess, we're in for some trouble." He smiled ruefully. She thought of the new *plural* responsibility. "They probably do, too." "But how?" she asked, puzzled. "Miriam," he said, trying to soften the blow, "where have you been all your *adult* life? *Detectives*. Everyone has them, baby, in situations like this."

Just like the movies, she thought. Dashiell Hammett. Sam Spade. But she didn't have any. Could lovers count instead? Would Stan stoop so low? A silver jet flew in the azure sky with great simplicity. As soon as she had asked the question, she chastised her own innocence. Even this phony hip crumb Fried knew that much last year, when he had warned her about her ex: "That's an angry man you've divorced, sweetheart. Remember that, for your future." She hadn't. *I mean, not the way you wanted me to remember it. Instead I thought about young and beautiful Ann Arbor Stan, or poor dependent Stan. It caused me such useless energy in anguish. Vengeful Stan, well, it was finally so uninteresting. Now I'm going to pay for it, is that what they're saying? All right, how high?* Sandy scolded mildly, "Well, what are you dreaming about?"

She stood to leave, the list of things down on paper about people who could testify as to her "moral character" and "capacity as a mother." Plus a calendar of dates. She let slip then, "They couldn't take them away from me, could they?" His deliberate pause and stare

161

shocked her. She realized suddenly how comforting were his usual threats and chatter. "I'm afraid they can. We're in the corner, let's see if we can get out of it. You get to work on some of those friends of yours. And meanwhile, Miriam, for godsakes, put some discretion into your private life! At least for the upcoming weeks during this thing. And let me see if I can get some useful dope on our friend Stanley."

Useful dope about Stanley? she wondered, getting into her car outside, in front of Stop & Shop. You mean his vices? Watching too much sports on television for a grown man? The two times during fourteen years that he had tried real Scotch? The too-quick temper? She'd concentrate on discretion then.

But what could she do when Jamie called to take her out to dinner? Was that illegal? Was she to call Sandy Fried to get his permission? She couldn't. She arranged a time with Jamie, and a baby-sitter. The word made her heart shake. Julia Havens, she explained to herself, repeating the name again and again.

She found it hard to concentrate on writing when she tried.

> Will I lose contact here too, where it's meant so much, maybe everything?
>
> All right, Mir, take it easy.
>
> Go slow, think, be practical. Seek affection.
>
> You overworry, you know that. Dr. L. has confirmed that.
>
> Should I write her? Ask her when she's coming back? One touch of trouble and look, Doctor, I'm shaking. Calling for you.
>
> Be reasonable, and get angry if there's an outlet and it's called for.
>
> Am I blowing this whole thing up out of proportion?

After a secluded weekend of trying to print pictures but constantly finding her mind wandering, she moved into Monday and Tuesday and discovered that horror in one's life forced one to administrate overtime. And it stopped serious work. She would see Nathalie Reibman, she had told Sandy, and Elizabeth Morrison, those friends with children and respectable husbands; Mrs. Mortimer, the head of the child day-care center; spinster Agatha Foley, schoolteacher at Peabody School; Dr. Goldmark, the pediatrician; who else? Harry did teach at Harvard occasionally and did know Stan. "You better have him see me for a chat first," warned Sandy skeptically. And concerning her mother and father being dead, Sandy interpreted for her the significant meaning, "You caught a bad break there, especially if they were friendly to you. Inside the courtroom, you can't beat a friendly mother or father, sitting and watching the judge." Yes, she had missed that aspect of their deaths.

When she tried for help, for aid, for advice, for companionship from friends like Sally P., the institute history professor, or Nathalie, she discovered that good will in Cambridge was hampered by busyness. Everyone was so *busy* in this town. (Was it Cambridge or adult life?) She phoned Nathalie, got no answer, then got that beep signal for the next half hour. She tried Sally, who explained that for the next few days she was loaded down with overnight guests arriving, and with an article that was overdue. Could she talk with Miriam next week or so? Miriam, embarrassed, said sure. Hating the telephone with a passion by now, despising her own need by now, she called Nathalie back. "Oh dear, Miriam, look I'm rushing like mad to make a meeting about teaching, could I call you back later, after ten-thirty, say?" "Of course." Ten-thirty came and went, eleven-thirty and twelve-thirty too. Miriam, knowing there was a reason, felt abandoned nevertheless. That absent phone call made her feel desperately foolish, alone.

It came the next morning at 8 a.m., however. "I'm sorry, Mir, but that damned meeting lasted longer than I thought, and I was so drained by it, I couldn't get up enough energy to phone then. And today, I'm afraid to say," her voice dying, "that we're heading for the Cape immediately after Arthur finishes his morning lecture. It's not an emergency, is it?" Miriam thought, No, no. Of course not. "How about Monday, can I call you then? You know how things are during the term." Miriam agreed. "Of course." She made a limp joke about sharks at the Cape and hung up. They were good girls, good women, it was not their fault, she told herself. Life kept you busy, ambitious or successful life kept you very busy. But it seemed like you almost had to make an appointment, weeks ahead of time, to keep friendship going.

Jonathan was calling, and Miriam got busy too.

On Thursday night she was at home, looking through Atget, having just gotten Jonathan a glass of water, when she began to cry. She cried for a minute, then two or three, finally for fifteen minutes, thinking of what Stan and the law and Sandy Fried were conspiring to do to her; she knew she was a *good* mother, a far better mother than Stan was a father, and she knew the children felt that way too. What *offended* her as much as the prospect of losing the children aggrieved her was the sense of the *lie* about it all. Stan knew how she and the kids felt; didn't Röchel, his new wife? She mustn't blame her, she was out of the picture. No displaced anger tantrums now. (But what was the good of being a psychiatric social worker if you let this go on?) It was Stanley, and that vengeance. And Flo, that Philadelphia Clytemnestra! Bringing out the revenge blood in her nephew-son! Stan! If she were in the living room now, Miriam would take up a gun. And use it.

The peace of the evening, of her reading and working, was disrupted. And when she lay down to sleep, she thought again of the *lies* and her own fears. She took two sleeping tablets, but they didn't work either.

Dear Dr. Levanda,
I'm getting in over my head, perhaps. You see, Stan . . .

She didn't know what to say here, and waited, pen-doodling . . .

has decided to sue for custody of the children, and things don't seem to be going right. Not breaking in my favor. Sorry, Doctor, for putting this so foolishly, but the trouble seems to be coming at me too fast. Something like that. (It's also v. late at night.) Anyway, what I wonder is, were you planning on coming back early for any reason? And if not, maybe you can recommend someone here for me to talk with for a short time?

I've had a very good and reassuring year, as you know from my past notes, and I'm sure this will pass.

No, Doctor, I don't know why I said that last. I'm not at all sure, that's why I'm writing you now, like this.

At about 4 a.m. she finally fell off to sleep, awakened at four-forty-five by Rosie crying. After breakfast, she reread the note and decided that it was . . . too rash just yet. Also, she sounded a little out of control. Was she? No, not yet; or, she couldn't be, this early on. She'd hold off on sending it. Compose it not so late at night, perhaps.

A curious thing happened that day at the lawyer's office. (The location of the office was also a matter of distress. In part to have a better address, Sandy Fried had moved out here, to a plush shopping-center area on route 9 in Chestnut Hill; for Miriam the fifteen-minute distance took thirty minutes each way in honking, rude traffic. And then she was forced to wait another twenty to thirty minutes [which she didn't have] in the orlon foyer, humiliated with the knowledge that one of these coiffured secretaries handled her "file.") Now what had

165

occurred this day was that Sandy got excited when it came out, in passing, that Miriam was going to have a show in City Hall in another month. "Now that's very interesting, very useful indeed." He sprang up. "Why didn't you tell me about this before? You don't know what's good for you, do you? That's exactly the kind of stuff we need to show you as solvent and successful in your career, alongside your maternal duties. What sort of pictures are they, by the way?" Hesitant about talking over her work with him, she grew easier as he seemed to be busying himself with more files. Suddenly he looked at her sideways and said, "What do you mean, erotic pictures?" It had slipped out, by mistake (for sure?), and he shook his head, lecturing a little child. "Forget those. Cut 'em out. Save 'em for your scrapbook. That's the last thing we want to show!" We? What was he talking about? What do you mean, you dumb prick! "I think that might be hard. They're my best photographs, I think. Along with—" "Forget it." He tapped the desk with his pencil. "They're out. That's hot stuff, get it? Out. Absolutely. Whaddya want, your kids or those pictures?" He swooped forward, across the desk, in gleeful fury. "Thank God, I got this out of you in time. Christ! Are you nuts or something?" Meaning it seriously. From the tip of his black buckled shoes to his absurd huge collar, she hated the mod squirt. Hated him fiercely. Hated his being *on her side*. But then, why don't you drop him? Because he knows the situation, because he was in on it from the beginning, more than a year ago, because I'm already *into him for money I don't have* and that figure'll double if I drop him now! "All right, now what other pictures do you intend for City Hall? Any children playing, for example? You know, that's not a bad idea. No"—he whirled back into his swivel chair, his pea brain struggling with his grand idea—"not bad at all. Groups of kids alongside your own. Their friends, if

166

need be. Sure." He shoved his forefinger at her. "Yeah, that's what we'll do. Now we're getting somewhere! Now, what did you say the date of this show was? Let's coordinate this thing properly." In ten minutes' time he had supplied not only the proper administration but the artistic idea too.

She left the office in blank despair and, swinging around, stopped up the highway at the first place she saw, Valle's Steak House. She didn't know what to do in the dark oval bar with the television screen flickering. A middle-aged woman sitting in a bucket chair was interviewing a comic writer and his Japanese wife, with an unwed mother waiting her turn. She'd put it all out of her mind, she thought, feeling the smooth liquor burn slowly down. Talk with Harry about it. Enjoy herself with Jamie tonight, and also talk to him about a different lawyer, maybe. Send that letter off, for sure, to Israel. The first scene of a melodrama, a man and his secretary and his wife, actors in close-up anguish on the television, had come on just as she was leaving. She was shocked to discover that the sun was high and blinding outside. She had never before emerged from a bar with the sun still shining.

Getting into the car in the parking lot, she realized something else. What was happening struck her as so old-fashioned, so out of date with the current Miriam S. It was an ordeal, a crisis, that befit Miriam Brown, say, but she, Scheinman? Hadn't she worked like mad this past year to escape just such old-fashioned frustrations and setbacks? Couldn't they—the men or society or whoever—figure out a more *modern* way of torturing her? Something more in keeping with her present *alive* life? She turned the key to start the engine. After all, did they think she felt guilty, or that they could hound her into that? No, she wouldn't let them! It was anger that drove her, and no! she was not going to muffle that, to convert it into guilt. No more of that, no!

167

Someone was tapping at her window suddenly. She rolled it down, unbelieving.

"Just thought I'd see if anything was wrong, the way you're revving that engine, you might wear it out."

She gazed at the pleasant face, released her foot, and thanked him.

Jamie looked sparkling that night in a light-blue denim shirt and silk tie, tan suit, and smart Caribbean tan. How appropriate that she should see her walking American advertisement, blond and optimistic, on her day of despair. She wore her best summer dress, worn only once or twice before, fuchsia flowers on deep-turquoise silk, reaching to the floor. "Why didn't you tell me you could look this way?" he effused, a bouquet of yellow roses in his hand. "What way?" He was at a loss for words, so she took the flowers and kissed him on the cheek. His face brightened. "Fashionably beautiful!" She laughed. "Should I change back into my hirsute sweaters and martyrdom jeans?" He shook his head. "Let's say goodbye to the kids. I promised Jonathan especially he'd get to see you." In the boy's room, Jonathan looked up from Julia Havens' building-block enterprise and elicited from Jamie a promise of a baseball game very soon. Hugging her son, Miriam felt the thick curly hair growing down his neck and knew she'd have to cut it. Too bad. When she was by the doorway, Jamie said, "Here, let's try one right now." And he slipped a single rose into her hair. She hooked his arm like a sweetheart date, and then went downstairs where Jamie helped her into the sporty Cougar. Before the observant eyes of two couples across the street, they sped off. A hotshot couple in the spring, huh? Two cheers for appearances! thought Miriam.

He took her back to her favorite Italian restaurant in the North End, that pair of rooms on the second floor with red-checkered tablecloths and Old World waiters.

(One of them was very hot for her, kissing her hand and kidding her that she reminded him of his first flame in Bologna. "Oh, when Paulo didn't have this!" holding his paunch.)

During the antipasto, she said, "Well, I made a mistake not going with you."

"You would have had a good time. And you deserve it. I warned you." He beamed widely and ate, with great enjoyment, as he lived.

"I know. I've just found out that I'm a moral degenerate anyway, so a week with a lover in the Caribbean wouldn't have hurt my reputation much more."

"What are you talking about?"

She explained the new legal charges with a certain brave coolness, aided by Bardolino. Closing with, "Maybe I can get a letter from you, validating that I passed up the trip because you wouldn't put a ring on my finger?"

"Sonofabitch," he muttered slowly to himself, aloud. He laughed low, in surprise; Jimmy Cagney in his twenties again. "So you're getting held up, huh?"

"Blackmailed for pleasure." She filled her second glass. "For my first year of good times. Oh well." She drank wine, and eyed her browned beauty. "And do you know the most ironic thing? He *can't stand* the children. He won't spend a solid morning or evening with either." He gazed at her, baffled. "Pride. Vengeance. Maybe *male* pride, vengeance . . . Sorry, my self-pity is showing."

They talked about the possibility of getting another lawyer, and Jamie said he'd look into it with the two lawyers he knew.

Then Jamie fixed her with a look. "He couldn't really get those kids, honestly."

"I've discovered that really he *can,* not quite honestly but legally. Which is what counts." She wiped her lips with the napkin. "Enough of Miriam S.'s *tsuris.* Tell me

169

about blue lagoons and scuba diving and coral reefs. Were there any Jamaican beauties? or just Manhattan secretaries?" She put her arms out, stretching. "And tell me about lying on a beach day after sunny day, with nothing to do."

"Sure. But first, what's *tsuris?*"

"Troubles," she said, running her finger along his good Wasp nose. "Now that your Yiddish is broadened by 75 percent, tell me about those beaches. And did you wind up taking a girl after all? I'm green with jealousy!"

As he talked, she filled in with her imagination. He was not a fascinating or humorous narrator. But she was all the more green that she had passed up the trip, knowing that the thing with her Cagney was not the word but the *deed:* diving, swimming, dressing, dancing, fucking. And as he spoke of a Penny Wilson from Sleepy Eye, Minnesota, he said, trying to admonish but really embarrassed, "Next time you'll listen to my suggestions, won't you?"

She nodded, wanting him to instruct her, to take her life over in fact, that life which seemed suddenly to be crumbling into little, little pieces, without her being quite able to keep things together; that life which had struck her as a perpetual brilliant noonday (without her quite calling it that), and which had suddenly turned around, or inside out, so that noon became midnight.

"Hey, watch that sauce!" and he wiped red from her dress.

After dinner they went to see *Last Tango in Paris,* which embarrassed Jamie—a fact which charmed Miriam almost as much as the movie itself, mainly those scenes between Brando and the young girl. "I don't know," Jamie said afterward, in deferential sincerity. "Is that art?" Miriam smoked a thin cigar in the car, driving back. "Who knows or cares whether it's art or not? It's a movie. I go to have a good time. And I did, did you?" He pondered that, in trouble. "I thought the photography of Paris and the color were fantastic," he came up with. She laughed heartily. "But maybe better with Gene Kelly dancing on some tables?" He broke into a smile, pleased. "Okay, you win. It's my fault, I'm sure. I just don't get all that jazzing up of sex. Fingers up asses, buggering with butter." He shrugged, deferring to her. She was glad one lover didn't know details about the other. Also, at another time she might have fulfilled her role better—the intellectual of the pair—and talked to him more about the picture, explaining just what she had liked and what she hadn't; but just now it didn't matter much. Not with Jamie so pretty, no. A good dinner, lots of wine, a beautiful man who takes you out for an evening and defers to you and wants to fuck you; what do you care if he's bored by buggering and prefers Brigadoons? Besides, who was she to say that fingers up asses or marmalade surprises were better than tap-dancing on tables?

She was mindful, of course, grateful, that behind Jamie's shy recoil from sexual explicitness or deviation, behind his embarrassment, was a splendid fuck. With his prick in her cunt he was all fine country boy, all straight man, erect for a long time and then, after coming, straightway hard again. At one point, later on in bed, she said, "Jamie, promise you'll never tell anyone?" He nodded, serious. "I like you better than I like Marlon, for sure." Miriam faced him on her side, Jamie locked between her legs. This straight blond lover boy who looked so refulgent and screwed so well was, she thought, a godsend that every woman should get for Christmas. He fucked as he looked and behaved: upright with competence, no elbows or chest fucking (like an athlete she had known), no deviations necessary or desired. A legitimate fucker, a true genital-intercourse man who would have made Dr. Siggy proud. So what if his virtue was perhaps also his limitation?—he finally wasn't as interesting all told in bed as Harry (or out, naturally), the less able fucker and more able player. Or kidder. (A nice aspect of *Tango*.) But that was what was all right about the present hours; Jamie relieved her mind of those outside complications and pressures, with his solid assertion of masculinity and his simple appeal to her own basic biology. This good fucking up there, light and easy, the penis doing the work with stiff patience, this capped off the evening splendidly, made Miriam think that the Caribbean had come to her, and allowed her to sleep, for the first time that week, with something like the old ease. With no will to record anything in print.

The gray light of morning put an end to that night ease, however. The next day, April 15, and the days following were a curious mixture of preparing for two very different sorts of trials, one legal and the other aesthetic. But the aesthetic was no longer an isolated issue, providing support and pleasure; it was now stained with the moral and practical considerations of her lawyer's demand for censorship. So whatever excitement she might have had in looking forward to the May show was undercut, especially with most of the day consumed by her effort to gather evidence on her behalf as a mother. This included setbacks that she hadn't expected. "Well, you know I've known Stanley for so long that I don't think I'd be able or willing to go to bat against him," said Helena Carlston, next-door neighbor, whose daughter Dina frequently played with Jonathan. Miriam responded, there in Helen's fashionable kitchen, "But you're not doing anything *against* him, so much as you're going to bat for me. Wait a minute, what am I saying?—I'm not asking you to go to bat *for* anyone, but simply to tell the fucking truth!"

172

The loss of temper did not sit well with pretty Helena, who never quite approved in the first place of Miriam's lack of formal politeness and her bohemianism. "I think you're getting a little out of control, Miriam," she said now, imitating her own Chevy Chase mother admonishing her. "If you'll excuse me, I have some work to do. But I really wouldn't count on me or Edward for help at the trial. Of course, if you should need any . . . moral support, then that's another matter." She wore a spotless floral dress, and Miriam was glad that her figure resembled a dog bone. "I'm sorry," Miriam said, recovering. "I only meant to convey to you just before that I didn't want to use you in any way, just to get at the truth. Thanks." She walked out of the apartment, spirit sinking, knowing it would take a few hours to get better. Going down the outside stairs, she found her hand gripping the banister too tightly. She remembered her anger vow and wondered when it was called for; now? Go back upstairs and say calmly, Fuck you? Scream it? She didn't know. She didn't know.

But in a few hours, Agatha Foley of Peabody School didn't help matters. She looked at Miriam from above bifocal glasses, which hung at the edge of her nose, and said, "I'm afraid I couldn't be of any help here, Mrs. Brown. I just see Jonathan in school and I wouldn't know a thing about him away from here." Miriam, raging against *Mrs. Brown*, replied, "But that would be enough, I think. For you to simply talk about how Jonathan is here, his behavior during the past year, his academic capacity." Miss Foley picked up a sheaf of loose-leaf papers. "To tell you the honest truth, Mrs. Brown, I am very much against a mother bringing up her children alone. I believe it's a very dangerous business. Especially when there's a boy involved. Of course, this is simply *my* opinion and has nothing to do with my feeling that I can't get involved in your legal situation. Although, as we both know,

173

Jonathan did display considerable antisocial behavior patterns when he first came into my hands." Miriam glanced at the long rigid face, at the narrow bony hands, and had a quick image of them sliding around her own neck; she took a step backward. *Mrs. Brown.* The classroom filled with children's pictures and happy decorations suddenly was another lie. She moved out, hurt, baffled. And the next day Elizabeth Morrison practically did her in when she said, in Miriam's kitchen, "Warner says we can't get involved at all, it wouldn't be fair to Stanley." Miriam saw the hurt on her friend's face, the hurt and the appeal, and she restrained herself from saying, "But you do what *you* want to do, Elizabeth. Don't let my life and my children's lives be decided by your husband's sense of decorum. Be a woman, stand up and tell the truth, that's all, for godsakes!" The freckle-faced dear friend stammered slightly, adding, "If, if, if you really think that you need my help, tell me, will you? I, I, I'll do it, anyway." She shook her head, trying to be strong, trying to practice for Warner, if it came to that. Miriam touched her arm, said thanks, ran the water from the faucet, and asked about the Commonwealth School.

It was worse when she called Sandy Fried that late afternoon, about the setbacks. "Miriam, what are you *doing* to these people and to *my* case?" She loved the pronoun. "Instead of making our case stronger, all I hear is how the case is weakened. C'mon, baby, if you want to keep those kids, get on the stick!" She clenched her fists, her teeth, and squeezed out, *"But what do you want me to do?"* "Stop alienating these people and get some witnesses to help us! And another thing, I don't like to talk this way to you, honey, but if I don't, who will? Keep away from *all adult, two-legged creatures who wear pants.* Buy a fucking chastity belt to use if you have to—but stop fucking around!" She promised herself that she'd get another lawyer, or take a gun to this one. Sandy seemed to hear her thoughts and changed his tone. "Miriam, look, kid, I say these things for your own good, for our good, for the cause. When this is over, live how you want. Christ, I'm no moralist or choir boy, Miriam. But the law is the law, and sometimes it's tough, okay?" *Say it and get it over with. But he has a point, doesn't he?* "Okay." "Atta girl, and I'll hear from you later in the week, then? Don't worry, we're not outa this ball game yet!" But when did the odds change? Miriam wondered. Putting down the receiver, shivering slightly, she saw the aerogram to Dr. Levanda on the mantelpiece and knew it was time to send that letter off. Which she did, that evening.

On Tuesday night at 11 p.m. she walked to the Sheraton Commander bar, careful, however, to stop first in Brigham's and Bailey's and the Booksmith to make sure she wasn't tailed. It was like a movie she had seen a hundred times, only now she was inside of it; what was once thrilling or cheap was now scary, unbelievable. And as she strolled off Brattle back up to Concord Avenue, the air April-scented, she thought how silly the little adventure was, and how futile—coming exactly one week late on the slim chance that he would too.

But he was there, her reddleman, at a corner table. He smiled wonderfully, and she wanted to kiss him for being there, for remembering her! She couldn't help leaning into his big shoulder, touching his wildly tousled hair. "Hi, your Eustacia has come," she whispered.

After they had ordered drinks, he said, "I thought something might have come up last week."

A few seconds after the sentence, she understood it, remembering to tune in to his low-accented mumble. She nodded. "It did." She shook her head. "I don't think I would have remembered tonight, but a friend called to remind me of my Wednesday women's meeting." She smiled. "Which reminded me of my *Tuesday* meeting."

"What did come up? Nothing too bad, I hope?"

She drank and told very briefly about her troubles, including the detectives. He was concerned. "We should be careful then, shouldn't we? Should I drop you off at home and forget this for the time being?" When she paused, in dilemma, he said, "Come on now, we'll do that."

And in five minutes, in a taxicab, they were approaching her apartment.

She asked, "Had you already booked a room back there?"

He shrugged. "As a matter of fact, yes, I had, but that's no problem."

"Let's use it then. Let's go back. No one's followed us that I've seen. Have you?"

He shook his head. "No, I don't think so," he mumbled, shaking his head. "I've actually kept an eye out, for someone's sake. But look here—"

"If no one's tailing us by the time we hit the Commander, let's make use of the room."

Her amusing verb only half-amused her as the taxi rerouted itself back to its site of origin, the young driver taking it all in stride. She found herself leaning into her friend, as if his size were better protection, a large warm nest.

Upstairs, he eyed her by the side of the bed and asked, "Why? If you don't mind my asking. Why'd you want to come up here?"

She didn't smile, taking off her blouse. "I wanted to, that's why." No brassière, Ms. Miriam. She went to work on her slacks. "I fought too hard to want things, to want my feelings, to give up the habit now. Also"— she smiled—"maybe I wanted to find out what it's like to make love like a real criminal. Or is it victim?" She

176

lifted a lampshade, put her finger to her mouth, and pointed to the bulb.

"By the way," she said, replacing the shade, "how's your wife?"

"You move too fast for me," he acknowledged. "She's rallied considerably since I saw you last." He untied his shoes, good shoes beaten up, laces ragged (she noted). "She's home now. Coming around, I think, getting her strength back."

Miriam eyed him. "I'm glad." She pulled the quilt back, getting down onto the bed, elbows on clean sheets. When she recovers, do I lose a lover? "Maybe I'll get to meet her one day."

"Quite possible."

"Quite improbable." She imitated his quick mumble and pulled him down to her. After kissing that neck, she said seriously, "Do you think I'm being unnecessarily self-destructive?"

He began to answer, but she cut him off. "No, no, I didn't come to drag you into my drab life. I came to . . . cheer us up, me and you. Let's start."

They started, and as they moved into a beginning rhythm, she was struck by this . . . sinking or dying sense, this fear of being taken down so far that this current activity would be forgotten about, discarded, and that old sexless Miriam Brown would rise up to take her place. She wondered, as he moved upon her in his gentle but firm way, whether he could have any idea that this might be her last fuck of pleasure, her final body-giving of will and spirit, and as she became driven by this fantasy, gripped by this interpretation, she moved her pelvis and vagina with all her accumulated knowledge and precision, at the same time that she felt the mane in the back of his head with as much tenderness as she had ever felt, loving this stranger out of a sheer burst of gratitude, and fucking

177

him out of fear, and she felt grateful too. She felt him get close, edge into a recognizable frenzy, and she hoped somewhere, prayed somewhere, that he would reach her, touch her soul, understand its grief and melancholy and be there, so that she wasn't alone, so terribly alone, and while she knew that she was bringing to this intercourse much more than it warranted or could support, she did it regardless, met his rising frenzy with her own wild need and longing, opening her eyes but seeing only his white cheek, closing hers and moving back into her urgent darkness, smelling lavender now and feeling herself filled and filling, drawing him into her farther, farther (her legs enfolding him), and finally forcing his eyes to hers for a moment only, seeing the green-gray of his iris like her mother's; and then she was satisfied and enjoyed the liquefaction, felt at home glued there, and didn't want him ever to depart; lay there filled with contentment and wholeness and felt solid at last (paradoxically), with him in her this way, having spoken and gotten her to speak without words, no words, words that were trying to do her in, just the trust of flesh and the faith of coming. She held him and held him, and was more grateful than he knew.

At the end he said, "You do cheer me up tremendously, you know." It made her feel useful, and she said, "That makes two of us."

But the next afternoon, playing with the two kids in the basement, she did remember her own question of self-damage. She wondered about it on that rainy Wednesday as Jonathan busied himself meticulously with the wooden railroad that Harry had helped him construct. His tiny hands moved with a deftness that always surprised her. Rosie was right in there, trying to keep up, and Jonathan, for want of a more able buddy, put up with her. Magnanimous soul. She had worked to convert that dim cold cellar into this bright, vivid playroom—at the Ping-pong table, the cobalt-blue walls, the new wooden floor painted canary yellow, on which were placed Hancock Street Station and the tracks. She wondered which she could stand, not putting those pictures up in the Show and not seeing her men, or giving up those two tiny operators here. When she thought of the courts of law taking away this boy and girl, because she was enjoying herself for the first time in her adult life, a temper filled her, a desire to murder, which shocked her. At Ann Arbor and afterward, she had thought of herself as a pacifist, personally and politically. And of course there was no guarantee whatsoever that relinquishing her pleasures and work successes would mean keeping her children. No guarantee; they wanted her to throw in the towel, anyway!

"Mom," asked Jon, "do you think Dad'll really keep his promise and play baseball with me this Saturday?"

She paused. "If he said so, why not?"

"Well, you know him, Mom, he's promised me that before. You remember the last time, he went off to play basketball by himself and *I*—"

"Jon," she said, on her knees, loading some lumber on a boxcar with him, "how would you like to go and live with Dad for a while?"

"Yeah, that'd be neat," he said, trying to hook up the locomotive to a boxcar. Miriam restrained sudden tears. "Like for a whole week or so, y'mean?"

She smiled. "Well, maybe for longer."

He fought down his frustration and tried again to hook up the engine. Working away, he said, "Where would *you* be?— Hey, Rosie, cut that out, will ya!"

"Well, here."

"But then, *why would I go there?*" he said, admonishing her logic, "or *have to* go there?"

You wouldn't have to, she wanted to say. But maybe he

would have to. "Would you like to . . . go with Daddy and Röchel for a while, maybe try it?"

His face lit up as he hooked them together. Animated, he decided, "Nah. I like it here, and seeing Dad and Röchel on weekends. Then I get to see Jamie and Harry and Ad this way too," he said, carefully listing them. "Nah," he decided for her, "this is the best arrangement."

"Arrangement"? Where'd he learn that from, television?

At story time that night, reading them *Peter Pan*, with Rosie drawing and Jonathan rapt in attention, she knew, she knew it would *kill her* to give them up. Over her dead body, or someone else's. *Peter Pan* and Babar records would never forgive her. Even if it meant kidnapping them somewhere, to Nova Scotia or to Santa Fe, New Mexico. No matter what theory she might have, about anything. "C'mon, Mom, you promised!" And Momma had to read up to the part where Peter asks the kids if they believe in fairies, so that he could leap from the bed and scream out, "YEAH WE DO, don't we, Rosie!" tossing two pillows about to prove his point, and trying to get Rosie to imitate his six-year-old superleap, knowing she wouldn't dare, and it would frustrate her. "Little big shot!" Miriam grabbed him with joy, possessive joy.

"Look, what's the problem?" asked Harry the next night in his loft. "Be a good girl for a few months, postpone the show if you have to, get this thing out of the way, and then get on with your life. Arrange the practical side right now, sweetie." The verb reminded her of Jonathan's new noun. Was that where he had gotten it from? "It's not that difficult, is it?"

She found it difficult expressing herself clearly lately, even with Harry. "Suppose I lose the kids anyway, in a drag-out fight? What then?"

"Then at least you've tried your best to keep them, and not done your life unnecessary damage."

Tried my best. Prudent Harry. I can't lose the kids, I won't . . . And the pictures.

"I worked hard to get those pictures. I've worked hard to get this show. It means a lot to me. *Two years of work,* and more maybe."

"I know, don't worry." He nodded. "Any chance of postponing it for a bit?"

"No. I called. They're booked solid for the next year. If I cop out now, I'm out, period."

He stood up and got a pack of cigarettes from his rolltop desk. "It's hard, I know. Very hard. By the way, have you thought of talking it out with Stan? Of confronting him now, before anything legal occurs."

She shook her head. "No, I guess I haven't. It wouldn't do any good. Besides, it would be too . . . humiliating. Intolerable. He'd—"

"Look, pal," he interrupted, looking at her, "you better get off any high horse you're riding these days. Any at all, especially with Stan. If it takes a temporary fall or humiliation just now, maybe you better take them, for the sake of the future."

Stan's gloating face floated before her, and she tried to smash it with liquor.

"Do you think there's a . . . law of some sort operating here?" she asked her counsel Harry. "A law that says, 'Watch out, sister, that you're not flying too high. Or trying to. Or we're gonna bring you down.' "

"Sure. Sophocles and his choruses." He drank. "Done by the Supremes, perhaps."

She tried to smile. Looking through the prism of her tumbler, she asked, "Does Stan know that you go to bed with me?"

He reflected.

"I'm not sure, though I rather doubt it. We talk very little about sex, and he's not exactly as open as Reich

181

about private matters. We play an occasional handball game and talk about politics, if we talk. It's easier that way."

She nodded, in resistance. "All right, I'll try falling a little."

Afterward, she sat down with her notebook, wanting to write. But she didn't know where to begin, there seemed to be so many things wrong. I'll wait until things settle down a bit, she decided, closing the notebook, until at least after the Stanley encounter.

She arrived at 9 p.m. sharp at the Pamplona. ("If you're not there promptly," he had warned her on the phone, beginning the campaign, "I'll be gone.") Stan was not yet there, and she found a small narrow table in the center of the low-ceilinged basement room. She decided to wait for him before ordering, not taking any chances. Fortunately, she had brought along a book, and now took it out to read. *An Anthropologist at Work: The Writings of Ruth Benedict* (ed. by M. Mead). In the dim light, she tried to concentrate, but her stomach was turning and her mind drifted . . .

Had she been a good Jewish girl and *balabos* type, they would have gotten along splendidly. Like the aunt of his upbringing (dead mother's twin sister) who till today teased and manipulated Stanley, who feigned illness and weariness to draw sympathy, who played upon his guilt and dependence like a pianist playing scales. And when she wanted to, she could, with the greatest of ease, draw blood, anger, pain, or else carve enormous anxiety, gut defeat, and baffled fury from her "dear beloved son" (always her opening salutation, combining lie with euphemism); and of course, through that same bedeviled son, she could wreak daughter-in-law vengeance. Upon Miriam. At the beginning, especially. The tricks that woman knew and delivered! Here in Cambridge and down there in Philadelphia, where she drew him like a little boy on a yo-yo, back and forth, through personal pleas, "crucial" ceremonies (a distant cousin's briss, an acquaintance's son's bar mitzvah, a sudden fear of mysterious illness). Or else she'd fly up to Cambridge—mostly Stan drove down to Philly, on those relaxing six-to-seven-hour Friday-night traffic jaunts, after work—and try her best to turn their apartment into the old Brown family cage. (Real father, a weak man, grew weaker when Flo took over after wife's death, went AWOL to Atlanta, where he married again and sent an annual New Year's card from his greeting-card business.) And dear Flo, complaining steadily but growing stronger with age and victories, had reared daughter Ethel to follow in her own footsteps. So that when Aunt Flo (called Mother) was not working on her adopted "beloved," it was half sister Ethel's turn, via telephone, to check in and plead / demand / reprimand. An emotion-washing process as good as the Chinese could rig up. No, he was not going to escape those ladies too easily. And when Miriam had suggested talking to a therapist about it, Stan, angry, accused her of open jealousy over his sister and aunt, who had "sacrificed" so much for him. (Ah, that magical word that served to camouflage sadists and maniacs and torturers as much as it described saints and sympathizers. *Sacrificed.* How Miriam had come to hate that word!) So there was Stanley, bearing an overbearing male brunt; it broke Miriam's heart. Even now, in the Pamplona, waiting. This sympathy, despite the indignity and humiliation she had had to put up with when Aunt Flo flew in and hounded Miriam about hygiene, diet, money, manner of setting the table or putting the children to sleep, lack of curtains and—"Open your mouth once again today, Flo," Miriam announced one afternoon, after three years of pent-up fury, "and you never get into this apartment again. I mean it. You, or I, will go."

Trembling, knowing that she was taking the chance that Flo wouldn't seek a showdown, since Miriam *wasn't at all sure* that Stan would be able to choose her over Flo; not at all sure. Subsequently, Flo shut down the obvious sabotage attacks and opened up a more furtive campaign, especially with the children. A strangler switching over to the poison game.

One of the great side benefits of the breakup was that Miriam didn't have to deal with that Overbrook Park virago any more. But this relief, alas, also brought remorse, for the thought of Stan still being there to take it from that woman and her daughter pained Miriam—even though she had long, long ago lost any love for him, or even liking. But the way they had him trapped, and continued the torture—money, career, comparisons with friends' sons, Aunt Flo's life of sacrifice! Though by now the major damage had been done, his fierce anger and aggressiveness mostly bottled up and inner-directed, escaping in tiny outbursts, against her mostly, or Jon. When she perceived the tragedy, this man of great intellectual power and gifts having the energy of his mind sapped and poisoned by his twisted needs and instincts, when she saw the cost to him of playing the good Wasp and proper academic, she almost hoped that he'd murder, *murder her*, Miriam—if that's what it would take to unleash those pent-up passions. When she stayed back and saw the tragedy from the distance, how could she help but nearly cry at his helplessness, the self-destructiveness, the wasting—

She stopped. It hurt too much. Sympathy for Stan, despite her distaste, despite his hate for her . . . it was all too complicated and tangled, it wearied her, living together with someone for so long and witnessing up close the helplessness and blind obsessions—

He appeared in the doorway, looked around until he saw her, and then approached with that sort of wel-

184

coming nod to society that he always offered. Society, his conqueror without a battle. By her table he looked around once more, keeping Miriam waiting yet another minute or two, before seating himself. A waiter in white shirt and black tie, a nice formality in this lovely informal restaurant, took their orders, a pot of oolong tea for him, cappuccino for her. She found herself scratching her calf, as she had when she was twelve and had a test in school. In the cozy, compact, square room, with the narrow black-marble tables set near to each other, other conversations seemed to eavesdrop upon her privacy. What looked like a TA or assistant professor and a female grad student were talking earnestly about whether "metaphysical" was the proper or improper term for John Donne and other poets. And just to Miriam's left, a tallish, long-haired girl was discussing her difficulties with a girl friend's boy friend. Stan sat upright, drinking his tea, waiting. He wore a sports jacket, with a white shirt, the collar placed neatly outside the jacket, fifties-style. And his brown hair was parted on the right side, like when he was a photogenic seven in his sailor suit. (Dear, dear Stan.) The features were prominent, dark and handsome, and the beard was characteristically neat, trimmed under the neck and on the cheeks. A Roman consul perhaps, but definitely a Citizen, an academic citizen of law, order, and propriety.

She tried to restrain herself, though she could feel that gigantic respectability, more than his obvious snubbing, rub at her. In a soft voice she said, "Do we have to go through all this? What is it you're after?"

He sipped his tea, pinky out. "I'm sure you can read well enough."

She hadn't wanted to start that way, she was going to ask first about Röchel and his new project and paper.

She asked about Röchel and the project, and he said, twice, "Well, thank you."

She took her hand away from her calf as she began again. "But why do you want to threaten me this way? You know you don't want those children, really. I mean, Röchel isn't pushing this, I know, and you, you don't even *like* them—"

Stan grabbed her wrist and twisted, delighting as well as paining her.

"If you talk this way once again"—the face tight with rage—"I'll leave immediately."

"You're hurting me," she managed.

His teeth unclenched, in line with his grip. "I'll hurt you worse if you say those things again. Those lies."

Her wrist hurt, but she understood that his fury had exhilarated her. That excited, out-of-control glint in his eyes had been one of her last pleasures as their marriage had gone downhill. Getting him to hurt her, to express himself toward her, had become their only real intimacy, her only real power with him; it opened the door to his anger, that life prisoner. At times she found herself likening her provocations to unzipping his fly and getting his member to stick out; and then watching him lord it over her—an overwhelming act of shame and power and release on his side. He was never happier than when he had just slapped her around, and never sweeter, never more helpless, never more boyish or more beautiful, afterward. When Sandy the lawyer had asked her, during the original divorce proceedings, if Stan had ever used force, she had passed it over, saying no. It was not merely a case of keeping dirty laundry within the family and out of the hands of the public, the courts and Sandy Fried. It was a case of their intimacy—and all intimacy—being a thousand times more complicated than the words "physical abuse" would indicate.

She rubbed her wrist—for real, for effect? "Why are you starting all this now, over again? Look, Stan, if you want the children for longer periods—more weekends, more of the summer or whatever, fine, let's talk about it. I'm not against that." She leaned forward, trying to reason quietly, to talk like grownups. "Why drag this back into court? Why bring up our dirty laundry again? Why waste money and time with those . . . parasites?"

He had moved back into an erect position, and brushed back a strand of hair that had come loose. "I don't think you're fit to bring the children up," he said simply. And then, to show he was reasonable and sane, added, "At this point in your life, at least."

"Are you crazy?" she asked slowly. "What are you talking about?"

"You know perfectly well what I'm talking about."

The sudden grating roar from the espresso machine mingled with the growing congestion in her heart.

"What?"

"Let's not get into the sordid details, Miriam. I didn't come here—"

"What sordid details? What did you come here for, to talk about your health?"

He poured himself more tea from the pot, meticulously. He checked to see that tea leaves hadn't fallen through to his cup.

"What sordid details?"

"Speaking frankly, since you insist upon it, I don't think you're fit morally, or psychologically, to raise those children properly. Perhaps at some point in the future—"

"What specific sordid details do you mean?" She forced the words out, against his attempt at casualness. "Tell me, specifically. And stop that *fucking piety,* it's *revolting.*"

The restaurant and passing waiter bridled his lust to hit her. He stared for a whole minute or two with murderous vengeance, forehead capillaries about to burst. It was the way he would die, she knew for sure, a stroke from trying to dam up his torrential anger. The effort produced beads of perspiration above the full, dark brows.

"We both know how you've been living," he said, with the restraint of a gentleman, "and I don't think we need go into it here."

"*How* have I been living? *How* do you know how I have been living? Did anyone on the outside ever know how *we* lived? And if we don't go into it here, then *where? when?* In fucking court?"

"No hysterics or filthy language, or I leave," he warned, finding the handle, setting the rules suddenly. "Your life is your business, agreed. But the children's lives and welfare are *my* business." He made "my" sound like a whole sentence.

She waited a few seconds. The assistant professor was definitely deciding that metaphysical was improper.

"Have you used detectives to spy on me?"

His chin edged sideways, his forefinger swept down his beard, in proper consideration of the question. It was a fair question, he decided. "If you must know, yes. To protect the children, Miriam, I've had to resort to . . . special officials, yes. And I would do it again." He leaned forward with the point. "Just to show you which one of us truly cares for the children."

When Sandy Fried had said it, it hadn't seemed to register. Or when she was with Colin in the taxi, it had meant something else, unreal. But this admission of spies in her life, hired by the man she had cooked for and made love with for nearly thirteen years, shocked and weakened her.

"Cut out those tears!" he ordered. "You didn't use those tears when you took those men into our apartment and *our bed*. No tears then, I presume." He leaned closer in fury. "So cut them out now!"

She felt her body trembling, she began to cough, she tried to control herself.

The espresso machine roared again.

"Miriam," Stan said, after a minute, cooler, "let's face the ugly fact for what it is. You want to live a certain way, that's your business. But *I will not have* the children subjected to . . . different johns every night."

She lifted her cup to her mouth, but his knowledge of her instincts was as good as hers, and as she was about to throw it into his face, he grabbed her wrist. The cup fell from her hand onto the marble table and off to the stone floor, where it cracked into pieces.

"You fool," he proclaimed aloud. "You *clumsy* fool, I'll let you pay for this."

A waiter was immediately there, cleaning up the mess.

"She'll pay for that cup," Stan said with authority.

"Oh, there's no need for that, it happens all the time." And to Miriam, "Would you like more coffee?"

She shook her head, confused. She felt as if she were dripping blood, menstrual.

"It's a hard fact to face, isn't it?" Stan said as the waiter moved off. "To see what you've become. You don't look at yourself in the mirror these days, or take pictures of yourself, do you? Is that why you don't know who you are any more? or what you look like?"

"No, maybe I don't," she said sincerely, depleted, wondering. "What do I look like, Stan? Who am I?"

He leaned his face forward, a mask of taut, strained glee. "A whore. A low-class whore. The whore of Cambridge. And no whore is going to bring up *my* children."

As evenly as she could muster her voice, she said, "It kills you, Stanley, that other men are fucking me, doesn't it? And that I *like* it. And you know that—"

As soon as she had begun here, she knew she had

189

gone too far. She knew it was too strong for him, he would never take it. Stanley didn't take it. He slapped her across the face, hard, twice, the sting making her eyes wet. And it flashed through her mind, *If he hits me harder, beats me up here, and then becomes shamed and helpless and confused, I'll be tender again, I won't be able to help it. God, please don't let it happen, please.*

After a long minute, legal advice spinning immediately in his head, he covered his tracks. "I did that," he said, a little too loud, breathing hard, "because I consider it an insult to my children for you to talk that way, and further evidence of what the language must be like around them. I won't hear it. And it's for that reason that I've taken the action I've taken, Miriam. This entire little provocation which you've set up confirms my worst fears about your moral state, and possibly mental health. Face yourself—you've become a slut!" He stood up, shaking the table, chin high in respectability.

Suddenly he smiled, for no one in particular, and in a moment of madness which she would remember, and for which she had originally fallen for him, he leaned down to her and whispered, "The children will be mine, I assure you." He was not a Roman consul now but a Dostoevsky gambler in a fever.

He loomed there above her like a little boy waiting to see a bridge collapse, the result of his having pulled a block away. She hadn't the strength to hit out at him; she heard the words like a death knell; she felt his breath in her ear with a splitting sadness, for she knew that he wasn't in control at all, that it was the neurotic demon of his personality on the loose and that it was that demon, neurotic and uncontrollable, frenzied, vulnerable, and disreputable, that had always appealed to her so strongly.

She smiled, weak, and ran her hand along his beard where his cheek used to be. He removed it with force and moved away to the register. He paid and departed, lowering his head to move through the low doorway and jauntily pumping up the stone stairs, returning to his social, respectable self.

Miriam sat there still. Stunned. Weak. Gasping for air. The frizzy-haired girl nearby was now hearing a confession of guilt from the second girl, and the teacher and grad student were now talking about "critical influences."

Head spinning wildly, she forced herself up and went to pay her bill, but was told that "the gentleman" had paid it already. Another courtroom detail, just in case.

She walked up the stairs slowly, into the spring night. Up curving Bow Street toward Mass. Avenue, for no particular reason. At the corner, Baskin-Robbins was mobbed by kids with streamers in their hair and new styles of overall jeans. She smiled at the pastel colors and buoyant pink faces. She turned and walked back down Bow Street, past Adams House, where Harvard students walked in and out, or lounged carelessly, on the walled terrace, talking. She felt heavy, her confusion like a chain on her leg. She wandered around the corner at Mt. Auburn, past Cahaly's and Lowell House and the Lampoon turret, then back around the narrow cobblestone street between Adams and the back side of Cahaly's. She found herself back on Bow Street, walking up it for the second time. Approaching her now was a young blond girl, who, when she came closer, turned out to be a blond boy, with a friend. At the ice-cream parlor she had a new impulse, and once again retraced her steps down Bow, this time with a purpose.

Down by the river she walked through the darkened arch of Eliot House, and up the rickety stone steps of the L-entrance; four flights up. She knocked on the door.

Adrien, in a silk bathrobe, was very surprised to see her.

"Well, uh, hello, I didn't know you knew where I lived, precisely."

She needed aid now, she wanted to tell him, to remind him of his offer. "May I come in?"

He looked uneasy. "Well . . . Ricky is here, you know."

Miriam saw a blond boy with shoulder-length hair in the background, the sounds of rock music floating through.

"It's all right with me," Miriam said, mustering control, "if it's all right with you."

Adrien looked back toward his friend. "We were going to . . . smoke a little, actually."

"That's fine with me," she said softly, feeling enormous strain and helplessness. She had an impulse to ask for his mask, for courage.

"Well, for godsakes, let her in," admonished Ricky, approaching in a Japanese kimono. He was thin and wore glasses and had fair skin. "No one could be *that* bad. Who is it?"

Adrien seemed to stumble.

"Hi. I'm Miriam Scheinman."

"Well," Ricky exclaimed, his pallid face lighting up with delight. "I've heard an awful lot about you. Adrien, where in heaven are your manners? *Do* come in, won't you? It's not the Plaza, I'm afraid."

"Why, thank you, that's nice of you."

Adrien, at the mercy of his surprise visitor and his eager friend, closed the door after her. A long room leading to another, decorated with Beardsley prints, peacock feathers, Oriental rugs, a velvet chaise longue, two Tiffany lamps throwing violet light.

The Harvard Plaza? she thought.

And all through their memorable hour-or-more get-together, in fact, it was Adrien who seemed the most continually surprised of the three—with Ricky running matters efficiently (and even cruelly with Adrien), and Miriam moving through the hash and tri-sex with the flow of a dream—as if Adrien had never known those two bodies at all, or as if they were altogether new, now that they were together.

But during the ride home, in the taxi that Ricky had called for her (accompanying her down in his kimono), Miriam felt her body drained, not light; and instead of her usual afterglow or high spirits from the sexuality, she felt peculiarly heavy, particularly despairing. She took out a cigarette, couldn't find a light, wanted to ask the driver, but there was the wire-mesh screen partition between them, and she didn't have the energy to break through all that. Enervated, she rode. Slowly the odd thought came over her that what had occurred (and was occurring) was actually a fitting second act, a fulfillment, to the earlier part of the evening; she did, in fact, feel like a whore now. Maybe she should have asked for money? But good for her body then! *It* would not be tricked by her will, her will for comfort and ease. She patted her flank admiringly. Yes, *it* knew well enough when she was using it for her own means, and perverse means; when she was loading the deck or pulling the strings; *it* was no puppet, and it offered her now no gratification. What it offered, on the contrary, was what it was offering now, mockery; paying her back in its way for her earlier exploitation. Ah, *it* was not a whore, even if *she* was! There was consolation in that, wasn't there? Yes. I'll have to make amends to it, for sure. Where? In New Mexico, perhaps? Around grass perhaps, not concrete? You needed the country and grass for amends, didn't you? Maybe Wausau. Maybe Jamie can take me canoeing down the Brule? But when the driver pulled up and she looked out, there was only the sidewalk and a clapboard house and that piece of tape announcing Scheinman (over Brown). That faithful body bore her inside.

It was the next morning before she had the will power to make a J entry. In her room at the institute, at her desk with coffee and quiet, she condemned herself to the task.

He's the stronger. I thought I was, but he is. And thinking I was, all during the last year, I restrained my impulses, lowered my guard. Once you, Dr. L., had steeled me against his offensive fury, he did a brilliant turnabout, and would come near tears, would beg and plead for me not to do it, and I'd give in, emotionally, even practically. I couldn't take that show of weakness. No matter what you warned then, I couldn't take seeing him vulnerable, hurt.

I cheated myself, betrayed my interests!

And making me more reasonable, or making me aspire toward reason, only weakened me further. I turned myself into his therapist, didn't I, trying *to understand* him, instead of seeing him clearly as my destroyer.

Doctor, can I become a reasonable murderer? Otherwise, he will torture me like last night, and I'm defenseless before it. Do you see, he without any doctor has free license to go on being a crazy bull, all fences down, to roam at will in my life and CRUSH. Why should I *pay* for trying to be reasonable, while he goes scot-free, is rewarded by the law, for avoiding it? Do you see the irony, Dr. Levanda? What is to be done?

I must get better control, I will. Of the "objective situation." Otherwise there'll be a body strewn on the ground—mine or his.

Forgive such extreme talk, Doctor. I'll get over it. Just now I can't seem to help it, like a victim bleeding slowly. When do I become a *patient* again?

194

The Show was to be mounted on Wednesday, and Harry was there to help with his pickup truck, while Kelly drove there herself. They got the materials over to City Hall in one trip, though they took two days to be mounted properly. First the long insulation-board panels, 18 by 4 feet, hung from rods embedded high in the concrete, had to be painted for proper background. (Beige was selected.) Then the individual photographs, already framed and under glass, had to be hung on nails on the panels, with some sense of order and purpose. The huge concrete rooms were lighted by overhead fluorescent, which was passable, and by the good natural light flowing in from large windows at the ends of the long rectangles. Nearly a hundred photographs were hung finally upon that awesome stage of massive concrete. "Looks good," observed Harry, sitting on an aluminum ladder, smoking. "Great to me," put in Kelly, in overalls. Miriam, tired, said flatly, "I think it's kind of ordinary and maybe even dull, to tell the truth. The best of Georgianna Hospers II." Their fictional family-portrait photographer. "You're exaggerating, by a lot," Harry said soberly. "They're fine, and strong, and it's a good Show. Better than three quarters of the professional photographers around."

That left the top 25 percent. She wanted more. "Ha. Thanks for the compliment. In three weeks' time, you could be better than three quarters too."

"Oh?" he said. "You don't say, Miss Superiority."

She gave in and smiled.

He tried to cheer her up over dinner—Kelly departed—and she went along with it, in charade. She felt as if she had just amputated her own arm.

Afterward, in the truck, she said, "Thanks, sweetie, for all the help." She kissed him. "I think I'll stay alone for the rest of the evening and relax." "All right. Be good now. And stop fretting, it's fine, honest." She

195

jumped down. "Nothing rash now, remember." She waved.

Upstairs, she sent Julia home and tried to read Proust, look at Atget, forget the Show. But her mind wandered back to several nights ago, to Adrien's suite. No energy to write about it, however. It was the first time she had ever gotten involved with two men at once. Had it not been for her depressed state, it would never have occurred, of course. The depression and the hash mixed well; her immediate gratification had seemed real enough. Having one young man do something to her in front, while another used another part of his anatomy on her backside, was terribly strange, exotically pleasurable. Oh, it could be powerful to have two younger men, themselves lovers, adoring you. Harry once asked her if she had ever fantasied making love with a pair of teenage boys (the way he did with his female models). Not yet, she had answered, smiling widely, thinking of the next century. Well, 2000 had come a little closer. Of course, the haze of dope made things easier. One could always make excuses to oneself, that extreme behavior was nothing more than a product of chemical stimulation. *If* one wanted, or *had to* make such excuses. Miriam did, she knew that. Yet she also knew that it was not the dope that inspired her to perform with two others. Or even now, concentrate on that instead of . . . And finally, there were the stunning moments when the two boys forgot her, or rather, put on a show for her and played among themselves. Those moments, in which she played hazy voyeur, were also like nothing she had ever seen or imagined. Like some underwater slow-motion performance, they moved together, around and upon each other, with knowing ritual and smooth skills. A new blue dream, choreographed by Picasso, sound track by the Jackson 5 and Diana Ross. (Where was her Leica then?) But it was not a dream, it was real, happening before her 20/20 eyes; the fantastic fantasy being acted out, in that Harvard dorm. She saw now, in retrospect, how cases of chronic hedonism were initiated. Addiction came easy . . . for some, anyway. In dreams were great pleasures, as well as severe payments. If only she didn't have to leave that dream for that taxicab, hangover, and drop down to reality. But could she have tried that trio under different circumstances?

In a fit of anger, she picked up her notebook.

Face it, kid. More and more you avoid the real for the daydream, the fantasy, the simple gratification. The real are the walls closing in on you. The real are those nice pictures on City Hall walls, while the best ones lie here in drawers. The real is being pinned up against the wall by alternatives which are razors, waiting for you to move an inch in either direction. How does it feel, Miry? How does it feel?

Come on, let's see how tough you really are, how low and subtle you can get—wanna masturbate, maybe? Or call the boys back for an encore?

She put her ball-point down, with an impulse to cross out the entire passage. The perversity was silly.

The ring of the telephone was a relief. In his Boston rasp, Sandy Fried told her that he had spoken that afternoon to Larry Jacobson, Stan's lawyer, and Sandy thought that Miriam ought to come around the next day and talk with him. "He's got the goods on us, baby. We oughta make a deal outa court. If what Larry said to me was true, we haven't got a Chinaman's chance if it goes before a judge. And he's not the kind to lie or bluff." She felt fatigued, wasted (Kelly's apt term). "But what goods?" she uttered. "Cameras in my bedroom or what?" There was a pause. "We'd better put our heads together and see what we can salvage. How's 10 a.m.?

Then maybe we can see Larry in the early afternoon or over lunch even."

Miriam tried to follow all this, but she was slow, she couldn't think. First the Show, then the thoughts of the two boys, now Sandy F. here, at 10 p.m., right in her living room.

"Miriam? Are you there?"

She prayed for someone to relieve her pounding head.

"Hey! Miriam?"

"Yes."

"Christ. Don't scare me like that, huh. Now, don't worry, we're not outa this yet. Can you make it at ten?"

"Okay."

He said something else, then something else, and hung up.

She had a strong, sudden desire to go out, to emerge, to walk about, to enter the Cambridge Common, say. To stroll amid the swaying trees and darkened paths and stone monuments of World War II soldiers and Puritan educators. And maybe bump into some nice black boys on the lookout for a strayed white girl. Or maybe some frenzied academic or harassed graduate student, gone the way of Charlie Manson, ready in his soul for a juicy night meeting with a woman stranger. And as the yearning for such adventures intensified, she smiled, looking at the pages of tight print in Proust. She drank her Wild Turkey for comfort. Notes to herself, written on the back of an envelope a long time ago, slipped from the book. "Superconscious woman, an emergent social type. Overactive woman, a burdensome role." What did she mean with those glib formulas or questions? She had to recover from Fried in her living room at night. From her leaving out her favorite shots. From the journal truths pressing in upon her. She took up two skirts that she had been meaning to sew for six months, went to her mother's old Singer, turned on CRB and classical music. It was a string quartet with a deranged violin. The Kreutzer? The Westclox ticked, and she sewed, her foot pressing the pedal, her hands and eyes moving meticulously, with old ease. She concentrated on the two hems like a madman or prisoner making belts in the activity room, before returning to his cell.

"I think that's the best deal we can hope for at this point, Miriam," Sandy said, the next morning, summing up his alternatives for dealing with her life and her children. The natty shyster had announced that she'd have to give the children up for a period of time, three to six months at least, he figured. And then, based upon Miriam's "good behavior," they'd ask for a new arrangement to be made and go to court if necessary. Miriam perked up. "What are you saying I'm to do, or act like, for those six months?" "Well, sweetheart, if Larry's info about the line of boy friends outside your doorstep is true, and you've not indicated otherwise, then you're going to have to change your ways, my friend." He thumbed his red-satin-vest chest. "Now, don't get me wrong, this has nothing to do with *me* or *my* opinions. I'm just giving you the . . . *facts of legal life*. And the main fact is that the picture of a young mother opening her house to a mob of men—" "A few boy friends," she interjected, for the third time that morning. "All right, a few. Except that more than one is not exactly an acceptable number to a divorce-court judge viewing a custody battle. And three's a *gang* to him," he pleaded with the obtuse child. "Where was I? Well, you're going to have to content yourself, I think, with one and only one steady boy friend. And if you can, if you want the best legal remedy, then you ought to think of making that boy friend over into a husband. Remember, I'm here to give you *legal* advice." He shook his head slowly, tapping his pencil, walking on his fire-orange carpet. "Lemme lay this thing on the line, pal. For it's right here that Stanley has the upper hand, at least in this state. This is still a society you're living in, and a commonwealth whose judicial rules you have to abide by; and in both cases, a single mother with no steady job and lots of lovers or boy friends is not a very salutary portrait in a custody question, against a husband who is solidly married again, who is a college professor, and who is a very reputable citizen in the society. That's the situation in a nutshell. Now, what you want to do about it is up to you, entirely up to you, but if you can't restrain your impulses for a . . . probationary period, at first, then you're simply not going to be able to bring up your own children." He moved his hands sideways, black hair protruding from the backs of the fingers. He shrugged, a kind of Reno dealer in his flashy vest, or a suburban parody of one. "Have it your own way. But as your legal adviser, I can only recommend strongly that you give up your . . . fun times and settle down to a more ordinary way of life. For the sake of your kids, for no other reason. For the same sake that we had to put a damper on those 'dirty' pictures of yours. Do you see what *I'm* up against in all this?"

This reasoning lasted for two hours. Miriam said she'd consider the "deal" he was suggesting.

When she wandered out of the office into that busy shopping center, with sun refracting off chrome and glass, and well-dressed citizens pulling in and out in huge Buicks and snappy Capris, and a teenage couple braking sharply before her in a sports car, she wondered what it was like for a woman who is suddenly told she has cancer, a malignant, possibly terminal growth inside her, and who has to decide between immediate surgery or starting radiation treatments. Sandy's propositions, his legal advice, added so much weight to her that she actually seemed lighter, in a curious way, and she was able to consider matters coolly, without hysterics; the situation was rock-bottom, say, and she was glad for that, for resolution in that direction. As she drove along Highway 9, turning down Chestnut Hill Avenue, past the spacious houses and vigorous trees of Brookline, she thought about herself "on probation," for three to six months, possibly longer. In fact, possibly for as long as she remained a "single woman," and maybe longer too. She smoked and listened to RKO. The top forty came and went in her head: "Yesterday Is Today," "Pillow Talk," "You'll Never Get to Heaven," "Bad Bad Leroy Brown," "Wrong Place, Wrong Time." And an oldie of the Beatles, "Love Is All You Need." She noticed that there was a line for every need in those pop tunes, if you listened to the lyrics. Might one live by their precepts?

By the time she got home, she found that she had made one decision, at least. Hardly knowing that she had done so. Once in the apartment, she moved with purpose. It took her nearly a half hour to gather up all those scrapbooks and manila folders and envelopes of pictures which she had censored from the Show, for prudence' sake. She then phoned Mrs. Gallagher, director of activities at City Hall, and asked if she might come by and work through the night, making some last-minute adjustments. "My, my," the woman laughed in admiration, "you certainly do work overtime at getting those exhibits right, don't you? Too bad no one's paying you for your time, eh?" Next Miriam called Julia and asked if she would pick up the kids, give them dinner and a bath, put them to bed, and maybe even think of staying over. Julia, after checking with her mother, said sure, and Miriam made a mental note of paying her an extra five dollars on top of the hourly wage. She called Harry next. But when he answered the phone, she slowly hung up. No matter how much she wanted his company and advice just now, it would only be that much harder with him there, telling her how foolishly and precipitately she was behaving. And that much she already knew, somewhere. Her head was reeling, she noted, and she was sniffling too. Simple stuff. In the bathroom she took a decongestant cold tablet, a four-hour one, and swallowed it with water. Popped two vitamin C's too, and put the bottle into her purse. Made a last-minute check of the drawers and file cabinet to make sure that she had gotten all the photos, and then, satisfied, scribbled a large printed note for the kids, with a marker pen. Too bad she wouldn't be around to see Jonathan read it to his pupil-sister, a lesson Miriam loved to observe.

DEAR PUMPKINS:
 BE GOOD, LISTEN TO JULIA. I HAD TO GO OUT TO WORK ON THE SHOW. I PROMISE TO GIVE YOU BOTH BIG KISSES AND HUGS WHEN I COME HOME, OR IN THE MORNING. JULIA WILL READ TO YOU FROM PETER PAN, IF YOU WANT IT, JON. ALSO, THERE'S A SMALL SURPRISE FOR BOTH OF YOU IN JON'S ROOM, HIDDEN SOMEWHERE.
                                    LOVE LOVE LOVE
                                    MAMA

She posted the note on the kitchen bulletin board, Jon's useful idea. Practical at six. And Miriam, near thirty-five?

Well, she was practical for the next half hour anyway, as she shopped for food in the Broadway Supermarket, and for that promised surprise. Soothing to Miriam to walk in that well-lit, spacious supermarket in the early afternoon, with few people around to distract her from the performance of the shelves, those stellar ingenuities by the thousands, the same toothpaste seven times over with slight variation, the same ginger ale done four times with minute nuance. America knew how to play, didn't it? It was not with power or moral purpose that it marked history, it was with 87 Varieties of everything. It teased history, just as it teased and convinced the small guy, the steelworker, housewife, accountant, shoe salesman, anyone who could afford to enter a supermarket. In short, Everyman. How could *Das Kapital* compete against capons on sale for 99¢ per pound? Her distracting revery was interrupted by a toy section (alongside household goods), where she found a baseball puzzle in a cardboard can. Jon would love putting together Willie Mays making a catch. And, on sale and irresistible, two pop-up story books for Rosie, *Jack in the Beanstalk* and *Little Red Riding Hood*. "Lambtzops" for Jon, Ovaltine and gumdrops for the Rose, fresh mushrooms and rare Bibb lettuce (frightfully expensive), and vine-ripened tomatoes for herself in case she wanted a salad with wine when she returned home later, and, finally, a half gallon of Paul Masson Chablis, on sale for the week. Going to the check-out counter, she had a quick insight into Jon's version of the supermarket as an exciting playground—the secret mirror doors above Meat, see-through refrigerators filled with soda pop, merry-go-round racks of spices and paperbacks to send turning (with help), oranges and grapefruits for baseballs, and lengthy boxes of Reynolds aluminum foil for bats, silvery steel carts for bumping cars (another six-year-old daredevil was needed for that game)—oh, he had a grand time when Miriam let him loose, off Stanley's leash. And ice cream—though here, to be sure, she ran into an obstacle—at age four Jonathan decided upon Brigham's, and wouldn't settle for anything else. And could spot a fake Bailey's or Breyer's immediately! So she paid for the packages, dropped them into the station wagon, and scooted through the underpass and up to the Square, where she took her chances on a ticket and parked in front of the ice-cream parlor. She ran inside and, inundated by this fairyland of color and scent, ordered a half pint of chocolate chip, scooped for her by a freckled, skinny boy whose nameplate read Sandy. Could she get him to handle her case in place of the other one? And could it be handled in here, instead of Third Middlesex Court? Outside again—no ticket, the car was still there, she was in luck.

She dropped off the goods and goodies in the apartment, hiding the Willie Mays canister amid three others on Jon's shelf, placing *Red Riding Hood* and *Jack* on his windowsill, behind the curtains (using Rosie's tiny combat boots for book ends). Satisfied, grateful again to Julia, she departed and drove across the Longfellow Bridge, with her hot goods, and arrived at City Hall near twilight. It took two trips to haul all her stuff inside. Upstairs, she immediately perceived a strategy for rearrangement. The simplest (safest?) thing was to hang all the new erotic pictures in the second, or inner room, which you didn't see when you first entered the gallery; while the first room would contain the more accessible and palatable material. She proceeded to work, taking nearly an hour to hang room 1, which now included the Celtic series, portraits of the old, and her two-year running studies of several Cambridge families. (Besides Joseph, her shtetl tailor, and Carrie Carouthers, her frantic friend, there were a divorced mother and her beautiful, dark, thirteen-year-old daughter, living amid plants and poverty down on Magazine Street; a Puerto Rican migrant family, who picked apples and grapes seasonally in Concord, and otherwise lived in the back of a store in East Cambridge; a Brattle Street publisher, with his sundecks, summer living rooms, sun-filled blond children.) The contrasts in dress, decoration, abodes, looks, faces, attitudes, spoke for themselves. Family studies, a product of Miriam's (earlier) social self, socialist memories, personal friendships. Cambridge through its mixed, broken, and antiquated families.

Hanging the new pictures in the interior room was another matter, more intense and more baffling. First of all, she had left hanging there a small series of pictures of the dead or near-dead, taken at the Boston morgue and Cambridge City Hospital, through the help of a friend in Emergency. Death and the erotic, they went together, didn't they? she remembered from somewhere. But she was less careful than she ought to be, she knew, about organization and proportion here. There were just so many pictures to be hung, and despite the danger of clutter, despite the absence of frames and glass for the new ones, she didn't know which to leave out. Overabundance of material, for sure. (But modern city life was overabundant too, wasn't it? Could you compare ancient Sparta or Athens with New York, or Cambridge today, when it came to demands on the intelligence or pressures on the ego?) Perspiring, sipping bourbon (a pint left over from the other day), listening to BCN and CRB alternately from a tiny transistor, she worked hard—driven, possessed— but also almost effortlessly, since this was no more than the culmination of her desires of the past few years. So the other half of her work was being put back into the Show, that labor of obsession as much as artistic intention, perhaps. She knew now it was obsessed, wild, angry, but that was okay, it was out of her control now, it was in the hands of some deeper, driven Scheinman, and this ordinary citizen simply followed the other's stronger dictates. Thus, all the erotic pictures went in, the several series of nude self-portraits along with the photographs of extreme erotica. She even included several photos of the Thorndike couple at play—the more abstract studies of anatomy rather than of actual people locked in coitus. Of course, the self-portraits were the hardest to hang, much more difficult than couples in intercourse or exhibitionists in hedges, because the exposure of naked self on public walls shocked and terrified her. But she did it, regardless, one Miriam nodding peacefully and ordering the other to go ahead with it, this was a truth too. All told, at the end, it was a room of (naked) turbulence, of woman anger, depression, transgression, of sexual madness and swollen impotent fury, a room of exposed self and a kind of public fantasy life, a long concrete rectangle resembling a cyclotron housing struggles of flesh and twisted instinct. About the lack of uniformed presentation, she could do nothing; there didn't seem to be any point to try to arrange neatly this explosion of anger, terror, confusion, and incredible pain.

When it was done, she was exhausted, not exhilarated.

She walked back and forth in that lengthy rectangle with windows at the end, a general looking over her cavalry before a charge. Or from recent reading, another image: a nuclear inspector assaying her inventory of U-235 and plutonium. A rock group flailing in the background, she was reminded of something else too, the famous Shakespeare sonnet beginning "The expense of spirit in a waste of shame / Is lust in action," reshaping it now to suit this present reality: "The expense of flesh in a service of spirit." A more modern dilemma than the older one, she thought, smoking, walking, airier. This was modern lust in action (still reshaping), lust not so shameful as powerful, inevitable, perhaps necessary. In place of murder, say. The lust of the spirit for contact, seeking meaning in a spiritual vacuum through the vehicle of the body. A new hunger-need of the self to reveal itself, in naked venom, in childlike blasphemy, in exasperated humiliation and injury . . . for purposes of? . . . She wasn't sure, she wasn't sure.

She sat on a high stool. The pulls and attractions of the city, its multiple meanings. Not in pretty nudes, magnificent houses, noble trees or mighty river, not in abstraction or remoteness, but in human beings acting out their longing for contact, their passion for eccentricity, their need for psychosexual release and recognition; this was Cambridge—only the noises were missing, those great noises of truck engines and pneumatic drills, and police and fire sirens which formed the sound track of the everyday, accepted insanities of the city.

And where was Miriam's voice?

She, the photographer, as unglamorous model, the middle-aged woman staring back at you, expressing premature aging, defeat, resignation, madness, renewal, struggle, health, new hope, did she fit into such a perspective? If she exposed the others, and her city, why not herself? The ethics were simple, on this level. And at this point the line between self and external order, between photographic art and personal drive-need, evaporated. Objectively, she could tell little, she saw. So much for that side of things. But she could *feel* rightness, honesty. *Feel* Miriam at thirty-four. Good.

She felt empty at the end, but an emptiness of work accomplished, and now, no longer a general or nuclear inspector, but a foot soldier or janitor asked to clean up, she cleaned up and left.

It was ten-thirty when she departed the medieval-looking City Hall, nodding to the uniformed guard downstairs, who said, letting her out, "Got it all done now?" "Keep your fingers crossed." He waved. The air outside was misty and gray, and she walked out upon the large open terrace of the building, hoping for a drink and maybe a snack across the street. Her head was warm, turning. The restaurant was dark, however. Boston at night was not Rome, she thought, or City Hall Plaza the Piazza Navona. So she walked the other way down Cambridge Street, toward her car. Midway between City Hall and the huge John F. Kennedy sky-scraper, she veered suddenly to the right and down the plaza steps toward the sprinkling fountain and wading pool. Down the few steps to the sunken pool, where she began to walk around, feeling the fountain spray mix with the windy mist, gradually forgetting the night and the place. She felt enormously tired, but also relieved, lighter. A burden released, somewhere. She had an impulse to remove all her clothing and lie down for a while in that glistening, splashing water. There didn't seem to be anyone around, just concrete, glass, water, and a large abstract sculpture, in front of the JFK building. A strange bronze creature, overlooking her. To her right, the plaza spread out into the night, empty, spacious, mysterious, promising the future. Without thinking, she removed her shoes, rolled up her jeans, and walked into the wading pool. The water was cold but comforting, and she had the feeling that if she were shot on the spot, she had done the best she could: all her photographs were now up on the wall, and her children were asleep, healthy, loved, watched over. It seemed so simple. *I won't have them, anyway.* She was thirty-four, and although she felt very young, perhaps half her actual age, it was all right for her to be shot now. In fact, she was concentrating so intently on execution and satisfaction that she didn't realize that she was walking round and round and round the center fountain, her clothes and face soaked from the sprinkling.

Nor did she hear the first shouts of the policeman approaching the pool. "I think you better get out of there now, young lady," he said, closer, "and explain yourself." She did get out, as if awakened from a dream, and began to search for identification; that stuff was in the car, however. So he escorted her up the stone steps to the waiting squad car, where a second policeman handed her a blanket, looking at her queerly (but not unkindly), and they drove slowly down Cambridge to her car. She produced credit cards with names and numbers, a Radcliffe Institute letter, her driver's license (the plastic cover breaking over that younger face), and a City Hall brochure announcing the Miriam Scheinman Show. This inspired good-looking Officer Higgins to say, "Are you in any real trouble, Miriam?" She shook her head. "Do you have a psychiatrist?" She shook her head. Why hadn't the doctor answered her yet? "What's in that bottle?" She stared at it. "Vitamin C." One policeman looked at the other and asked, "Mind?" She shook her head. He opened it, sniffed, and gave it back to her. "These days . . ." "That's all right," she said. "Thank you . . . for getting me dry," she offered, the words more feeble than the expression. "It just sounds screwy to me," said the second cop. She thought of a line, shrugging, "It was just one of those things." Oh? What did that mean? And all the way home, shivering, she thought of that old popular song.

She had no strength or inclination to make any J(ournal) entry when she got home.

For the next few days that late-night fountain dipping stayed in her head through her regular routine, making her wonder what it meant, if anything. She felt the spray and the cool water on her feet as she went shopping, fed the kids, washed the dishes, talked to Harry and Kelly and Adrien and Jamie. She had never done anything like that in her life, anything so clearly silly and unreasonable, and she wondered, What next? The fact that the event didn't bother her that much, didn't terrorize her, was also a surprise. Harry had said one evening on the phone, "You seem a bit light-hearted, is it true?" She didn't answer, because she didn't know, though light*headed* seemed more to the point. The days before the Show were like bracing ocean waves, lifting and carrying her through.

It was not the waves, however, but an airplane that brought a letter from Dr. Levanda the morning before the Show. In small, clear handwriting, on Tel Aviv University stationery, she apologized for the delay, explaining how she had been away at kibbutzim, seeing women there, and she had just now arrived back in town. No, she was not coming home early; in fact, would probably have to stay on an extra six weeks or so, into deep July. She did have a doctor friend in Cambridge, however, with whom Miriam could speak, and gave her her name. Also, she knew a good female lawyer in Boston, if that was of use now. At the end she wrote:

If it is a crisis it will be instructive to see how you deal with it, Miriam. To tell you the truth, if I hadn't thought you were strong enough to handle it on your own, I wouldn't have suggested a stop to our regular meetings. Surely you know this, I hope. You've more strength in your ego than you sometimes give yourself credit for. On the other hand, Dr. Rudnick is a fine woman and doctor, and by all means use her for support and counsel if you need her, until I can see you again.

P.S. Here the situation of women in general is one of permanent crisis, as I told you, and I find it tragic indeed. It is far too complicated to go into now, this curious, unique piece of history, but I shall, when I return.

With fondest regards,
Esther Levanda

She'd call this Dr. Rudnick as soon as the Show was over, Monday perhaps. And maybe she ought to think of going over to Israel for a while, to bring her own version of crisis? *Stronger*, she repeated to herself, *stronger than you know. Dr. L. wouldn't hand you a line.* She bucked up. She was right for sure about putting those pictures in. She remembered the spare, plain face . . . the slow determined voice with the accent

210

. . . the well-tailored clothes the doctor always wore. Oh, she did like that woman a lot! She knew whom and how to criticize, when and how to offer sympathy.

By Friday evening at seven-thirty "Miriam at Thirty-four"—that solitary accomplishment (with the help of her town)—was ready for public inspection. Society was going to come around, to look in on what Miriam was up to these past few years, months, weeks. Okay, she thought, putting on her beige cotton suit, old-fashioned, with skirt taken up, heels and nylons, navy blouse with wide collar. A big girl tonight. Make Dr. L. proud. Applying natural lipstick in front of the mirror, Harry in the living room with the kids and Julia Havens, she imagined for a moment what it would be like doing this, preparing for the Show, knowing that her *best photographs were locked away in her file,* not on the wall. She stopped, the sense of rape chilling her. She smiled, at peace with her knowledge. They *were* on the wall, her will had not been seduced, tricked, or betrayed. Looking in the mirror, knowing this, she thought she looked more womanly, more real, more ripe. (*Ripe and sexy as hell* returned.) Could her flesh really show that she had done what she had wanted to? Her lips, were they really fuller? did the cheeks look smoother, with color? She'd come through okay, she felt suddenly. And confirm Dr. L.'s opinion. Exert her will. Flex it regularly. Impose her deepest self upon the self that society desires. Stick with it. Miriam Scheinman over Miriam Brown, Miriam the photographer over Miriam the wounded. No more double exposures. Come together . . .

She felt more solid and substantial than she had for weeks, as she walked out of the bathroom and into the living room. Harry, with Rosie and pieces of Tinkertoy on the floor, looked up, and, on his knees, stared. "What's the matter?" she asked, alarmed. "You're a

211

beauty," he said. "Oh, is that all?" "Yeah, that's all. A knockout." Fib or not, it felt good. Maybe she was? Hah. He stood up, to Rosie's chagrin. Miriam kissed and hugged the kids, said goodbye to Julia, and as she started to go downstairs, Jon ran to her and, looking very serious, his finger lecturing, said, "Now, just remember, Momma, you're a knockout!" He cheered, and she wanted to cry at his cleverness.

Downstairs with Harry, she saw Jamie pulling up to the curb, whistling a wolf call. "Oh God, are you both going to give me the works all night?" The men, who had met before, greeted each other. "Just get in the back and behave," advised Jamie, and Harry was right there, opening the door and pushing the seat back. In the back she got, behaving, tears forming in her eyes as Jamie and Harry compared Cougar with Chevy pickup, taking for granted their escort service. Couldn't we all go for a drive first? she wanted to ask. The three of us and the kids, to New Mexico or Wausau? Or to Israel? She'd bring enough men to ease *that* crisis. She wanted to plant a kiss on that blond neck, that dark-brown hair, the way they made her a queen like this.

Kelly and Nathalie were already there, with Mrs. Gallagher of City Hall, having set up punch bowls (whiskey sour and something? plus orange peels), platters of cheese and cashews, Fritos and Triscuits, ginger ale and Bitter Lemon, and some marvelous Israeli dates and figs. After explaining all this, Nathalie exclaimed, "Working for you, Miry, means we might be too tired to see the actual show." "Maybe you shouldn't," Miriam replied seriously. Why put this dear kind girl through another embarrassing encounter, *Deep Throat*–style? "Cheesus, you're a number in that outfit, aren't you?" jumped in Kelly, excited. "You really ought to step out of those jeans and into this sort of gear more often, doll!" Miriam again wondered who was standing there, which Miriam? Would she be in a display case all night? If so, what would happen to it during the next few hours? And as the first guests started arriving, Jamie and Harry and the girl friends produced a half dozen bottles of Great Western champagne and two dozen long-stemmed yellow roses. Corks popped and she had to turn away to get something out of her eye. The kindness was hurting her, embarrassing her. Be a big girl, Daddy had said. She shifted back, clear-eyed, forcing a smile, lifting up her glass for Harry's toast.

People began arriving steadily now, a safari forming perhaps; couples, strangers, odd groups and single girls, photographers and cool dudes, official men and society women. A movie set? Harry's tape deck and corner speakers produced early Dylan, trio sonatas (Tartini? Bach?), the Beatles. As she moved around the room, getting slightly dizzy from the champagne, earlier Wild Turkey, and celebration, comments began to circulate, directly and indirectly. Dr. Goldmark, her tall, angular pediatrician, told her, "I never knew photography was an art form before this." She nodded, thinking, she didn't know it exactly either, but it meant he was liking it, her; okay. Then old Lena was there, with two hard-looking chicks, Lena in jeans and sloppy sweater. "I wouldn't've missed it for the world—the sisters storming the gates of piggy power! Glad you're laying it on, Miriam." All right, everyone had their form of liking. (Or disliking.) She smiled, grateful for the booze rolling around. Elizabeth Morrison greeted her warmly, with husband Warner squeezing out his little waspish greeting and approval. Elizabeth said, "They're so beautiful," shaking her head to indicate the poverty of words next to the photos. "Just don't forget that little date my son has with your daughter next week," she responded. Elizabeth smiled and said, "We bet-bet-better see the other room," and moved off.

213

And here came Sandy Fried—*checking up, huh? Good, glad you're here to take it all in*—in a mod flare suit, with wife Trudy, tossed hairdo and sweet demeanor. "Congratulations, looks sensational from what I've seen of it!" Sandy winked. "So you know Havlicek and Silas, that *might be useful*." Miriam nodded, and said hello to Trudy. "I hear that Larry Jacobson is coming down," Sandy added, in self-congratulation. "This'll give him something to think about concerning your competence and success." He beamed at *their* accomplishment. The name and the message stopped her, for ten seconds; but why not, the more the merrier. Sure, why not get down to legalities and away from . . . pictures, pleasures? And then there was Stan, invited too, with Röchel, a pair of spruced-up book ends approaching. ("Watch the bitchiness, Superiority," cautioned Harry, reading her mind.) Stan took a step forward and put out his hand to his ex-wife. "I want to wish you every success, Miriam," he pronounced aloud, for every witness; Röchel, the Jewish Orthodox social worker wearing a formal black dress, obediently stood next to him, uncomfortable. "Have you tried the punch, Röchel? It's really quite good." Röchel smiled, looked easier. Stan thanked Miriam and explained that Röchel didn't drink. "There're soft drinks too," Miriam said, wanting to throw her drink at him, grateful that she could move off, free. Right into Sandy's arms. "Ah, here you are. Miriam, let me introduce Larry Jacobson, uh, Stan's attorney." A slim, nice-looking man, dark-complected, smiled. A smile which surprised her with its sensitivity, warmth. "I'm impressed with what I've seen thus far, I can tell you that. In fact, I wouldn't mind buying a few prints, if they're for sale." Why did certain enemies have to turn out attractive, allies gross? He reminded her of her old movie flame, Montgomery Clift. "Thank you. I think there's a price list around somewhere."

214

How much more unreal could the whole affair get? In the midst of the peeping Toms looking in on her private life (Now, Superiority . . .), she caught sight of Jamie, blue stalk of corn, and Harry, beard, turtleneck, glasses, her Brooklyn Pollock. And where, where—ah there, Adrien stood, drink in hand, necklace of beads, earring; her pirate dandy. Sly boy, didn't even say hello, or did he? Dramatis personae all accounted for. (Wait, another pirate type stood next to him: Ricky, in tight Renaissance trousers and shirt. A good pair to introduce to Stan and Röchel?) Her trio of bedfellows, ready to stand by her. Would they confess to Stan, to Larry, or inform Sandy, what they did to her and she to them? Tell about marmalade and masks? About her passion for one particular ass? Go ahead, Stan dear, ask Ad how he likes to climb on from behind. Or Harry, what I'm willing to do for his testicles. Ask Stan, Sandy, show some real balls. Was she getting drunk on liquor or resentment? or vengeful pleasure? "Hello there." She heard a familiar mumble and looked up to see the smooth, ruddy face of Colin looming above her. Wordless at first, she then said, "What are you doing here? It's not Tuesday night, is it?" "Your brochure looked inviting," he murmured, wearing a tie as if it were a piece of rope. She reached up and pecked him. "You're sweet for coming." "I haven't given you my verdict yet, so don't be so friendly. Besides, my wife may be jealous." "Your—" "She was feeling much better and you did say something about wanting to meet her?" Miriam was dumfounded. But before she could think, Colin had brought over a tallish, trim lady with a prominent chin and a pixie face. She said, "I envy your photographs, they're smashing. Congratulations." The voice was solid, and Miriam thanked her. She eyed Miriam candidly and with curiosity. How candidly? wondered Miriam. "We'll buzz off now and look around a bit more," Colin said, and Mary Edmundson smiled a goodbye. Miriam observed their backs, the carved bony one she knew and that of the tall, straight lady, and was curious herself about what Mary knew or imagined.

Mrs. Peterson of the institute was saying something about what a difference a whole show of pictures meant, rather than a single picture or two. And about what women were doing these days. The chatter was calming. Her head drifted to her men, these lovers who were now looking in on another part of Miriam. Three lovers, and a Tuesday-nighter (plus an ex), wandering about. What did it all mean? Anything? Did she have a photograph or series to suggest each experience—aggression, fear, curiosity, ambivalence, indifference, adventure, sport, impudence, risk, lust, love, lunacy? Something to remember her by, to remember them by, when her own body was gone? Could she have a photo for every love affair, every lover she would have in life? *Why?* Her men, her intimate band, mingling with these strangers, made her feel poignant, less lonely, sportive. It was a horse race of sorts, you bet on this man, on that emotion, over a distance of time, and then you won or lost. (As you bet on this picture or photographer, say?) So this was an exhibition in more ways than one, wasn't it? It showed her who the players were and what they were like at this point in her life. *Or are you simply getting stoned, my friend?*

But now she knew her next project, the photographing of those lovers. With their approval, or not. And herself in it too, in action with them. That was the next logical step.

That first hour-plus of champagne, roses, ceremony, and flattery-high ended when the pediatrician Goldmark came around for the second time. "That's a . . . bit strong in that *other* room, I'm afraid. A different kettle of fish. And not for me, Miss Scheinman." That

216

somber disillusion brought her mind back to the second room, and was the forerunner of many remarks on that erotic inner sanctum. (There were exceptions. Big redheaded Kelly was right there, of course, "Baby, like wow! When did you sneak those pics in?" She jerked her thumb. "That's *hot stuff* in there!" And old man Tyson, youthful in dark turtleneck, observed, "It appears as if Kelly and I have been performing in the wrong locations," making Miriam grateful. And Adrien drawled, "And to think that while I baby-sat you were doing *those*. I'm a little bit awed." Her muttonchop baby-sitter.) Harry, however, presented a different view. "They're good. Better than good. But it may have been dumb and not worth it. I don't know. I'll keep my fingers crossed." He squeezed her arm, in faith, but it didn't lessen the sting of his realism.

The sense of realism shifted perceptibly as a voice said, "Hello, remember us?" A familiar man in smart white turtleneck and dark blazer, with a pretty, recognizable woman. But their names? "Bruce and Mary Ann Thorndike." "Sure," Miriam said, "I'm sorry." Bruce shook it off and went on, "We saw the brochure and couldn't resist coming in. I had thought that our pictures were something, but next to *those*—" He gestured in that hot direction and smiled. "It's a far-out show, *really far out*." "If that's good," Miriam replied, curiously interested in his attitude, "then good." Mary Ann in her small, twangy voice burst in with, "You do have a great deal of courage to show them!" Miriam gave a look of appreciation. "It's more than *simple courage* that's impressive"—Bruce corrected the old-fashioned naïveté—"it's the fact that you've really *gotten into yourself*, and maybe even *beyond* somewhere. Only a person deeply in touch with her subconscious could have produced those." He shook his head. "It's not unlike Laing's schizophrenic model, where the sick take their journeys to a dark territory unknown to the rest of us and come back with new knowledge. In your case, the *actual evidence*." He paused, and seemed to move closer in, the blue in his eyes growing bluer, more gemlike. "You really owe it to yourself to attend one of our group sessions soon, and see what comes of it. I'm convinced now that you—and we—will profit greatly by it." For some reason, this blue-eyed Thorndike, programmer and therapist, with boyish dimples and hard mouth, with his mixed language and salvation wisdom, made Miriam shiver slightly. And his terms, which in the past had served only to amuse, now lodged themselves in her head, like bullets; and as they pressed upon her, she smiled. *Schizophrenic, sick, dark territory.* She half-laughed in the midst of her seriousness. "Yes, that might be nice," she said finally. "Would you call me?" And then someone was taking her arm.

The shift in sense of reality and tone continued as the majority of guests and even some friends sided with the pediatrician. Why? Because, Miriam answered herself, it was one thing to see impersonal sexy pictures on a wall, quite another to know the photographer is a friend, *and* a woman. They wanted the everyday Miriam back, the predictable element, the "bohemian" but respectable woman; not this *other creature.* She offended. She embarrassed. She flaunted bad taste. *She humiliated herself as well as others.* Blushing deeply, Elizabeth Morrison came up, after the second room, while husband Warner, usually the model of politeness, walked off to the exit without so much as a nod. The red-faced girl moved her lips, shook her shoulders, smiled awkwardly. "It's all right, dear," said Miriam, "you don't have to like them." "I, I, I . . . I guess they take some getting used to." Miriam nodded and patted her arm.

Stanley contained his fury, his desire to hit her. Although she wasn't attached to him now, she *once* was. "I consider those pictures vulgar and revolting. But, to your credit, you've picked an excellent time to reveal yourself. You've become, among other things, an ego-maniac." He shook his head slowly. "Those pictures won't do you any good, but they may very well do you *considerable harm*." He rolled the words as if they were licorice, which he loved. Miriam smoked, seeing the face of the man who had never really *liked* her, but his new name for her stayed. "Stan, you sound as if we're still married. You don't have to worry any more about your *vulgar wife* dragging you down, dear. And as for 'considerable *harm*,' shall we drink to it?" Reflexively, he grabbed her forearm, but then Mrs. Peterson came up and he let go, squeezing his hate into a tight smile. He greeted the institute lady and moved off. *Egomaniac*. Yes, it was true, she thought, Stan is right. My ego is out of control, yes, yes. So now she had picked up two names at the show tonight, to go with Scheinman.

Mrs. Peterson, wearing a long, brightly flowered dress, a patron of Good Taste and Propriety in her art, was gazing at Miriam strangely, as if she were a ghost, and Miriam stared back, friendly. "I can tell you that I much prefer the pictures in here, Miss Scheinman," she said politely, with firmness, returning to old formality with Miriam. "I don't think the institute realized . . . exactly what . . . sort of work they've been encouraging in this past year." Miriam replied to that schoolmarmish displeasure, "I thought they were encouraging *me*, Mrs. Peterson." Mrs. Peterson didn't smile, her long chin jutting into the air, and she walked off and out the door with a recognizable Harvard professor.

Now they were coming out of that inner sanctum at Miriam fast and thick, and Miriam was glad, so glad for the manufacture of alcohol. Sandy Fried looked as if he'd burst a capillary. "You're a stubborn fool, and worse, a *bad* client. And *a spoiled child*. You wouldn't listen, would you? How could you dare to put those photos up in the midst of our negotiations? How could you *dare* to?" "The legal case was hopeless, as I understood it," she said, imagining champagne pouring down his face. "I was lost before I started." "You mean *now* it's hopeless. When Larry Jacobson sees . . . oh Christ . . . Why'd you do it, *why?* . . . Oh Christ!" He scratched his head, an appealing gesture for a change. "Let's just hope that some art critic will call them *artistic*. That's our only hope." Miriam nodded. "I'll keep my fingers crossed, Sandy. Meanwhile, don't worry too much." And she moved off, seeing his face shift back to anger. And then there was the Legal Enemy, her movie-star beau. But he was smiling, good-naturedly, she thought. "You certainly are distinctive, I'll say that. I think they're . . . very unusual pictures." He moved his hands together and laughed. "I'm not a photography freak, you understand. But I just couldn't stop looking at them. I'm speaking as a layman now, of course." "Not as an art critic, or lawyer?" He smiled. "Not as either, that's right." She wanted to say, "You've a very sensual face, do you know that? May I touch it? In fact, can we go out sometime? And maybe touch each other?" He was staring at her, wondering. "I must say," he began, his voice flutelike, his long thin face dark and Clift-ish, "that I have great admiration for artists. I never know where they get their inspiration to work on their own, the way you do." She shook her head ever so slightly and said, "Maybe you ought to represent me too." He laughed. "One's enough in a situation like this, thank you. Besides, you have a top-notch lawyer already. I'm glad I don't have to face him in court over this, as he's indicated." He put out his hand. "Well, thank you, the pleasure's been mine."

So it was settled, almost, huh? Almost.

But you seem decent, you seem sane, you're so beautiful, why do you want to do this to me? Why can't you switch places with Sandy? Why, why, why?

He was gone, and in his place, as if a line had formed, were others. A well-known local photographer, from M.I.T.: "I think I see what you're trying to revolt against, Miriam, and I applaud that. But I can't say I applaud what you've come up with in its place. A little too much content, actually, for my taste, and I think it distracted you from compositional qualities." Next, old standby Lena, who did have a knack for turning up in certain situations. "I better lay it on you straight. Those pics back there are retrogressive, alienated, sick. I think there's a lot of self-hate and confusion fucking up your head. They *objectify* women a great deal. You have a lot of work ahead of you to get rid of your shit." Miriam took it silently, which seemed to soften Lena. "Sorry to put it this way, but I have a principle of honesty at stake when dealing with sisters. Some of us could see you were on the wrong track way back." Miriam controlled herself, stared, then turned away. Could the M.I.T. photographer testify about her art for Sandy? And Lena testify to the movement about her head? Mrs. Gallagher of City Hall then pointed out to her the local critic from the Boston newspaper, a middle-aged man in a flashy suit, ascot, goatee. He was busy chatting, except at one moment, when someone pointed Miriam out to him. He immediately turned away when he caught her eye. Oh well, so much for the artistic side, Sandy.

Suddenly Joseph was there, her saintly tailor. "It was not very nice in there." He shook his head. "Miriam, I'm surprised, very surprised. You're a fine girl . . ." and he spread his hands wide, in puzzlement. He moved off, and Miriam was pained. *But you knew the show wasn't for him, anyway, didn't you?*

Even dear Jamie said to her at one point, shaking his head, "Why'd you want to put all those unflattering pictures of yourself in? I don't get it. It took a lot of guts, I know that. But it bewilders me. Look at you

221

now, here, and look at you inside—" "Not a knockout, huh?" He didn't get the reference, just shook his head. "Sorry," she said, realizing it was Harry's word.

There emerged emphatically the pattern of spectators going into that inner room with praise and enthusiasm and coming out disappointed, offended, embarrassed, angry. And although Miriam had anticipated this, in theory, and though she had a good high on, she was nevertheless shocked by the palpable hostility and dislike. Shocked in her system, beyond her reason or logic. It *hurt*. It was a betrayal of sorts, an ironic betrayal. The work which she knew to be her best, her strongest, which took so much time, skill, and finally silly courage (to take *and* to put up), this work was being treated as if it were a vulgar disgrace, sensationalist and cheap, dirty blasphemy. Dirty, that was it really. (It was the word that Nathalie had used, with irony, laughing but serious too. "Dirty pictures, you've invited us to an exhibit of dirty pictures!" And went on to say how she wasn't sure *how* to take them, yet; they were "too unusual.") Miriam drank, and peered through her wineglass at the guests continuing to emerge from that chamber of horror. A ginger kaleidoscope of color and dress turned, as Dylan sang "Positively Fourth Street." And she began to see that the spectators were fatter and grosser now, their figures bloated, distorted (Max Beckmann portraitures?)—as if they were cannibals who had just feasted on human flesh with no time yet for digestion. And the flesh was herself, Miriam.

And the flesh was herself, Miriam.

The glass slipped from her hand and crashed to the floor.

Guests flocked around to attend to it and to her, asking if she was all right. Jamie and Harry were there too, and that made her feel easier. "Sure, I'm fine," she said, forcing a smile. "It just slipped out of my hand."

222

Someone brought a chair, and she sat in it. And slowly the last hour of the opening dissolved, like a movie fadeout. There was no more surprise or shock at the revulsion nerve she had touched, there was only the down feeling and the occasional surprise bordering on disbelief when someone came up to say that he had *liked* what he had seen in there. (Like an old Boston teacher who said, "Those pictures were a great leap forward for you. They're risk-taking, and, quite possibly, original. I'll come back when things are a little more quiet around here to get a closer look at actual composition. Meanwhile, congratulations, Miriam.") Ah, that was soothing, and sweetened her for a bit. Until the next cannibal couple emerged, gross and bloated, and Sally Rosen said, "In all candor, I didn't know you were interested in pornography, Miriam. Too bad Bob and I are not up to the times." Miriam's head and throat now began to ache again, sorer, and she longed for air, clean air, after this coffin of tortures and congested horrors.

She felt grateful for her removal by Jamie and Harry, who drove her across the river to Hancock Street. The baby-sitter, Julia, had fallen asleep, and when Miriam asked her if she wanted to go home, the girl turned her head sleepily on the convertible sofa, back to the pillow. The boy friends together like that were newly chivalric and paternal, like a pair of perfect daddies. Sugar and real, tidying up for her. Harry kept reminding her to forget the cheap shots and vulgar criticism, he himself had been through that act before and all it did was to drain useful energy. "Besides, most of it is jealousy or fear about what you've done." She wanted to remind him of his own critique, or Jamie of his bewilderment, but it didn't matter. They were affectionate now; that mattered. They even made sure that she was ready for bed—11:15 p.m. seemed like 4 a.m. from the drink and the excitement—and actually stood by the sides of the bed, each kissing a cheek. The most comforting moments of the long cannibalistic evening. "Sweet dreams, Mir," Jamie whispered, and Harry offered, "Sleep like a Cambridge log." Gosh, she thought, after their departure, that sort of *good night* is as good as photographing or sex. All that solicitude made her forget, temporarily . . . She was a little girl again.

She didn't sleep, however. She tried, she tried honestly, taking a capsule too, then two, for she sensed that not sleeping would be somewhat dangerous for her just then, that she would descend back into the swirling evening and inevitably sink down to that sickly feeling in her flesh. So she tossed and turned and put the light on and read—a travel piece on the Caribbean in a magazine; then she tried a short story in *The New Yorker*— but it did no good, and after an interminable time (an hour and a half?), she stopped and listened. Recalled. Faces, situations, couples, the evening. And then it returned to her again, beginning with the Fellini pageant of guests leaving that room and then swelling into cannibals, and she felt her skin shudder and sickness take her. *Schizophrenic, sick.* Those faces began to eat at her voraciously—the pediatrician, Stanley, Sandy, Mrs. Peterson, Lena, the Rosens, and Warner and Elizabeth Morrison, the newspaper critic and the local photographer, blue-eyed Bruce, and who else, tomorrow or later this week? She perspired, coughed, knew she had to sleep, but also knew she had to steel herself, and got out from under the covers, the attackers.

In the darkened dining room she poured herself whiskey with a little water, washed her face with cold water while the liquor warmed her, checked the sleeping children and then Julia. As she slipped on her clothes, old familiar ones, she thought, What more do I have to lose? What is loss, or pain? Where is its depth, so that I can sink there fast, sink down and know that it's bottom at last? She wandered around the bedroom, smoking, noticing the familiar shadows, objects. Her Bronc Burnett books. A watercolor of Jonathan. On her desk top, amid the clutter of papers and books, she found her old Waterman's fountain pen, from Dad. And, across the room, on a mirror finial, hung her baseball cap. She picked it off, and fingered its blue felt, frayed and almost out of shape. She tried it on, pulling the brim down firmly, in control. She was twelve, and an Indian again. Boudreau at short. The tomboy who played catch with Daddy. It had been a very long time since she had been an Indian. She walked out of the bedroom and again checked the kids in their rooms. They'd be fine, now, or in the future. With Jon she forgot about her cap, and the brim pricked his neck, and he turned over abruptly, frightening her. But he rolled over, back into sleep. In the living room she saw her notebook on the mantel and, standing, scribbled in it.

I didn't make it, did I, Doctor?
I chose right, but it turned out wrong. But the other right would have been wrong too, wouldn't it?
Why do I feel twelve, and frantic, out of control?
Why does the cost of living seem to go up as you go on?
Why aren't you here now, to keep me talking, to keep me

She stopped there and put the pen down. Useless. It was time to go out and . . . make amends. Like the silly song said. Suddenly she turned back and stared bitterly, derisively, at her old friend: sure, why not take little Notebook for a walk too, little Dr. Know-It-All and Hear-It-All? Safe and sound it was, pages intact—

as she leafed through them, the year's work—while she and her photos were getting dirtied. Okay, wise guy, come along with Schizzy for some night air.

She made her way down the stairs, closed the door softly, strolled out into the streets. Not now the terrified ingenue of a few weeks ago but an animal of sorts, a driven, wounded animal. The trees rustled here and there, isolated cars whisked by; otherwise the little town slept, tucked away for the night. Like any sleepy town in Ohio or Indiana, say, except this was Cambridge. She sashayed along Harvard toward the Square until Trowbridge, where she turned, swinging Notebook like another lady perhaps flashing to prospective johns her rhinestone purse. She moved noiselessly, expectantly, over the small red hills of sidewalk brick, but her pals of the other night were not at their station. Too bad. So she walked across Broadway to the public library park area, but there were just the big maples and silvery beeches and still darkness. Perhaps I should deposit you for safekeeping in that Return book slot? she said to Notebook, using a temptress's voice. You'd *love that*, wouldn't you? Oh no, you just come along with me for now, tapping it like a tambourine against her hip. Egomaniac will take care of you just fine.

Her body felt unreal, loose-limbed, wily, yearning; she was overtired, she knew, near worn out. That was okay, there was a task to do. (Oh, what? she wondered.) Her brain leaped with jumbled memories from childhood, recent days, her marriage, crisscrossing. She had taken pictures of what was out here, what shadows and what truths skirmished beneath the polite surface of brick and bush and clapboard, but when she had displayed them on the City Hall walls, the citizens grew angry and rejected them. Rejected her. Simple. Maybe she'd walk over to the Paperback Booksmith to find another pickup (why not go over to Colin's house near the Square, she had missed saying good night to him at the Show and could now have that chat with his wife, perhaps?), or else why not return to the plaza fountain for a little midnight skinny-dipping? She could do anything now, right? Now that there was nothing left to lose, she was free, right? A liberated woman at last, correct? Was this new freedom schizophrenia, sickness? Good. She'd find new territory then. Her boy friends understood, her children at some point would understand too. The pictures were the pictures and spoke for themselves. Who, or what else, was there?

Approaching the Square, she saw the squadron of cabs lined up in the distance, ready for action, and the buzzing game of autos speeding this way and that on the one-way streets. She noted a green sign, pointing out the routes to Winchester, Somerville, Medford. The names traveled through her brain, stopping at Medford. She smiled, following the sign and strolling the long way around, through the underpass to the Cambridge Commons. And as she wandered here, she had a vision, a dream . . .

She was walking on the other side of town, to a friend's apartment. At the door Judith Lesser smiled, and Miriam asked, "Can I borrow your revolver, Judy? I've been getting these kook phone calls, and I'm afraid for the children's sake."

Judy L., who had obtained the gun after her apartment was burgled last year, got the .32 caliber for her and showed her how to use it, just in case. And then Miriam was in one of those yellow chariots, chauffeured to the suburbs, near Tufts. She loved sitting in the back of that cab, feeling the violent little Colt in her shoulder bag, heading for peaceful Medford. Sitting there, gliding along, the air blowing cool, she was poised, scared, slightly thrilled. An explosion of repressions, a release of anger, a triggering of dammed-up desire; all this accomplished in a single swift action! Hooray for technological man, angry woman.

She advised the driver to stop at the corner and told him to wait. He was skeptical and she gave him five dollars. Quietly she turned the corner and walked up the narrow sidewalk, passing two perfect lawns and houses until number 1121. The house was clapboard Cape Cod, white, set back maybe a hundred feet and bordered by shrubs, with a lawn in front and a garden area in back. She walked back and forth on that front lawn, thinking of him in there. The yellow light from his upstairs study reflecting Seriousness, the lantern light by the front door signaling Order and Suburban Propriety. Yes, Stan, yes, my dear, you've traded in Dmitri K. for a tame Jewish Rabbit, and I'm going to change you back again. The lawn was clipped and freshly planted in certain places, and the white Cape reminded her of Easter bonnets on little girls. She crisscrossed the lawn, at first circling, then making a cross, finally a six-pointed star. Fascinated by the strange power of this suburban attraction, which could camouflage a Salk or deter one. But, Stanley, why did you then have to deter my life?

Should she call him out and ask him?

"Stan? Hey, Stan?" she called up, to the lighted room, like a child calling a friend out to play. "It's me, Stan, it's Miriam. Come and see!"

The window was raised abruptly, and Stan's bearded face poked through. Already she could see the effect on his face at her intrusion on his lawn, standing there in hunting shirt, little temptress skirt, sneakers.

"I'm coming down, Miriam, but you better get off that grass if you want to see me."

Off the grass, Miriam. But why hadn't she brought some of her own? Well, she did have her Hitachi transistor; she flicked it on, to rock on BCN. A sound track. She got down on her haunches and felt the grass. It smelled good, respectable. Upstairs she thought she saw the curtain move, and she waved,

228

saying, "It's okay, Röchel, I'm just passing through, thought I'd stop for a minute."

Stan opened the door, white shirt open at the neck, chinos, hair combed. Lilacs blooming in the doorway. "I thought I told you to get off—"

"The grass, dear? No, no, you come over here and see what I have for you."

"Are you crazy? Don't you think you've disgraced yourself enough? Cut out that music, do you know the time? What's this all about?"

She felt humble. "About this, Stanley." She took out her pistol and pointed it in front of her, chin height. "Come over onto the lawn, Stan, won't you?"

Stan smiled devilishly; it was proper that she should be so juvenile and perverse, he had won in his way.

But it was happening on his front lawn. "You're sick," he said.

"God, those lilacs smell wonderful. Come over here, Stan, in front of the flower box. I want to ask you something. Really, Stan, please do."

"Turn off that crazy music, will you!"

She waved the gun, near tears with tension. "I'm not kidding."

Nodding, he moved, five, six steps to the flower-box area, in front of the bay window.

"Why did you force me here, to do this?" she asked sincerely. "Why do you want to strangle me?"

His eyes narrowed, lips grew thinner. "You're confirming everything I've charged you with. You're not fit, Miriam. This proves it conclusively, can you yourself have any doubt after this? Now put that childish protest down, before you truly hurt someone. You're only embarrassing yourself more. Röchel," he called upstairs, "put some tea—"

"Leave her out of this, you rat."

Stan lifted his head, stroked his beard. "Hadn't you better turn that radio down before the neighbors come along? And put that pistol, whether it's a toy or not, back into your bag."

229

He was still the same, even here, this way.

Suddenly she felt helpless, like she was falling, and she turned the radio up higher; yes, the neighbors would come soon now, good; she felt space moving in and upon her body as she prepared to squeeze, and Stan sensed it too, and his face softened, dilated, oozed. And she whispered, "Why'd you do it, Stan? Couldn't you live without my blood?" Stan was helpless too, stunned, shaking his head, not a man but a guilty boy, a naughty boy. But it was too late, it was too confusing, the Stones, or somebody, were yelling for action, for squeezing, and someone was calling out the window about the noise now, and it was all as she had anticipated except that here at the end something was going wrong, haywire at the last second; she saw Jonathan and Rosie playing with Röchel and knew that she was good with them, and that if she couldn't do what she had come to do, she could—must—do something else but along the same lines, and she gulped air as she turned the gun around and for a second, a long long second, she observed that minute round aperture of nozzle, a devastation not photography hole, and she heard a low scream (hers?) and suddenly was stunned, falling hurting . . .

The hedges of the Commons pricked her and half-propped her up. A couple was there, asking if she was okay? Stung, perspiring, she said yes, she was, the scent of lilac in the air. They were afraid to let her go, said she had just sort of toppled over and screamed out. "No, I'm okay. Really." And walked off from them, away.

Toward the center of the darkened Commons, thinking how she couldn't even kill him there in the fantasy. *Globe* and *Crimson* nightmare tales came to mind, about the two Cliffies raped here, the B.U. coed murdered, the secretary mugged. The recall heightened her spirit, a delirious wind upon her fevered body. Walking and smoking, she noticed her apparel for the evening stroll: an old pleated skirt, a ribbed rose sweater, worn (Top-sider) sneakers, her checked hunter's shirt, brimmed cap. Old friends, with that other one in her hand. What did her body know that she didn't? she wondered. And as she strolled, she speculated, carefree. This is it. *This is mystery, adventure. Cambridge Commons is my Belgian Congo. Or my Wounded Knee. Will I meet Mr. Kurtz in the park here? Be massacred? Please, God, tell me, will there be an upshot to it all? In the long run, a contribution to some collective unconscious?*

Three teenage kids approached from around the large center statue and her heart jumped. They bounced closer on the balls of their feet, grinning and joking, two boys and a girl; the boy noticed her, said something about her cap being cool, and made a show of standing to the side, bowing, for Miriam to pass. She was strongly tempted to hand over her notebook and say, "Here's my homework, would you like to check it?" Taking a deep breath, she passed, and then walked on, free once more to be stupid . . . reckless . . . abandoned.

Hot and moving, she realized now that a man had been tailing her, practically since she had come into the park, and she scratched at her calf and breathed deeply. The light from the lampposts cast a fine violet glow upon the green, like a miniature golf course or perhaps a night softball game. She forced herself to walk more slowly, though it was difficult and her heart beat wildly; she had a vision suddenly of a meadow and a silo and a hired hand waiting. Was it Notebook who said, now, *You're crazy for sure. Fantasying, Sick. Come on, heroine, stop and face him. Or are you bluffing?* She turned the corner of the thick hedge, and his step crunched closer on the gravel. She stood and waited. Waited. Seconds became hours. Perspired. Steeled by her practice with the Leica and those special encounters, she waited for a strange animal to appear out of the woods. What happened was stranger, however. The man turned the hedge corner in a hurry, but when he came upon her standing there—a deer waiting for the hunter—he looked at her startled, age about thirty, fair, slight, faltered in speech, managed a "Pardon me!" and bolted. She could do nothing but stand there and catch her breath in bewilderment and letdown. Even desperation. Couldn't the Commons use a psychiatrist on duty at night? Couldn't she have her Leica on duty too?

The letdowns were cooling her off by now, taking the juice out of her urgent, ambiguous desires. She couldn't care less as she stepped back onto the path, just as the next pair of strangers came around the curve. One was a tall, mustached black wearing a large-brimmed leather cowboy hat, the other a shorter boy, white, in sports jacket and white shirt, with a red bandanna. An odd couple. She walked ahead easily now, and when the tall fellow stopped to ask her for a light, she obliged casually, almost happy for the return to an ordinary occurrence. Wearing an expensive yellow frontier jacket, he grinned widely with fine white teeth, looking exotic, rich, a pale-brown cowboy. In the flash of the yellow flame, she looked more closely at his light-skinned, handsome face and knew then that this was it. It was going to happen after all. The short fellow was suddenly gone, his breath at the back of her neck, cutting off escape. The brain recorded all this within a few seconds. The tall fellow lit his cigarette and exhaled, nicely; his face was peaceful with resolve and she noted (admired?) the smooth, sensuous brown of his chest and neck. Then she saw in his face that *he saw that she knew.* (Missing her other strange flickering desire.) There was no smile, and on her part a certain involuntary trembling began. She thought in terms of three words; "robbery," "rape," "murder." Which was it to be, she *longed* to ask him, one, two, or all three? These reflections and the brief mutual glances occurred during the space of perhaps fifteen or twenty seconds, during which she didn't move; they, in turn, were evidently casing the territory and judging the timing. And she knew now the meaning of that movie term.

In a low, husky voice, tinged Southern, he said, "Don't scream or it'll be worse for you."

She didn't scream, or speak, or think, the moment expanding into something like an underwater adventure, a new and breathtaking element. She wished only that a friend like Kelly or Nathalie could be there, not to help, but just *to be there,* so that she didn't feel so absolutely alone, so terribly alone.

Belief in the new element intensified when the boy behind her grabbed hold of her neck, near the windpipe, and began dragging her off the path.

By the hedge, the tall boy whispered sharply, "Watch this shit, man! C'mon, move it."

Dragged through the branches, she managed to jerk at the boy's strangling grip, and somehow he understood, in discreet agreement between victim and attacker, and loosened his arm to let her breathe better. Like a stretcher patient, she was lifted through the hedge—a twig knocking her cap off and scratching her cheek, forcing her hands (and Notebook) up for shield—and then she heard, "Ovah heah, man, right heah, c'mon, boy!" They jerked her to the side; the ground came up suddenly to meet her, making her gasp. In a few seconds, however, the smells of earth and grass filled her sensuously.

"Man, she ain't got no underpants on!" exclaimed the tall boy now, reaching up her leg, discovering the fact for all three of them.

And then she was age eight or nine, a man in an overcoat in another park was smiling and saying something about "Little girl, didn't your momma give you any pants to wear . . ." Feeling her with his hand, she holding the tears in.

233

Now, as he began to mount her, her body, up till then compliant and at one with her wishes, surprised her. It rebelled. It began to struggle. And somewhere or other, through the first scent of lilac from a wind, she realized again the body's secret knowledge, how it knew more than the brain would grant it, or could understand. (*But then who was understanding this now?*) It began to struggle, as if it had had a brain or soul of its own all these years, or this transforming year, one that she hadn't quite acknowledged fully. And as it struggled more fiercely, she grew more proud than she had ever been of her flesh, and she observed it almost as a spectator, in admiration. It fought against her too, against the irresistible perverse desire which had brought her here, and she found herself swinging and catching the boy above the eye with Notebook, causing him to howl low, like a cat scratched! For that swing of pleasure, she was paid back with sharp pain in the arm and neck. (*And as he paid back her desired blows, she saw, mysteriously, his face change and he was Stan; change again, and he was Sandy; change again, and he was Thorndike; and yet again, and he was that stranger from long ago.*) It was now her legs versus the boy's body, and she found that there, too, she was stronger than she had imagined as she bucked and tossed furiously in an effort to shift her feet to his chest suddenly and kick him off, melodrama-style. "A fightin' squaw, with a weapon yet, whaddya know!" the black boy declared, joining her in admiration. *Though where was Judy's gun now?* And then she must have done an awful thing, with her one free hand or leg, she wasn't sure, for the lanky yearling above her moaned, and in a second or two he came right back at her with an awful blow, a boot heel upon her vagina which made her gasp with pain and go blank for a few seconds. Then she was begging him in her mind not to do it to her right now, not now, and

234

out loud finally she was saying, "Not now, please, not now. Just a minute, wait." Laughing low and wildly, he said something about her getting what she asked for, and then he was between her legs, wale-cord trousers down, jockey briefs still on, and black snake out and stiffly pushing up against her, turning into iron as her body's fury yielded in its shock and pain.

The rape itself was neither pleasure nor real hurt. But maybe that was because during it all those other faces and bodies from the Show seemed to change places with the boys', forcing her to concentrate on the persistent apparitions—of the pediatrician, the lawyer, the ex, the critic. This was the Commons—not Medford—where everyone could come, right? The tall boy did his work in a few minutes, and she saw him working upon her, through the crystal of shock tears, with mechanical duty, no more. Every now and then she caught his large eyes, beneath his bad hat, and he said to her, "Close 'em." And she did, for fear of a blow. He smelled nice, leaning over her, a male odor. He did not excite her, she had no fantasies for his pistoning friction, it was closer to banal or pathetic than traumatic. Helplessly pathetic, because she wouldn't have minded in real life making love to him; on the contrary he smelled that sexy way, she even touched his kinky hair at one point, and his smile—his only smile—was terribly handsome, but here she was, feeling nothing and responding nowhere, her cunt and his prick involving them perhaps in legal disputes rather than sexy pleasures. Then this fine-looking boy lunged and said something like "Gash!" and he was done and there was nothing, no interest or sensation except dull shrinking wetness; and the lilac in the air was better and finer than the boy, and that hurt her. It occurred to her, too, how boyish he looked now; instead of looking like a man just then, the way he ought to have, he looked younger than ever, more helpless and at a loss, momentarily. Sadness enfolded her, and she said, "Poor Stan."

He shook his head, saying, "Man, you are *too much.*"

Next came the white sidekick: a fair, slight face with wire-rim glasses, the ascetic look of a studious grad student (biochemistry? mathematics?), a ball-point pen clipped to his pocket, that silly bandanna around his neck to keep up with his cowboy friend. Fear was penetrating his eyes, however, and he was having trouble, Miriam realized somewhere, getting an erection. "C'mon, man, get humping!" hissed the black boy, holding her neck and arms now, accentuating his friend's inadequacy. She saw, however, that the white boy was stalemated for sure, and that pressure on him was building, and it worried her too. When his teeth began to scrape his lips in panic, she knew she had to act. So she reached under him and began very slowly to fondle his testicles, her sure-fire trick with Stanley. She prayed to him, from her eyes to his. But he squeezed his eyes shut—and pictured what fantasy, she wondered?—and then this poor young mad boy began to get hard, and she took a deep breath of lilac, and it wasn't a minute before he ejaculated against her (never actually getting inside of her) and was small again. A tiny satisfaction which may have averted a large violence. She was grateful and immeasurably easier. And for his proven virility, he thanked her with his eyes, moving off.

Lying there on the ground, looking up at the flickering birthday sky, she heard their words, plans. And as she did, thoughts passed through her mind. Why did her body have to suffer for the spirit's desires? for the will's pictures? Why couldn't her body simply let go and really go to town with these boys? Why not make her body over from moral to free, and the boys over from dangerous to playful? "Did you see a purse, man?" "Nah. C'mon." "Cool it," the black boy advised. "Hey, you—got any bread?" She shrugged, not caring. Her lumberjacket shirt was searched; then a hand reached roughly into her skirt pockets and came up with change and dollar bills. "Shit. This ain't even worth the fight she put up, is it?" Crouching by her, the black boy stared, interested. "I oughta bust you," he half-teased. "C'mon, Marcus!" the white boy urged, scared. But Marcus stared at her, and she stared back, cool herself. She reached out her hand slowly and touched the baby-smooth coffee cheek, surprising him. She had touched other boys that way, hadn't she? "You got spirit all right"—he smiled—"jes like a tough little filly that needs to be broken, tha's all." He smiled ambiguously and began to reach across her with his huge basketball hand. She flinched, and closed her eyes and prayed to God. Gradually he half-ripped, half-pulled her brief skirt down off her body, exposing the warm belly and below. She watched him fold the skirt up neatly into the size of a quality paperback and tuck it away in his jacket pocket. "Something to remember you by," he said, accent Southern again, "And vice versa." Then he leaned very near—like some other madman in her life somewhere?—closing her eyes with his fingers, and whispered, "Now you jes forget my pretty face, baby, or I'll come back and cut yer pretty one up into *little, little pieces*. You heah?" She thought of the smoothness of his skin, the feel of his long fingers. He grabbed her hair at her silence, and she immediately grabbed him back. He laughed wonderfully, showing pleasure for the first time during the encounter, and used real force, saying, "You heah?" She nodded, hurting, and released him. "You betta believe it," he added.

As he rose, however, she had an idea, to make a J entry just then, and she raised herself. To her surprise, there was the white boy, on his haunches, leafing

237

through the pages of the notebook like he was studying at the Widener. She said, as if talking to a schoolmate who had taken her toy, "You give that back to me, now!" "Are you crazy!" cried the black fellow—to her or to his friend?—and then, *You dumb fucking crazy raped girl!*" She was whacked high on the head with his big hand, sending her reeling back, more off balance than in great pain. He was right, she thought, she was dumb, she was dumb.

Her head went around, stung sharply, and when she opened her eyes in a minute or two, they had stolen away, vigilantes in the night. She looked over, and it, Notebook, was gone too. Good. Serves you right, she said privately to orphaned Notebook, driving me that way. She reached behind her head with her arms and rested on them; she felt easier, released; the sky was jet black and blinking brightly with stars, and she thought how it would be a good day tomorrow, and how she had promised Jonathan that she'd take him to the Upland Road ball field. The moon shone pale white and remote, an unknowing eye. She found her Marlboro pack on the ground, lit one, and inhaled deeply, cherishing the slight bitterness. The whole thing had taken maybe fifteen or twenty minutes, and had, strangely enough, cleared her head. (By clearing her desires?) She felt weak, fatigued, but okay. Surprisingly okay. One way of coming up perhaps after the show letdown?

When she stood up, however, she almost toppled over. She steadied herself, her knees rubbery. Her naked behind felt as if it had been pierced with icy needles, and she rubbed the stuck grass off her, massaging the cold cheeks. That felt good. She kneeled, grabbed a handful of grass, and wiped her thighs and pubic area with it. The smell on her hands and body was strange but good. Her nakedness, from sweater down, was striking, and she had an urge to walk out of

238

the park that way. A sign of some sort. She decided instead on tying her lumbershirt around her waist like a towel; it fit like a sarong. Holding it with one hand, she made her way to the hedge, where she bent and found her baseball cap, getting nicked again by the branches. She brushed it off and put it on, feeling better. The path was dark and empty and serene, and her sense was of a deserted battlefield at night. She began to walk toward the center war memorial statue of the park, her body light, smoking her last cigarette, feeling as if she were returning from a long journey. On the far side of the war memorial, on the path at the edge of the Commons, two couples were returning from the Square.

One of the women happened to notice her, and stopped in disbelief. In canary-yellow dress, nylons, and heels, she nudged her friends to stop and look. Strangely, Miriam didn't (couldn't?) change direction, and walked on toward them; the four stood like tourists watching a primitive approach. (Or four jurors observing a leper, a convicted body?) The second lady stared in open embarrassment, while her friend, long-faced and strong-boned, stood her ground, hand on hip, smoking. As Miriam approached, she observed aloud, "Lost something, dearie?" The man with her, in a seersucker jacket, touched her arm. A short distance away from them Miriam stopped and peered at the woman, who was observing her with intense interest, an anthropologist looking at a new species. The man said, "Come on, Tizzie, let's go." Tizzie didn't budge, however. The second man said to Miriam, "You okay, sister?" Miriam waited for a wind to move her, to get her going. It didn't come. "Sure she is, John," Tizzie replied, exhaling smoke slowly. "Little Miss Riding Hood has simply been playing some baseball with the wolf, right, dearie?"

Miriam wiped the perspiration from her forehead and eyes with her fingertips. She raised the brim of her

239

cap slightly. The woman, about Miriam's age, who might have had a child in the same day-care center, wore a gold pin on her blouse and her bobbed hair was decorated with a yellow cotton ribbon; beneath the blouse were the obvious outlines of underwear, the straps of respectability. It was Stanley all over again, now taking the form of this well-groomed Cambridge lady. Miriam felt suddenly exhausted, impossibly fatigued, as if she could never budge again, blocked forever by this woman's conventional force. "Come on, Tizzie," said the man finally, pulling her off gently. Yielding to pressure she didn't really respect, she allowed herself to be taken off slowly, saying emphatically, "Those kind *kill* me."

But *what* kind? Miriam immediately wondered. The raped kind?

A slight wind curled up her thighs, forcing her legs forward, toward Broadway and the darkened way home. But as she crossed over, she suddenly had a great, irresistible yearning for ice cream and, as if nothing had happened, began to retrace her steps. Crossing diagonally from the dangerous wedge of parking area in the Square, she forced a car to swerve, barely missing her, and she felt sorry, wanting to apologize as the man cursed, looking back. On Mass. Avenue she headed for the ice-cream parlor. The late-night pedestrians between the Unitarian Church and the Harvard Square theater turned only intermittently to see her; after all, she was just another freak preening along Freak Row by night, between the theater and Coop corner. The thick glass door of Brigham's was held open for her, and she stepped inside, stunned momentarily by the white dazzle of fluorescence and the bright universe of ice cream. It was as if she had never been there before. Then she made her way to an open horseshoe counter and sat on a stool. She gazed up at the bands of pastel pinks and sky blues, and the brilliant explosions of frappes, sundaes, banana splits, cones dripping with jimmies. A waitress approached warily, exchanging glances with other customers, and Miriam said, "A dish of vanilla, please." The girl set down her water and eyed her uneasily before moving off, shaking her head. Miriam was grateful for the cap's visor, which cut down on the blinding artificial light. In a few seconds a sideburned tough, about nineteen, sat down alongside her. "Hi," he said with a modified leer, "I'm Tony Moreno. Would you like to go for a cycle ride when you get your order?" She shook her head, not looking at him but following the merry colors and heady, fruity suggestions. The boy continued to talk with his pronounced Boston accent, wheedling and propositioning as if she were dumb or retarded, saying how she could "trust him," wondering if she wanted the Cleveland team to move to Cambridge, and she hoped with all her heart that he would stop, that someone would make him stop, that someone would take him away.

"Aw, look, I'm sorry, I didn't mean anything," he begged off, as tears rolled down her cheeks. "Aw, look, I was just trying . . ." He stood up, his pals jeering at him. "She's too weird, man, too weird . . ."

The ice cream came and it tasted as perfect as the first mouthfuls of ice cream she had been given after her tonsillectomy, at age six, in the hospital. It was the same magic all over again, and she was six again, with pigtails. Or Jonathan, delirious in anticipation of chocolate chip and Brigham's colors and smells. His own private Harvard Square circus.

She was on her fourth spoonful when the policeman said, "I think you better come with us, miss. We're going to have to take you in."

Raising her cap brim, she looked up at the policeman, older than the Boston one, and wondered aloud, "Can't I finish it?" She wasn't sure why they wanted her, but she didn't mind, it was all right. In fact, she felt like going along, residing in their care. Yes, it would be nice, actually.

The policeman got the waitress to bring Miriam a sugar cone, with vanilla. Then he and his partner helped her up. A horseshoe of people had formed, curious, ogling, remarking on the crazy and the naked. What were they talking about? Who? As if she were a movie star at an opening, she was escorted out, helped by the uniformed men. In passing, she eyed fondly the candy case and counter at the left, a paradise of cookie jars filled with candied apples, twisted pretzels, chocolate caramels, peppermint sticks, peanut-brittle clusters, English toffee ("Come on, now," the man urged softly), and the rows of all-day suckers, swirl pops, strips of candy buttons, licorice laces. In a way she didn't want to leave all these rich goodies and bright colors, but she knew too that she wouldn't have been able to handle all this abundance for too long in her shaky condition. Finally, outside, the circus was replaced by ordinary night air; and a blue-and-white squad car, with the telephone number UN 4–1212 on its side and two blue domes on top, was waiting by the curb. Just as they opened the door for her, however, a flash went off like a glass smashing. "C'mon, move off now," said the policeman to a newspaper photographer. Shocked, she then thought, What a nice change, to have her picture taken by someone else. They settled her in the back seat firmly but gently.

A grid of metal rods—a catcher's mask?—

Caged in that way, she thought of something. "Have I done something wrong?"

One policeman looked at the other, and then back at her. "Do you always forget to put your clothes on, miss, when you leave the house?"

"The laws call it 'indecent exposure,'" added the second.

They pulled away from the curb and her admirers, and Miriam licked the vanilla cone and thought of *National Geographic* volcanoes, Cotopaxi, Chimborazo, Cayambe.

It was cozy in the car, being chauffeured through the city this way, finishing her cone, and she wondered where the sirens were that she usually hated so much? She felt cheated by their absence and asked about them.

"No emergency here," the policeman driving said.

They had curved around Eliot Street and were now heading up Mt. Auburn, toward Central Square and the police station. Reports were coming in from the police radio, a monotonous voice amid the breaking static. An alarm had gone off mysteriously at 2412 Mass. Avenue. A woman was complaining of a prowler on Sacramento Street.

"What's your name and address, miss? Might as well get started."

She considered the questions. She told them about Miriam Scheinman, and where she lived.

They passed the Orson Welles Theater, and turned up Hancock toward Broadway. "We'll just check this address out, if you don't mind. It's on the way."

She turned her head from the passing shops. "I don't mind, no."

The officer in the passenger seat looked back at her. "You okay?"

It was like the man at the path. "I think I'm bleeding a little." She smiled.

The driver looked briefly at her and said, "Well, not over the friggin' seat, lady!"

The accusation hurt her, and her own words slipped out, "I was raped about a half hour ago in the Commons."

The officer driving said, angry, "What did you just say?"

243

She remembered it clearly. "I was raped about a half hour ago in the Commons." She thought of something else. "And they took my notebook." But maybe they'd return it, it had her and Dr. Levanda's address. Or maybe they'd just turn up to see her sometime?

The second policeman turned to her, glanced at his buddy, who shook his shoulders in uncertainty about this kook. He looked back at Miriam, who was eating the last of the sugar cone.

"Why didn't you say that earlier?" the driver fired. "And take off that idiotic cap!"

"Where did you say it happened, Miriam?"

She really hadn't wanted to say it, it had slipped out, the chastisement had brought it out of her. Actually she liked the policemen and their car, and she looked forward to the station and to a cell of her own.

She removed her baseball cap and held it in her lap, not wanting to make the policeman more angry.

She had started telling about the Cambridge Commons at night when the driver asked, "Is anyone upstairs now to verify this address?"

"The baby-sitter, who's asleep." She smiled. "And the children. They'll know me."

The two cops exchanged another glance.

"Better change that call, Frank," advised the one at the wheel in an irritated voice.

They pulled over by her house.

Frank lifted the phone and called in.

Will they know me? Will they stick by me now? "Would you, Jon?" "Oh, Momma, don't be silly!" playing with his frog. "No, Jon, I'm different now. I'm not . . . who you think I am . . . I'm . . . I'm . . ."

The driver was talking to Miriam. "You know, I'm gonna tell you something, sister. This job is tough enough without girls like you going out and *creating* more work for us." His face was swarthy and full-featured, with a prominent nose, and Miriam wondered,

244

mildly startled, Jewish? as the malice rose in his deep-set eyes. "What the hell do you mean by being in that park alone at night with your children asleep here? Christ, if you was my daughter and this happened, I'd give you a little *something* to remind you of your *responsibilities!*" He glared, and she thought for a moment that that something was going to come right now. "Where the hell is your husband, what's he think of this? Or is he gone long ago? Jesus. Your type makes me wonder what I'm doing in this job!"

She seemed to be angering everyone tonight, she thought, regretful.

Frank was off the telephone now. "Come on, Lou, lay off. You check the name out on the bell, and I'll get some facts. Are you up to answering a few questions?"

"If she can get herself laid—"

Frank hit his partner's arm, saying, "Go on, will ya!"

He got out of the car with resistance, and Frank said to Miriam, "Don't mind him." He shrugged. "He has a daughter about your age and she's caused some trouble for him . . ." His hands gestured vaguely.

The questions from Frank came as the police radio monotoned on. What was she doing in the park at that time? Two dogs were making a disturbance on Green Street. Had anyone seen her on the Commons before or after the rape? Another call about the loudness of the rock music at Jack's on Mass. Avenue. Could she identify the rapists? Well enough to recognize a mug shot? Two cars had been in an accident at Kendall Square, no major injuries. Why'd she go to Brigham's after the incident? And what about that notebook, was it important?

Lou, getting his bulk back into the squad car, said, disappointed, "Yeah, she's for real."

She thought for some reason of Harry and Jamie, Adrien and Colin. They seemed far, far away. Were they for real?

Officer Lou said, "You have a lawyer, lady? That's who I'd call if I was you. You'll need one before this mess is cleared up."

A lawyer, for me? Sandy, call Sandy Fried for getting raped?

She felt the wool of her cap.

"So that's funny, eh?"

Frank interceded again. "Why don't you get us going?" And to Miriam, "Do you have a private doctor you'd like to have meet you at Cambridge City?"

"Cambridge City?"

"Cambridge City Hospital, Miriam. The law demands it in rape cases. And Mrs. Hennigan from headquarters will be there, to talk with you."

"*Alleged* rape cases," Lou inserted. "To check them out."

The hospital? Yes, that would be nice. Doctors, nurses, white rooms, fresh sheets. But her only doctor was Goldmark, and he hated her pictures.

"Wait a minute," Frank said, and a door opened and closed, and then another door opened and closed.

The engine turned over, the blue lights and a daydream crept into her mind. Stretched out luxuriously in a hot bath, soaped and scrubbed down by her Wausau Apollo and her affectionate painter. But the serenity kept being interrupted by Lou's incessant reprimand about her need for a lawyer, and about paying the price for her little stroll in the park. *Little Red Riding Hood* came back to her, and that word, "paying." She repeated it to herself: paying, paying, paying. She realized now that Policeman Frank, her friend, had moved to the back seat, to comfort her somehow, as the car swung away from the curb and out Hancock. She returned to her daydream, struggling through the police radio announcements and Lou's cutting criticisms, imagining the scrubbing and warm soaking, and it was only when Frank said to her, "There, there, you'll be all right, it's just the delayed shock," and put his handkerchief to her face, that she knew that she was crying again, shaking. Just tearing away while trying not to think about it all, or about what just happened, it was all so silly and trivial; but she couldn't seem to stop and her wet face leaned into the crook of the midnight-blue uniform that was suddenly there now, as the squad car this time used the siren, which screamed and twisted and screeched until Miriam was clutching the blue arm of the law for dear life, her cap falling off her lap, and she sensed now that there was an emergency somewhere.